I0536713

THE TREASURE OF THE SEAS

THE TREASURE OF THE SEAS

JAMES DE MILLE

WILDSIDE PRESS

Published by Wildside Press LLC.
www.wildsidebooks.com

I.

The aged Schooner.—The Ancient Mariner.—The Waste of Waters.—Perplexity.—Solomon and the Saw-dust Soup.— The decrepit Compass.—The baffled Navigator.—The despondent Boys.—A sudden Squall.—The Sails come to Grief.—Captain Corbet to the Rescue.—No Use! Too far gone!—The Antelope at the Mercy of the Winds and Waves.

The waters of the Atlantic Ocean were reddened far and wide by the rays of the rising sun. The glorious beams had flashed over tract after tract of the watery expanse as they came from the east, until at length they poured in a full blaze upon a certain gay and gallant bark which lay tossing upon the tide somewhere within a hundred miles or so of the shore of the western world.

Yet though undeniably gay and gallant, the hand of time was visible on that bounding bark. For her buoyant hull was worn, and torn, and aged, and weather-beaten, and in fact decrepit. Aloft, over that battered hull, whose dilapidated sides, covered with bruises and bare of paint, showed gaping seams, from which the oakum protruded, rose the rickety masts and rotten old rigging. The sails, all torn, and worn, and rent, and patched, were spread to catch the breeze, while on high floated a gallant but dingy flag, bearing the blazonry of a now undecipherable emblem, together with letters now half effaced, which looked like "B. O. W. C."

Yet though undeniably gay and gallant, the hand of time was visible on that bounding bark. For her buoyant hull was worn, and torn, and aged, and weather-beaten, and in fact decrepit. Aloft, over that battered hull, whose dilapidated sides, covered with bruises and bare of paint, showed gaping seams, from which the oakum protruded, rose the rickety masts and rotten old rigging. The sails, all torn, and worn, and rent, and patched, were spread to catch the breeze, while on high floated a gallant but dingy flag, bearing the blazonry of a now undecipherable emblem, together with letters now half effaced, which looked like "B. O. W. C."

Such a disreputable craft, and such preposterous sails, had surely never before met the eye of the astonished sun in these waters, and great must have been the hardihood, or else the ignorance, of those who dared commit themselves and her to the merciless ocean. Whether bold or ignorant, however, there they were, all of them—Captain Corbet, the mate, Solomon, and the boys of the "B. O. W. C.;" and these now all stood on the deck of the Antelope, looking at the reddening dawn.

At the helm of his gallant bark stood her bold commander, as wise, as vigilant, and as care-worn as ever, shading his venerable brow with his hand, while, with eagle eye, he sought to make out some floating object or some friendly shore. But to that eagle eye the wide waste of waters showed nothing of the kind; and so it came to pass that, at length, the aged Corbet heaved a gentle sigh, and his eyes rested with mournful meaning upon his young companions.

"Well, captain," said Bart, who was standing near him, "we don't seem to have made land yet—do we?"

The captain shook his head slowly and solemnly.

"Kine o' curous, too," he ejaculated, after a thoughtful pause.

"I don't suppose you have any more idea of where we are than you had yesterday."

"Wal," said Captain Corbet, "not to say much of an idea; but I'm kine o' comin round, an mebbe I'll get the hang of it yet."

"Well, why not head her west? We'll be sure to come in sight of land then."

Again the captain shook his head.

"Wal, I don't know," said he, "about that. Thar's currents, an thar's eddies; an thar's the Gulf Stream to be considered. Now, if we'd kep straight on at fust, when we got out o' Canso, we'd been all right; or even after we left Louisbourg, ef we'd only kep along the coast, in sight—but thar's the mischief of it. I let her git out o' sight o' land that night, an she got kine o' slewed round, and 's kep kine o' cantin round every which way, until at last she's in this here onfort'nit position. An now I'm all teetotally aderrift!"

"O, I shouldn't think that we can be more than a hundred miles or so south-east of the Nova Scotia coast."

"Wal, I don't know; seems to me we may jest as well be off Bermudy as anywhars else."

"Bermuda!" exclaimed Bart, in amazement. "You don't mean that."

"Wal, I don't see why not. Here we air, after a kerrewsin around a whole fortnight every which way, driven up an down by wind an tide, an canterin along with the Gulf Stream; an whenever we ventured to hail a passin vessel, only gettin the finger o' scorn a pinted at us for our pains, an the laughter of frivolous an light-minded men. So what's to hender us from bein anywhars?"

"Well," said Bart, "don't you think it would be better to take some one course, and stick to it?"

"Ain't I done it?" said the captain. "Ain't I done it every day? Every day I took some definite course, and stuck to it; an what's the result? Young sir, if you seek a answer, look around."

"But something must be done," said Bart, "or else we'll find the Antelope becoming a second edition of the Flying Dutchman. A fortnight of this sort of thing's no joke."

"Who ever said it was?" said Captain Corbet. "An what's wuss, every passin vessel will pussist in makin it a joke. They think we're a fishin schooner, bound to the banks; an if we ask a honest question, they won't do anything but yell out jokes that ain't got any pint that ever I can see. Wal, this sarves me right, for ever ventrin outside of old Fundy. Put me in old Fundy an I'm all right; out here I ain't any good, an hadn't ought ever to dreamt of comin."

From this it will be seen that the ill-fated Antelope was once more in a most unpleasant predicament, and the company on board appeared in danger of encountering adventures of as unpleasant a kind as they had known in the Gulf of St. Lawrence, if not worse. And certainly the prospect was dark indeed, when the captain himself could go so far as to hint at Bermuda as being by any possibility in their neighborhood. So Bart thought; and as he walked away there was a shade of anxiety on his brow.

As he walked forward he saw Solomon drawing some water for breakfast out of one of the barrels.

"Solomon," asked Bart, "how are we off for provisions this time?"

The sable functionary raised his aged form, and, holding the water-pail in one hand, with the other he slowly scratched his venerable wool.

"Wal, Masr Bart," said he, "dis yar time we ain't got no 'tiklar cause for 'ziety. Dar's a barl of salt pork, an two barls of biscuit, an dat ar's 'ficient for de 'quirements of dis yar company. Lucky for us, too, dat Cap'n Fuggeson cars for us. He put this pork an biscuit aboard for extry, an say dat we all boun to come to roonatium some how. An dat ar am de very 'visiums dat we got to lib on now."

"But haven't we got anything better than salt pork and biscuit left?" asked Bart, in a rueful tone.

"Well, notin 'tiklar. Dar's a drawin or two ob tea—an a grain or two ob flour—an some red her'n; but, law sakes! child alive—what you mean by frettin and pinin so long's dar's lot to eat? Nebber you mind. I'll cook up dis yar pork so's you'll blieve it's roast turkey. Will so. You don't know me yet. Tell you what,—wait till you see how I cook up dis yar."

"O, I know," said Bart; "I believe you could feed us on saw-dust soup, if you hadn't anything else. It wasn't that."

"Saw-dust soup!" cried Solomon. His eyes rolled fearfully. His aged figure bent double. He put the pail of water down, and then seated himself on the deck, where he proceeded to shake his venerable sides; and swing his body backward and forward, while chuckles, and giggles, and choking laughter burst from him. Every little while, as he could get his breath, he would roll up the whites of his eyes with a look of ecstasy, and whisper to himself, "Saw-dust soup!—saw-dust soup!—dat's so. Tell you what! takes ole Solomon to do it. He's de boy. Is so! Yah, yah, yah!"

From this outburst of African sentiment Bart turned mournfully away, and stood apart, looking pensively upon the water. The other boys seemed to feel as he did, for they all had on their faces an expression of anxiety and disappointment. They all knew how they were situated, and the situation was not agreeable to any one of them. Whatever novelty there may have been in it had gone off long ago, and there was nothing now left but impatience and vexation of spirit.

The wind had been freshening during the night; and now, as the day advanced, it grew more and more boisterous.

"It's blowin a leetle mite too fresh," said Captain Corbet to Bruce, "for to contennew on this course; so I'll jest come round, an run afore it. Arter all, it's the best course,—for it's west, an had ought to fetch us up somewhar eventooly, though I ain't got overly much confidence in this here compass."

"Compass! Why, what's the matter with the compass?" asked Bruce.

"Wal, yesterday at sunrise," said Captain Corbet, in a gentle tone of regret, "I noticed that, accordin to the compass, the sun was a risin in the nothe, an that was agin natur. So I knowed that either the sun was wrong or the compass, and nat'r'ly concluded that it was the compass. So I jest examined it, an sure enough, I found the needle all rusted up; an I'm a leetle mite afeared it ain't no more good, jest now, than a rusty nail. Consequently, I don't feel like settin any very great confidence on her. Wal, for that matter, I never thought much of compasses, an don't gen'rally go by them when I'm in old Fundy, though hereabouts they might p'aps be some use."

At this fresh instance of Captain Corbet's way of navigating, Bruce was so overwhelmed that he could not say a single word. A flush passed over his face. His lips parted as though he was about to speak; but he checked the rising remark, and walked forward, where he began to talk earnestly with the other boys.

But suddenly their conversation was interrupted. There was a sharp crash, a wild flap, a dark shadow, and in an instant a large object floated away through the air on the wings of the wind, while the noise of flapping, snapping and cracking still filled their ears. A hurried, startled glance showed them all. As the Antelope was coming round, a gust of wind more violent than usual had struck her. The old sails were too weak to stand it. The mainsail yielded utterly, and was torn clean off, and flung away upon the waters. The foresail had suffered but little less injury, for it had been torn completely asunder, and now showed a huge rent, while the two portions flapped wildly and furiously in the blast.

"Wal," said Captain Corbet, "ef—this—here—don't—beat—all!"

He was silent for a moment, and stood contemplating the ruin before him.

"Wal," he continued, drawing a long breath, "what's got to be must be. I knowed it would come some day. You can't fight agin the wind an storm for more'n seventeen year without feelin it; and these sails has been an had their day. I knowed it. I told you, boys, once—I dar say you mind the time—that them sails might be stronger, and that they wasn't adapted to be hung on to a ship of a thousand ton. Still I did hope that they'd stand this here vyge."

"But what are we going to do now, captain?" asked Tom.

"Do?" said the captain. "O, wal, 'tain't so bad's it might be. We've got the foresail yet; an me and Wade'll fix her; we'll take her, an sew her up, and make her as good as new; an we'll work along some how. You needn't be troubled; it ain't goin to make a mite of difference; an I don't know, after all, but what in the long run p'aps it's a goin to be better for us. We ain't ben a doin much with the two sails, that sartain; p'aps now we'll do better with only one."

And now the venerable captain and his noble mate prepared to obtain possession of the sail. This was done without any very great effort, the boys all assisting. Then the two navigators (master and mate), having armed themselves with sail-needles and twine, proceeded to sew up the rent, to patch, to mend, and, in general, to renovate the old, old wornout sail. At length this last was happily accomplished; the sail was restored to its place, and as it swelled out at the pressure of the ocean blast, it seemed as efficient as ever. But either, in this case, appearances were deceptive, or else its previous condition had been deplorably weak. Certain it is, that after having sustained the blast for about half an hour, the old rag of a sail began to give way again in a dozen different places, and at length split up almost close beside the former rent. At this Captain Corbet surveyed the tattered canvas with melancholy resignation.

"This here wind," said he, "is a leetle too stiff for her jest now. I think we'd better save her from another time. She'll do very well in milder weather."

By "she" Captain Corbet meant the sail, which he thus personified with affectionate familiarity. As he said this, he proceeded to lower the tattered canvas, and examine it in a pitying, compassionate, and caressing sort of way, quite oblivious of any other duty.

Meanwhile the Antelope tossed and pitched about at the mercy of the waves. There was nothing that deserved the name of a storm; yet, nevertheless, the wind was boisterous, and the sea somewhat rough. The position of the Antelope became, therefore, in the highest degree unpleasant, and this last example of Captain Corbet's helplessness and incapacity served to complete the despondency of the boys. It now seemed as though their last hope had gone. The compass was useless; the sails were reduced to rags; they had no means of flight from their present misery; and the only comfort remaining was, that the danger which menaced them was not immediate, and might yet be evaded.

Nothing now was left to the boys but to watch with eager eyes the scene around—to search over the waste of waters with the hope of seeing some sail, or perhaps some sign of land. And to this they devoted themselves. It was indeed a cheerless task, and one, too, which gave them but little hope. Hours passed, yet no sail appeared. Dinner time came, and the dinner was spread; yet the boys showed but little appetite. They had been in far worse circumstances than this, yet still this was sufficiently unpleasant to destroy all relish for Solomon's cookery, even if the banquet had been composed of greater dainties than salt pork and sea biscuit.

Thus the guests at that banquet were not at all appreciative; and they sat there in the schooner's hold, not to eat, but merely to pass the time, which hung so heavy on their hands. Yet even thus their impatience did not allow them to spend much time at the dinner, for they soon retreated, and took up their stations on deck once more, to stare around, to scan the horizon, and to peer into empty space.

Hours passed. On that afternoon, the wind gradually went down, and there seemed a prospect of calmer weather. Captain Corbet began to talk of mending the sail, and hoisting it again; and at length, calling upon Wade, he and his mate proceeded with needles and sail twine to patch up as before. Into this occupation these two plunged, but the boys still stood on the lookout.

At length, Bart directed Bruce's attention to something which appeared on the margin of the sea, far away on the horizon.

"Bruce," said he, "don't you see something out there that looks like the mast of a vessel?"

Bruce looked eagerly in the direction where Bart was pointing, and the others, who had heard the remark, did the same.

II.

A strange and startling Sight.—A Mast in Mid-ocean.—Land.—A Land of Terror.—A Panic.—The worst Place in all the World.—Tom drives away the Panic.—Drifting.—The Anchor dropped.—The Dawn of Day.—The low Land on the Horizon.—Preparing to go ashore.—The Confidences of the unfortunate Solomon.

As they all stood looking in the direction where Bart was pointing,—

"I see it," said Bruce. "It's certainly the mast, and the mast of a ship, for there is the yard and the rigging; but there's only one mast."

"It's a sloop," said Phil.

"No," said Tom; "it's a square-rigged vessel of some sort."

"Sure an it ain't got no more 'n one mast," said Pat; "an be the same token, there's no hull at all at all. Be the powers, but it would be a quare thing intirely if it was to turrun out to be another wather-logged ship. An if it is, it's meself that'll not set fut aboord of her; not me, so it isn't."

"There's something," said Bruce, "that may be a hull. I can see it sometimes quite plain. Now look, boys, carefully, all of you, as we rise on the top of a wave."

All this time Arthur had been examining the object through the spy-glass. As Bruce said this, he handed the glass to him.

"It's not a ship," said he, "nor a vessel of any kind. It's land."

"Land!" cried all the boys.

"Yes," said Arthur.

All were silent. Bruce took a look through the glass, and then passed it to Bart, who, after looking through it, passed it on to the others.

"It's a fact," said Bruce. "It's land; and that's a flag-staff."

"It's very low land," said Arthur.

"It's a mere sand-bank," said Bruce.

"A sand-bank," said Bart, "with a flag-staff in the middle of the ocean! It's queer."

"Yes," said Bruce; "and remember this, too, that this sand-bank in the ocean, with this flag-staff, is probably not very far away from the coast of Nova Scotia. Now, put this and that together, boys, and where do you think we are?"

At this question they all looked at one another in silence, and for a time no answer was made.

"Well," said Tom, at length, "I'll tell you what it is, boys. I believe that another prophecy of Captain Ferguson's is turning out true. He prophesied that we'd be thrown upon Anticosti, and so we were. He prophesied that we'd be thrown on another place, and this is that place. You all know what I mean. I mean Sable Island."

The boys made no remark. This thought had been in the minds of all of them. It was a thought that brought the deepest anxiety and gloom. For, bad as Anticosti was, there was one worse place; and that place was the very sand-bank before them—Sable Island!

The boys had all along been hoping for deliverance, either in the shape of some passing vessel or some sign of land. But this land, which they had approached unwittingly, seemed to be surrounded by a terror far worse than anything that was connected with their present situation. For Sable Island—that treacherous sand-bank in the midst of the sea—had always been known to all of them as the dread of seamen, the trap of ships, and the graveyard of shipwrecked sailors. The solitary flag-staff rose there out of the low island, as though to warn them away, like a signal of danger; and yet it was impossible for them to move away. Without sails, and without a compass, they were helpless; and there seemed now no prospect, except to go ashore there and meet their doom.

Tom was the first to rouse himself.

"Captain," said he, "here's Sable Island. Come and take a good look at it, for we're going ashore."

Captain Corbet had been so intent upon his work of patching the old sail, that he had heard and seen nothing of this excitement among the boys. These words of Tom came, therefore, suddenly and abruptly, and filled him with a terror equal to theirs. He started as though he had been shot. His needle dropped from his hands. For a few moments he sat staring at Tom; and then he rose slowly to his feet, and going over to where the boys stood, he looked out over the waters to where their eyes were directed. He stood staring for a long time in perfect silence.

"Sable Island!" he at length said, in a low voice. "Wal, boys,—I didn't ever think—I'd ever live—to see—this here day. I've ben a tryin all my life, boys, to keep clar of this here island; but fate's stronger than the hand of man,—an here we air!"

"O, see here now," said Tom. "Come, now, captain, this here sort of thing won't do at all, you know. There can't be any very great danger. The wind's gone down, you know. The sea's ever so much smoother than it was, and it's going to be smoother still. All sorts of vessels visit this island. The Nova Scotia government send supplies here regularly; and so I don't see what danger there is. For my part, I think we'd all better go ashore. The more I think of it, the more convinced I am that we'll be better off ashore on Sable Island than we are drifting about on board of the Antelope. And so I say, Hurrah, boys, for Sable Island! Let's go ashore, and get a decent sail for this vessel, and some supplies."

These words cheered the boys amazingly. A reaction at once took place. Tom was right. The sea was calm enough here to admit of a landing anywhere; and in the face of this fact thoughts of danger were not to be entertained.

Yet the panic which had been inspired by the very name of Sable Island may easily be explained; and, in circumstances like these, it was quite justifiable. For of all places in the world, Sable Island is, perhaps, most dreaded by seamen. It is a low sand-bank, about twenty miles long and one mile wide. This much is above water. But besides what is visible to the eye, there is much more invisible, treacherous, beneath the sea, extending all around it. Sable Island is, in fact, the crest of a vast sand-bank or shoal, which rises out of the ocean depths, about a hundred miles south-east of the coast of Nova Scotia, in the very track of the vast commerce between England and America. Though the island itself is not more than twenty miles long, the shoal extends much farther; and it has been calculated that, for a distance of fifty miles, there is danger to the ship which ventures too near. Moreover, this shoal runs in a curved line, and may be said to enclose in a segment of a dangerous circle all vessels sailing north of it, or between it and the main land. Approach to it in a storm is always dangerous; and with certain winds it is positive destruction; wherefore ships always give it a wide berth. Many are the vessels which are known to have been lost there; but many more, by far, are supposed to have perished on the outlying shoals, without leaving a vestige behind to tell of their fate.

Now, however, there was nothing like a storm. The wind, that had prevailed all day, was gone; and it only needed Tom's cheery words to drive away from all of them the terror that for a time had taken possession of their souls. They therefore roused themselves from the silence and the gloom into which they had fallen, and began to talk over the probabilities of a landing. Each one brought forth all that he knew about Sable Island, and added it to the common stock of knowledge, until at length a very favorable idea of the place was formed. Bart knew that there was a regular overseer, or governor, or superintendent of the island, placed there by the Nova Scotia government. Bruce knew that a vessel was sent there four times a year to convey supplies, and to take away any shipwrecked people who might be there. Arthur knew that there were huts, built for the purposes of refuge, in different parts of the island. Tom was sure that a landing could be made in ordinary weather, without much trouble; and Phil was eloquent on the subject of the ponies which live and thrive on the island, constituting a peculiar breed, well known in Nova Scotia, where a batch of Sable Island ponies are brought every year, sold at auction, and dispersed through the country. The result of this interchange of ideas was, that the boys at length began to look upon Sable Island as rather a desirable place, and to feel impatient for the time to come when they might drift near enough to make a landing.

But this was a thing for which they had to wait. The Antelope was certainly drifting; yet her progress was slow, and there was no way of hastening it. For hour after hour they watched the flag-staff, and the low line of land away on the horizon, without finding themselves near enough to think of going ashore. By the shifting and changing position of the flag-staff, they knew that they were drifting past it; and yet there was no way by which they could prevent this. In the first moments of their panic, the possibility of drifting clear of Sable Island would have seemed most welcome to all of them; but now that they had formed the plan of landing there, such a prospect seemed not at all desirable; and the slow drift of the schooner, while it baffled their hopes, filled them all with impatience.

In this way the hours of the day passed away. It was about three o'clock in the afternoon when they first saw Sable Island. The hours went by, and sunset came; still they were not near enough. Night was impending, yet the weather was too calm to allow of uneasiness, and they could only hope that on the following day they might be able to make the landing which they all desired so earnestly.

Passing the night in the vicinity of such a place as Sable Island is what few would choose for any amount of money. On this occasion, most fortunately, the weather was calm. The wind had died away to a gentle breeze, and the water was quite smooth. The only motion experienced by those on board the Antelope was that long rise and fall which is always felt out at sea, owing to the never-ending undulation of the ocean waters.

The boys went below and slept. Captain Corbet, however, remained on deck, and kept his lonely vigil far into the night. The first mention of Sable Island had produced upon him a profound effect. His first words exhibited something like a panic terror, which might have communicated itself to the boys, had it not been for Tom's cheery exhortation. From that first terror the captain had managed to extricate himself; yet still there remained, deep within his soul, the gloomiest anticipations. The night was not particularly dark. The sky was dotted with innumerable stars; yet so low was the island, and so destitute of any conspicuous landmark, that it passed out of view with the early twilight; nor was the eagle eye of the watchful Corbet able to detect any sign of the vanished land. At length he determined to guard against the danger of any further drifting, and accordingly proceeded to let fall the anchor. It was about two hours after midnight when this was done, and the rattle of the chains awaked the sleepers below, and announced that at last their long wanderings were arrested.

On the following morning they were all on deck with the dawn of day, and looking out eagerly upon the waters. The sight which met their eyes was one which could have given nothing like pleasure to any others; yet to them it was indeed pleasant, so far as it went. They saw rising out of the sea a low, sandy shore, which extended as far as the eye could reach. About opposite them rose a flag-staff, which they supposed to be the one that they had seen on the previous evening, though there was a difference of a most important character between what they saw then and now. For here they saw buildings which looked like comfortable residences, perhaps the abode of the keeper of the island. Except this house and its belongings, nothing else was visible along that sandy shore.

The Antelope had come to anchor in good time, and the shore was not quite two miles away from this place. Still, so shallow were the waters, and so treacherous the sea bottom, that it was not at all advisable to attempt to approach nearer. If they wished to land, they would have to do so in the boat. The boat floated astern, all ready, being no other than that one which they had saved from the ship Petrel. Into this they prepared to go.

For this voyage all the boys volunteered, and Captain Corbet also. Wade was to be left aboard with Solomon. Bart noticed that the venerable African was looking at the island with a pensive gaze, and thought that he saw disappointment in his face.

"Would you like to come ashore, too, Solomon?" he asked, kindly.

Solomon shook his head.

"Darsn't," said he. "Darsn't, no how."

"Pooh, nonsense! Why not? Come along," said Bart, who thought that this was some of Solomon's superstitious fancies which were now affecting him.

"Darsn't," said Solomon, again. "Couldn't ebber leave it agin. An don you go an try to 'suade dis yer ole man, Mas'r Bart, if you don want to lose him. Tell you what—dat ar island's too safe; an ef I foun myself dar, I wouldn't ebber leave it."

"Safe? What from?" asked Bart.

Solomon looked all around with the glance of one who fears pursuit and capture by some mysterious enemy.

"De ole complaint," said he at last, with a groan.

"What, rheumatism?" asked Bart, innocently.

"No, sah," said Solomon. "It's Broomatiz—an acute Broomatiz too— what I cotches from de ole woman whenebber she finds a broomstick handy. It generally attacks me over de back and shoulders. An what's wuss, dar ain't a medicine, or a liniment, or a wash, or a poultice, dat does a mite ob good. De only cure is for me to go an hunt up some desert island in de middle ob de ocean, an habit it for de ress ob my days; an so, ef I was to go shore dar, I might hide, an nebber come back. Too great 'tractium; couldn't resist it. Safe dar forebbermo from dat ar ole woman; safe an free; no more knocks an bruises; no more terror. O, Mas'r Bart, p'raps, after all, dis here ole man better go asho dar, an hab peace."

"Nonsense, Solomon," said Bart, who was astonished at learning the real cause of Solomon's strange fancy for Sable Island. "Nonsense. Don't get that notion into your head. Your wife'll never find you. You come to Grand Pré, and Dr. Porter will protect you."

"Dat ar place is de berry place whar I kin nebber be safe. She's dar now, a waitin, an a watchin, an a waitin for me. I know it. I feel it in my ole bones. Dey allers aches when I think ob her. Ebery mile we go brings me nearer to her broom-handle; an de longer I stay away, de wuss I'm goin to cotch it. So, p'raps, Mas'r Bart, I'd better go asho on Sable Island."

The idea seemed to have taken full possession of Solomon's mind, and to such an extent, that Bart found all efforts to banish it utterly useless. He therefore gave it up, and concluded, under the circumstances, that it was better for Solomon to remain on board.

The boat was now ready. The boys and Captain Corbet were calling for Bart to hurry up. Bart got on board, and they pulled away. It was a long pull; but the water was smooth, and they made good progress. At length the boat touched the shore, and they all leaped out upon the sand.

III.

Landing.—A friendly Reception, and a bounteous Repast.—Sable Island.—The strange Soil.—The sandy Ridge.—The Lake.— The long Walk.—A wonderful Sight.—The ancient Ship.—The Governor's Story.—A tremendous Storm and its Effects.—A great Surprise.—Examination and Exhumation.—Disappointment.— Theories.—The Governor rides a Hobby-horse.

When they stepped ashore upon Sable Island they found themselves in the presence of the whole of the population. This population amounted to about eleven souls; namely, the governor, or keeper, or guardian, or regent, or whatever else he may be called, of the island, six of the members of his family of various ages, and four able-bodied men. The governor was a bluff, broad-shouldered, red-faced, bearded personage, with a bright gray eye and a cheery smile. He had a reefing-jacket and "sou'-wester" hat; while his four satellites were dressed, two in reefers, and two in Guernsey jackets. The intercourse of the Sable Islanders with the outside world was very infrequent, and usually very exciting, so that on the present occasion they had turned out in force to greet their extraordinary visitors.

Not far off was a substantial and comfortable-looking house, that seemed well adapted to withstand the Atlantic storms, and shelter its inmates from the severity of the weather. A few small out-houses adjoined it, and in the distance, where the ground rose a little higher than usual, was the signal-staff already mentioned.

Whatever doubts the visitors might have had about the reception which they would meet with were dispelled at once and utterly by the first words of the potentate, whom I will call the "Governor." Without any remark as to the suddenness of their appearance, and without any question about their errand, he at once shook hands with them all round, and invited them to the house to breakfast, which, he informed them, was all ready, and waiting for them. A long and dreary voyage and monotonous sea life made a meal on shore seem attractive beyond expression to all of them, and the kind invitation was most thankfully accepted. Whereupon the governor led the way to the house above-mentioned, and ushered his visitors into a large but low room, where a long table was spread, and lay invitingly before their eyes. Here they seated themselves, and partook of the governor's Sable Island hospitality, in the shape of fragrant coffee, and hot rolls, and baked potatoes, and corned beef and tongue, with other articles too numerous to mention; all of which served to efface from the minds of the guests the memory of late hardships, and to diffuse among them a general feeling of peace and calm, of cheerfulness and content.

In the course of this repast the visitors made known to the governor their whole story, and that story was heard by him with an astonishment which he did not attempt to conceal. The fact that they should have been drifting blindly about without finding any place of refuge, and that they had finally been forced to seek for help from him in this place, of all others, was so overwhelming, that at first he seemed unable to believe it; and even after he had been compelled to yield his faith, his reason remained unsatisfied. The thing was true, yet unintelligible, and to his mind simply preposterous. Yet there was the fact, and here were the factors, that went to constitute that fact. The governor was dumfounded. Captain Corbet was clearly beyond him.

At length, like a wise man, he gave up the attempt to fathom what was inscrutable, and devoted himself rather to the practical duties of hospitality. He promised to let Captain Corbet have what he wanted, and also he offered to do the honors of Sable Island, and show the boys all that was worth seeing.

The governor was thus not only hospitable, but also very communicative. He told them all about Sable Island, and gave them much information, in addition to what they had already learned about this singular place.

The little colony was placed here for the purpose of giving aid and comfort to any who might be unfortunate enough to be shipwrecked here. Full supplies of all sorts of stores and provisions were placed on the island under his care. In addition to the buildings at this place there were two other houses of refuge, farther away towards the east, and also two other signal-staffs. In the other houses of refuge no one lived, but supplies of food and fuel were laid up there for the benefit of those who might need them. There was no lighthouse, because it was believed that a light might have a tendency to mislead, and because all seamen sought to keep as far away as possible from the island.

Sable Island, in fact, is nothing more than the ridge of a vast sand-bank, which rises from the ocean depths, and at this place emerges for a few feet above its surface. The sandy ridge is over twenty miles in length, and is curved in its form. The shallows at either extremity also follow this curved line, so that the whole extent of this place of danger, including the shoals as well as the island, is not much less than fifty miles. Its concave side is towards the north-west, and ships on that side in stormy weather are in great peril whenever they come within twenty miles of the place. As a consequence, many wrecks occur, some of which are known, while more are never heard of, and can only be conjectured.

Caught, so to speak, between the long-extended arms of this treacherous sand-bank, they are swept helplessly to destruction among the waters that rage over these far-reaching shoals.

Once every three months a vessel comes here from Nova Scotia to bring supplies and to take off any who may have been cast ashore. The landing is often difficult, and sometimes impossible, so that the vessel has to keep away for a long time before daring to venture near.

The governor informed them that life here, on the whole, was not unpleasant, but that in winter there were times when it was impossible to venture forth out of the house. The cold was never excessive, for the surrounding waters made the temperature milder than that of the adjacent main land; but the storms were terrific, and sometimes the sea seemed to make a clean sweep over the island, and all the air was filled with clouds of driving spray. After such storms as these it was always their practice to explore the island in search of shipwrecks. Sometimes they found human beings, who had been cast ashore, huddled for shelter behind hillocks, or in the other houses of refuge and brought them back; but more frequently the only result of their search was the sight of some fragments of a lost ship which the furious waves had washed ashore; or, worse still, the lifeless bodies of those who had perished amid the raging waters. These last were always conveyed to the burial-ground of the island, where they were committed to the grave with solemn ceremony, the governor reading over them the burial service of the church.

This information and much more was communicated at breakfast; and after the repast was over, the governor proceeded to fulfil his promise by taking the boys out to show them Sable Island.

It did not appear as though there could be much to see. On leaving the house there spread away a sandy waste, whereon grew some coarse grass. This grass grew not close enough to form anything like turf, yet in sufficient abundance to afford pasturage to herds of wild ponies which belong to the island. These ponies were put here many years ago, and in successive generations have become developed into a wonderfully intelligent and hardy little animal, ugly, woolly, yet strong, and capable of feeding on anything. They endure the severity of the winter season here without any shelter whatever; and when snow is on the ground they get at the grass underneath with the same ready instinct that is exhibited by the buffaloes on the western prairies.

After walking some distance, they reached the crest of the sand ridge, and from this place they saw a long, narrow sheet of water. This they were informed was a lake, which took up half of the length of the island, being more than ten miles in length; the formation of the island being what may be called a long, irregular oval, enclosing this sheet of water.

The eastern half of the island is, however, a solid, continuous sand-bank, and the lake lies rather towards its western end.

It is the eastern end which is most affected by storms. Here the herbage is scanter, and the hillocks more frequent; here, too, the sand shifts and changes with every storm. The governor informed them that after every very great storm, important changes might be seen in this direction, and mentioned that one of a very interesting nature had occurred a few months previously in a tremendous equinoctial gale, which had been by far the wildest that had taken place since his residence on the island. This he promised to show them, and led the way to the place where the object to which he referred might be seen.

They walked about four miles, and at length reached a pond which was about in the middle of the island, and at an equal distance from either side. Here a black object arose, which the boys at first took for some sort of a rock. As they drew nearer, it looked more like a hut; but finally, on coming close, they saw, to their utter amazement, that it was nothing else than the hull of a ship.

That ship had a most singular form. The timbers had been greatly broken, and the decks had vanished long ago; but the outlines were visible by the broken beams, and it seemed to have been about five or six hundred tons burden. But what most impressed them was the quaint and singular appearance of the stern. This part had been less injured than the rest. It rose to a height of over sixteen feet, and much more was still buried in the sand. The uppermost portion was battered and broken; but beneath this there was a second deck and a third. Between this second deck and the third was what might once have been a cabin, and the broken port-holes astern, that once gave light, were still plainly visible. The great height of the stern and its division into successive stories, reminded the boys of the pictures which they had seen of the ships of three centuries back, and filled their minds with intense excitement.

"This ship," said the governor, "was uncovered by the great gale of last March. Until that time it had been completely covered by the sand, which formed around it the biggest hillock on the island. I never had any idea that inside of that hillock there was anything of this sort. I attributed the formation of the hillock to the accidental concurrence of the winds which had gathered the sand up here. You would scarcely believe how large it was. Why, for hundreds of yards all around here that hill extended, and it was over thirty feet higher than where we now are.

"Well, a few days after the great gale, I came out in this direction, and noticed, to my amazement, that the hill was gone! That didn't surprise me much, for I had known other such changes to take place in every storm, though I had never known any on such an extensive scale. But when I came nearer, and saw this old hull, you may depend upon it I was astonished enough. Here it was,—all laid bare, all the sand blown away just as you see it now, except the cabin there, which I proceeded to clear out as soon as I could.

"Now, the first glance showed me that this old hull must be at least a couple of hundred years old; and I took it for one of the old French or English ships that had been wrecked here in the early days of American colonization. I accounted for its position so far inland in the easiest manner in the world. The fact is, this whole island is all the time shifting and changing. I don't believe it is in the least like what it used to be. When this ship got here, I believe this was a shoal where she drove ashore in some tremendous gale, and was soon covered up with sand. Gradually the sand gathered about her more and more, and the island changed its shape, and the shoal rose above the water, till at last this place became the middle of the island. Two or three hundred years from this, I dare say there'll be miles of land away off there to the north, all along, and this'll be considered the South Shore."

"But didn't you find anything aboard of her?" asked Bart, in eager curiosity.

"Well, that was the very first thing I thought of. This old-fashioned ship reminded me of the Spanish galleons that used to take cargoes of gold and silver across the water, and I was full of the idea that there might be some immense treasure still on board. The sand had preserved the wood from decay, and gold was still more likely to be preserved. So I hurried back at once, and got a shovel, and came here alone. I cleared out the whole cabin there that day, and to my deep disappointment, I found not one single thing. I found it, in fact, just as you see it now— completely cleaned out by the waves. Everything had gone, except the timbers and some of the deck work. Doors had been torn off, and the whole front of the quarterdeck had been forced away. There were no movables of any kind, nothing, in fact, except those beams and planks, that had been strong enough to resist the fury of the waves.

"I went back that day in deep disappointment, and gave up all hope of finding anything. On the following day I called all hands together, and we all came here to examine the hull. We worked for about a week, and dug out most of the sand,—it's all back again, though, you see,—and in other places we thrust in poles to see if anything was there. We found nothing, however; no gold or silver, no precious stones; nothing, in fact, but a rusty, demoralized, and depraved old cannon, that looked as though it had been cast for the Spanish Armada. The old piece is over there in the house, preserved as a curiosity."

"And so you didn't get anything?" said Bruce, in a tone of disappointment.

"Not a thing, except the cannon," said the governor; "and I leave you to imagine my disappointment. I was at first sure of making my fortune, retiring from the island at once, and going home to live on my wealth. But I'm afraid I shall have to postpone that for a long time."

"Do you suppose there ever was any treasure on board of her?" asked Arthur.

"Well, yes. I not only suppose so, but I almost feel certain that at one time there was a good deal of gold and silver aboard of this very ship. I've examined her, and studied her very attentively. Look at her now for yourselves. Notice how high that stern is. I don't think those high sterns were used later than the days of Queen Elizabeth. It was in just such ships as this that the Spaniards brought their gold and silver across the water. In fact, boys, I believe that this is neither more nor less than a Spanish galleon. Believe? in fact I know it. For on that old gun that I spoke of, there is a cast that's precisely the same that you see on the old Spanish dollars—the arms of Spain.

"Now I'll tell you what the idea is that I've formed about this ship. You know that in the days of Elizabeth the Spanish Main swarmed with buccaneers, who seized the treasure ships whenever they could. Among these, English sailors were the worst. You know that well enough. Well, my idea is, that some of these buccaneers seized this very galleon, plundered her of everything, and let her go. I don't think that a Spanish ship would have been likely to be driven up here from the West Indies, or to drift here. I think it most likely that she was seized and brought here."

"But perhaps," said Bart, "the buccaneers were lost in her."

"It's possible, certainly," said the governor, "but I don't quite think it. I think, if there had been any gold left, some of it would have been left hereabouts in the hull. No. I think it most likely that she has been plundered by the buccaneers, who then let her go,—for a big, clumsy ship, like this, was no good for their purposes. They may have let the Spanish sailors go in her,—not unlikely; and if so, the poor wretches left their bones in these sands."

"But what would buccaneers come here for?" asked Bart,—"so far to the north. I thought they all lived around the Spanish Main."

"Ah," said the governor, "that brings up the very point that proves my whole theory."

IV.

The Buccaneers.—The Traditions of Mahone Bay.—The Spanish Galleon.—The buried Treasure of the Buccaneers.— The Plunder of the Spanish Main.—The lost Ship.—The Arms of the royal House of Spain.—Convincing Proof—Further Wanderings.—Undisciplined Ponies.—A last Farewell.— The Antelope departs.—The Plan of the Boys.—Corbet grieves, but yields.—Out of the Reach of Danger.

"You must be aware, in the first place," said the governor, "that over the whole Atlantic coast of Nova Scotia there are traditions of the buccaneers. There is one place, however, where these traditions seem to have a centre, and that is Mahone Bay. The people there have handed these traditions on from father to son ever since the country was settled; and the belief at this time, is as strong as ever, if not stronger. The only change that they have made is in the name. They do not speak of the buccaneers but of one certain man, whose name all over America seems to have lent itself to every tradition that the past has handed down about pirates and piracy. This is Captain Kidd. So at Mahone Bay the traditions all refer to him.

"Now I don't believe that these traditions originated in nothing, but that they grew out of actual facts. The buccaneers, when they infested the Spanish Main, needed some place in which to store their plunder. They wanted a place which was at once safe from pursuit, and so remote that the Spaniards would never think of following them. Well, this they could gain by sailing far enough to the north, and Nova Scotia naturally seemed the best stopping-place; first, because it seemed to them like the last point of the coast of the main land, and secondly, because it was convenient for a run over to Europe. Besides, Nova Scotia afforded a greater number of first-rate harbors than could be found in any part, not only of America, but of the world. It was therefore out of the way of pursuit and discovery, and the best place that they could wish to have.

"Well, now, among all the harbors that line the coast of Nova Scotia, there isn't any that can be compared to Mahone Bay for the purposes of the buccaneers. Once in it, and discovery or capture is next to impossible. The bay is spacious and deep, without shoals or currents, and, above all, dotted with three hundred and sixty-five islands of every sort and size. Among these a hiding-place could be found, that for safety and seclusion could not be equalled anywhere else. And what are the facts?

Why, the tradition of the country ever since asserts that this very bay was a chosen haunt of pirates in the old piratical days.

"And what's more," continued the governor, "this tradition isn't vague and general, but it's direct and specific. It points to some one place there,—one of those islands in particular that is distinguished from all the other islands. I don't know the name of it; I don't know that I ever heard it; but I do know that there is such an island,—one of those three hundred and sixty-five, that is pointed out and well known as the place frequented by the buccaneers. Everybody says, that on this island they lived, and that in this island, deep down,—under the level of the sea, in fact,—the buccaneers buried the plunder of the Spanish Main.

"Of course, as I said, they don't speak of the buccaneers, but of Captain Kidd. They call it Kidd's treasure. But it's all the same. The fact remains whatever changes mere names may undergo. Now, mind you, I don't say that there's any treasure there now,—it may have been all dug up by the very men who buried it, or by others who knew about it. It's a long time since it was buried, and Mahone Bay had no settlements for generations. At the same time it's quite probable that it may be there still; and I, for my part, shouldn't be a bit surprised to hear at any time that some lucky fellow has got hold of it all."

"I suppose you never went to Mahone Bay yourself," said Bart.

"Well, no," said the governor. "The fact is, I never thought much about it until lately, after the old galleon set me speculating about it; and then I remembered old things that I had heard. Go there?—O, no!—I'm too old. If I were a young man, without a family, I'd make a dash at it; but now it's impossible. I'd have to give up my situation. O, no! I dare say somebody'll make his fortune there one day; but that'll never be my luck. And as for treasure, I believe that there's lots of it deep under these sands, all about, if one only knew where to dig—but that's the difficulty.

"And so, you see, that's the conclusion I've come to—putting this and that together. This is a Spanish galleon. Here she is,—ever so far out of the course which the treasure ships of the Indies usually followed,— up here in these seas, in close proximity to the most notorious haunt of the old buccaneers. Do you suppose they had nothing to do with this? Of course they had—everything. In those days no ship in these waters could have escaped their eyes, much less a big Spanish ship full of gold and silver. Mark my words. As I said at first, they captured her, brought her here, unloaded her, buried her gold and her silver in Mahone Bay somewhere—on that island that I spoke of, and then let the ship go."

This notion of the governor's might have been critically examined and utterly disproved by a competent person; but for such a task the boys were too ignorant and inexperienced. The firm belief of the governor in his extraordinary theory affected every one of the boys most profoundly; nor could any of them see a reason why it should not be perfectly true in every particular. Every word that he had uttered sank deep into their souls, and every one of them felt himself filled with an irresistible desire to hurry off at once to Mahone Bay, and seek for the island where the buccaneers had buried the plunder of the Spanish Main.

On the present occasion they poured upon him a torrent of questions of all sorts, every one of which showed how attentively they had listened to his story, and how eager the curiosity was which they all felt. The governor answered everything with the minuteness and the exactness that characterize a man when he finds that his own particular hobby meets with respectful appreciation from others.

At length they turned back to the house, talking all the way about Spanish galleons, treasure ships, the buccaneers, gold, silver, diamonds, the Spanish Main, and the various haunts of the old marauders—subjects fascinating above all things to these boys, as they are to all boys, so fascinating indeed, that they were sorry when they came back to the house. Here, however, another pleasure awaited them, for the governor showed them the very gun that he had found on the old ship, and pointed with respectful pride to certain marks upon it. The gun was terribly rusty, and the marks had been so effaced that they were capable of being interpreted to mean anything; but the governor assured them that they were the escutcheon of the Royal House of Spain, and the boys believed it implicitly. Other and more critical inquirers would have asked what the governor meant by the arms of the Royal House of Spain, and inquired whether he meant the house of Arragon, or of Hapsburg, or of Bourbon. To the boys, however, such a question never occurred.

The water was still calm; but Sable Island is a place where no one can stay long. The governor therefore hurried up the venerable Corbet,—who, on this as on other occasions, seemed to give indications of a dilatory disposition,—and furnished him with some sails, which, with a little alteration, would suit the Antelope very well. Upon this Corbet returned in his boat to the schooner, carrying the sails with him, and one of the Sable Islanders to help him rig the sails. The boys were to be put aboard by the governor later in the day.

They then went off with their genial host to other parts of the island. This journey was made on ponies which had been broken, yet not so much but that they retained a very fair share of their original wildness. The riding was not very conducive to speed. All of the boys were thrown, but none of them were hurt on the sandy soil, and the governor made himself merry over their horsemanship. As to scenery, there was nothing different from what they had already encountered, except numerous wild fowl that frequented the lake.

By the time that they returned they saw the Antelope with her sails filled, and a boat drawn up on the beach to convey them aboard. The governor shook hands with them all most heartily on bidding them good by.

"Good by, my lads," said he. "I'm the most unhappy of men in one way. Although I keep shipwrecked guests an immense time, I dare not be hospitable to visitors. I would press you to stay all night, but I'm afraid to. If you had a better craft, and a better captain, I might venture to do it; but even then, it wouldn't be safe. As it is, it would be madness, and my only parting word to you is, to hurry away as fast as you can, and get away as for as possible from Sable Island."

The boys got on board; the sturdy Sable Islanders bent to their oars, and soon their vigorous strokes drove the boat far out to sea. But all the way the boys could see the little group on the shore watching them. On reaching the Antelope, they found all ready for a start. The Sable Islander who had accompanied Captain Corbet returned with his companions; and as the Antelope moved away, the flag of the B. O. W. C. went up and down rapidly, and three ringing cheers burst forth from the boys.

So ended their very remarkable and eventful visit to the most fearful and dangerous of all the islands of the sea. Few, indeed, are the vessels which, having drifted upon this perilous coast, are able to leave it so safely, and so pleasantly. For Sable Island generally surrounds itself with destroying terrors for those who chance upon it; and more than Anticosti, more, indeed, than any other place, deserves the dread name of—"the graveyard of ships and sailors."

In turning away, there was now but one thought in the minds of all the boys, and that was, of course, Mahone Bay. In any case they would sail straight for the coast of Nova Scotia; and Mahone Bay was the only place at which they were willing to land. There was now no further difficulty about making their way, for the governor, in addition to the sails, had furnished a compass also.

"The Nova Scotia coast," said Captain Corbet, "air doo north by west, an it ain't more'n a hundred mile. The wind's fair, an we ought to sight it before—well, before three days."

"O, we'll do it long before that," said Bart, "if this wind lasts. But why can't you head due west for Mahone Bay?"

"Wal," said Captain Corbet, "there air severial reasons why: fust an furmost, because, ef I sail west, I'll have to coast along this here shore, which is the very thing I don't want to do. I want to get as far away as I kin, an as quick as I kin. Second, I don't want to go in the dark no longer. I want to sight the Nova Scotia coast, and then to keep it in sight till I die. Never agin do I want to git out o' sight o' Nova Scotia. Then, third, I don't want to stop at no more places, but to contennew along my windin way, till I git to Minas. An, fourthly, I don't want to go to Mahone Bay at all."

"Not go to Mahone Bay!" cried Bruce. "Why not? Why, we want to hunt up that island that the buccaneers buried the treasure in."

Captain Corbet looked at all the boys with an expression of solemn regret, mingled with mild reproach upon his venerable face. Then shaking his head mournfully, he slowly ejaculated,—

"O, boys, boys!"

"Well, why not?" asked Tom.

"O, boys! O, boys!" continued the captain, in a dismal tone. "An has it come to this? Air this the end an the melankilly result of the bitter teachins that you've ben an had by sea an land?"

"Bitter teachings?" said Bart; "what bitter teachings?"

"The teachins, an the warnins, an the experiences," said Captain Corbet, "that's ben a heaped upon you's all. Why this thirst for perishable treasures? Why this yearnin for money-holes? Hain't you had enough of treasures, and dreams of wealth? Look at me, boys. Behold this wretched victuim of Avarice. Think how the demon of Avarice got possession of me in the Gulf of St. Lawrence, an drawed me away captive to his chariot wheels. Think how he tempted me to desert you, an leave you in tremenjous danger. Bar all this in mind, I humbly beg, and then desist. Say no more. Temp me not. Leave the aged Corbet be. Don't inflame this beaten heart. Be wise in time. You'll only suffer for it ef you don't. That thar treasure is onhallowed. Didn't we try diggin for buried treasures once afore? Answer me that. We did. An what was the result? I pause for a reply."

"O, but this is different," said Bart. "That money-hole on the hill was all nonsense; and, besides, what was it then frightened us, except a miserable little donkey? This is a different matter. There ought to be something there, out of all the plunder of the Spanish Main.

"Don't talk about plunder, and the Spanish Main," said the captain. "The way that that governor had of rollin out them words of his was somethin that made a man feel a tinglin all over. It's the thirst for gold, boys; don't kindle it up to a flame; don't temp me agin my better natur; don't, don't."

"O, see here now, captain," said Bart; "don't look at things in that way. When you left us on the ship, it wasn't Avarice; it was because you hadn't any idea that we were in danger."

Captain Corbet shook his head. "No," said he, "It was Avarice, the Demon of Gold—nothing else. It blinded my eye, an hardened my heart. It's the way it allus does."

"Well, I don't see how you can call it Avarice. You only wanted money for your baby—you know."

At the mention of his tender offspring, Captain Corbet's face changed; a mild and mellow light beamed in his aged eye, and a tender parental fondness was visible in the expression of his venerable face.

"Terew!" said he; "terew—as gospel!"

"Well, then, you must feel as anxious about him now as you were then. You failed that time; perhaps this time you'll succeed. And only think how jolly it would be, if you could make his fortune, and give him a college education."

At this crafty allusion to Captain Corbet's fondest hope, the aged navigator was overcome. His eyes became moistened with tears; a gentle sigh escaped him; he said no more, and all the boys saw that his silence meant consent.

The Antelope was heading towards the nearest point on the Nova Scotia shore. That shore lay almost north, or north by west, and it was about a hundred miles distant. The wind was fair; there was no prospect whatever of a change for the worse; and so the Antelope walked the waters, as usual, like a thing of life, while the boys amused themselves with recalling the strange story of the governor of Sable Island, and in speculating about the probable appearance of that island of the buccaneers, which, according to him, had been the deposit and the burial-place of the plunder of the Spanish Main.

The Antelope did her best. The wind was not very strong, yet it bore her along as fast as she was capable of going; no very great rate of speed, to be sure, yet fast enough to assure them, by sunset, that they were already far enough away from Sable Island to be out of the reach of danger; out of the grasp of its far-reaching arms, and in a pathway which brought them every moment nearer to a friendly shore.

V.

Land again.—A Line of Coast.—How to navigate.—Plans for finding the Island of Treasure.—The Bays.—The populous Island.—The old Man and his Ox Cart.—Ironbound.— Tancook.—The cautious Questions of Bruce.—An obtuse old Man.—A Confidence from Solomon.—A useless Search.—A Change of Policy.—How to find the Island.

The wind continued fair, and during the following night the Antelope kept on her course. On the following day, by noon, they came within sight of land, and the distant coast-line running along the horizon showed them now what course they should take. Captain Corbet now headed her a few points farther to the west.

"I'm all right now," said he. "Jest you let me see the Nova Scotia coast, and I'll foller it. Here we go now, an our motter air, On'ard an up'ard."

"Downward, rather than upward, is my motto," said Bart; "for I'm bound to get to the bottom of the treasure of the buccaneers. At any rate we ought to find out the truth about it; for the saying is, that truth lies at the bottom of a well, and a money-hole isn't very far different."

"Do you think you can manage to find Mahone Bay, captain?" asked Bruce, with a very natural doubt about Captain Corbet's capacity to find his way to a strange place.

"Wal," said he, "'pears to me easy enough, with this here coast-line to guide us. You see all we've got to do is, to keep on along this here coast till we come to Halifax harbor. Wal, we don't go in thar, but keep straight on. Wal, the next place is Margaret's Bay. That's easy enough; and then the next place is Mahone Bay. So you see it's so plain that a child might guide his tender canoe in safety to such a place as that."

"O, I dare say we'll work our way sooner or later to Mahone Bay," said Phil; "but what we are to do after we get there is a thing which, I confess, puzzles me a little."

"O, we'll hunt about for the island," said Bart.

"Hunt about?" said Phil. "But how can we find it? Shall we ask people?"

"O, no," said Bruce; "that would never do. It wouldn't do at all to let a single soul know what we are after. They'd all follow us, and interfere with us. No; we've got to be very cautious."

"That's a fact," said Tom; "we must keep dark."

"O, I dare say," said Phil; "but how can we find the island?"

"O, we'll hunt it up," said Bart.

"But how can we tell it from Adam, or from any other island?"

"Sure an that's aisy enough," said Pat. "We're lookin for an island that's got a hole inside of it; an if there's a hole, sure we'll know it by the heap it makes."

"At any rate," said Arthur, "we can look about, and if we can't find any marks to guide us, why, then we can make inquiries among the people."

With such vague plans as these, then, the boys looked forward to Mahone Bay, feeling that it was necessary to keep their purpose a profound secret, and yet not knowing how to find the island. They were unwilling to betray their errand by asking questions, and yet without asking how could they hope to learn anything? This was a difficulty which they all felt, and in the presence of it they could only conclude to be guided by circumstances.

A few days passed and the Antelope reached the entrance to Halifax harbor, which the bold captain recognized, not by any knowledge of his own, for he had never been here before; not by any chart or observation, for he did not own the former, and had not made the latter; but simply from seeing a steamer go up into the land towards a place where the sky was black with the smoke of bituminous coal. When he saw that, he said, "This is Halifax;" and, saying this, he felt secure of his position, and kept the vessel on due west.

It was morning when they passed Halifax. By noon they passed a broad bay, which they decided to be Margaret's Bay. By evening they had reached another broad bay. At its mouth, and well out in the ocean, lay an island, with black and rocky sides, and wooded top. On sailing inside of this, they noticed that it was inhabited, and from this point of view showed houses and farms. A few miles farther on was another island, which was cultivated from one end to the other, and appeared to be thickly populated. Farther on there appeared other islands, and wooded shores, and cultivated fields, and high hills.

This, they felt sure, was their destination—Mahone Bay. The Antelope passed inside of the second island, and here dropped anchor.

It was yet more than an hour before sundown, and the boys went ashore upon the island nearest to make inquiries, not about the plunder of the Spanish Main, but merely of a general nature. The island was thickly inhabited, and on walking a short distance from the beach where they had left their boat, they found a road which seemed well travelled, and appeared to run from one end of the island to the other. In a little while an old man came along on an ox-cart, who bowed with a good-natured smile, and remarked that it was a fine evening. To this they assented.

"What's the name of this island?" asked Bruce.

Upon being thus questioned, the old man stopped his oxen, and, looking around upon the young faces before him, he said,—

"What?"

"What's the name of this island?"

"Tancook," said the old man.

"Tancook?" repeated Bruce; "and what's the name of that other one?"—pointing to the outer island, which they had first encountered.

"That thar?" said the old man, looking where Bruce pointed,—"that thar? Why, we call that thar island by the name of Ironbound.",

It was a fine name, a sonorous and at the same time an appropriate name, and deeply impressed the boys.

"Fine farming country this," said Bruce, once more plunging into the conversation.

"Wal, pooty so so," said the old man. "We ain't got no reason to complain; though, what with diphthery, an sich, it's mighty hard on children."

"A good many people here, apparently," continued Bruce, in a lively key.

"Wal, pooty tol'ble," said the old man; "'bout a hundred families on this here."

"Farmers or fishermen?" asked Bruce.

"Wal, a leetle of the one, an a leetle of the tother."

"You've got a church here too," continued Bruce.

"Yas—a meetin-house."

"What persuasion is that meeting-house?" asked Bruce, in an anxious tone of voice, as though the fortunes of the whole party depended on the answer.

"Wal, mostly Baptist," said the old man, "though not all. Were kine o' cut off, an live mostly to ourselves. But Tancook ain't sich a bad place, arter all, and we manage to grub along."

"It's a fine bay around here," said Bruce, with a grand, patronizing sweep of his right arm, which seemed meant to include all creation.

"Yas," said the old man; "there ain't nothin like it nowhar. We've got three hundred and sixty-five islands, of all shapes an sizes, in this here bay—one for every day in the year. This here's the biggest, an the smallest isn't more than a yard long. Yas, it's a fine bay, an a great harbor."

"Three hundred and sixty-five islands!" exclaimed Bruce, in a tone of surprise. "Is it possible? And one for every day in the year! How extraordinary! But is there really that exact number, or is it only fancy?"

"Really an truly," said the old man, with whom this was evidently the deepest conviction of his mind. "O, yas, thar's no mistake or doubt about it. They've all been counted, over an over; yas, over an over—over an over."

"It's very strange," said Bruce. "It's most extraordinary; and now I dare say," he continued, in an insinuating way, "I dare say that, among so many islands, some of them are well worth a visit. This island of yours is a perfect wonder—so fertile, so beautiful! Are there any others that are like this?"

"Wal, not to say jest like this; but they're fine islands, many of them, an curous, too. Thar's some that's only islands at high tide, bein connected with the main land by narrer beaches an shoals at low tide; an then, agin, thar's others that's only islands at low tide, bein completely kivered up by the water at high tide; and so it goes; an some's cleared an inhabited, like this; an some's wild, an kivered with woods; an some has only one family on it; an some's cultivated, but has no one livin on them; an so we've got all sorts, you see, an they're all well wuth visitin. Thar's Dead Man's Island, an Quaker Island, an Oak Island, an Maple Island, an Ironbound;" and the old man went on to enumerate dozens of names in addition to these, out of which no individual one made any impression on the minds of his hearers.

Thus far Bruce had been questioning the old man chiefly with the hope that he might drop some remark which might be of use to them in their search after the treasure island. But no such remark was forthcoming, and the string of names which was enumerated conveyed no information whatever. So Bruce made one more effort, and ventured to come a little more to the point.

"This bay," said he, "has been a great place for buccaneers—so I've heard. Do you know anything about them? Can you tell me of any island in particular that people talk of as being visited by them? There's one, I think, that the buccaneers used to visit. Perhaps you've heard about them, and can tell us the name of the island, and where it is."

Now, this was pretty direct; indeed, all the other boys thought that it was altogether too direct, especially since they had all concluded that it was best not to ask any questions, except those of a general character. Bart and Tom both nudged Bruce very violently, to rebuke his rashness; but their nudges had no effect.

The old man stared, then frowned, then looked blank, and then frowned again. Then he looked at Bruce, and said, in an uncertain, hesitating way,—

"Bucker nears?"

"Yes," said Bruce. "Buccaneers. They used to come here, you know. Lots of them."

The old man wagged his old head up and down several times.

"O, yas; I dar say. Buccar nears—an lots of other fish, that's left us. They used to come here in shoals—likewise mackerel; but them days is over. Sometimes shad an her'n comes here now; but things ain't as they used to be, an it's gittin harder an harder every year for us fishermen. It's as much as a man can do, with farmin and fishin together, to find bread an butter for himself an his children. As to them—buck—buck—buckfish, I don't know. I don't mind ever hearin of them, leastways not under that thar name. P'raps they're a kine' o' mackerel; an I only wish they'd come now, as they used to when I was young."

At this extraordinary misapprehension of his meaning, Bruce stared, and seemed, for a moment, about to explain himself; but the other boys checked him, and the old man himself seemed to become suddenly lost in his remembrances of those days of youth, which might never be equalled now.

"Won't you jump in, an take a ride?" said he, at length. "Air you goin my way? Ef so, you may as well git a lift as not."

The boys thanked him, and excused themselves. They were not going his way, but in another direction. A few more words passed, and at length the old man bade them good by, whistled up his oxen, and moved forward. As for the boys, they did not feel inclined to pursue their investigations any further just then.

"The next time we ask," said Tom, "we'll have to talk about Captain Kidd, plump and plain, and then perhaps they'll understand."

"Well," said Bart, "I don't see what use there is in proclaiming to the whole world our business. We'd better cruise about for a while, and examine for ourselves."

"O, well," said Bruce, "there's nothing like dropping a quiet hint, interrogatively. It may bear fruit in the shape of useful information."

"Like the old man's information about the buccaneer mackerel," said Tom, with a laugh.

Bruce deigned no reply. They waited here a little longer, and, after strolling about some distance farther, they went back to the boat, and returned to the Antelope.

That evening Solomon addressed himself to Bart, secretly and in confidence, as the latter happened to be sitting on the windlass, trying to concoct some plan by which they might find the mysterious island that contained the buried treasure of the buccaneers,—the wonderful, the stupendous, the incalculable plunder of the Spanish Main. To him, thus meditating, cogitating, and reflecting, the aged Solomon thus addressed himself:—

"What's all dis yar new 'posal, Mas'r Bart, 'bout buried treasures, an tings? 'Pears to me youn all goin mad, an rushin head fo'most into de jaws ob 'structium. Better look out, I say. Dars no knowin whar dis yar's goin to end. Dem dar pirates' ghosts keep allus a flyin an a flittin roun de place whar dey bury de treasure, and it'll take more'n you boys to tar dat ar plunder out of deir keepin. Dis yar scursion 'bout dis yar bay ain't goin to end in no good. Dar ain't a succumstance dat kin favor you; eberyting's clean agin you; an if you fine' de hole whar de treasure's buried, it'll only bring roonatium an 'structium."

"Solomon," said Bart, "my aged, venerable, and revered friend, I am deeply pained at this exhibition of superstition in one who ought to have a soul above ghosts. A man like you, Solomon, who has real evils to suffer, who is afflicted by such real calamities as rheumatism, and what you call "broomatism," ought to have a soul above ghosts. Isn't it enough for you to live in perpetual terror about the reappearance of that Gorgon who calls you husband, and beats you over the head with a poker, that you must take the trouble to get up a new set of afflictions, and trot out your superstitious fancies."

"Mas'r Bart," said Solomon, earnestly, "look heah; dis yar ain't no common 'currence. Dar's death an roonatium afore us all. You're goin to 'sturb de 'pose ob de dead—an de worst sort ob dead. Dem's de sort dat won't stand no nonsense. I've had 'nough ob money-holes, an diggin in em, for my time. De ghost ob a dead pirate ain't to be laughed at. Dey'll hab vengeance—sure's you're born. Dar's no sort ob use in temptin fate. Sure's you go down into dat ar money-hole, so sure you hab down on your shoulders de ghosts ob all de pirates dat eber was hung, an dem dat was unhung, too. So, Mas'r Bart, don't you go foolin round here dis yar way. I'se a ole man, Mas'r Bart, an I'se seen much ob de world, an I 'vise you to clar out, an not temp de ghosts ob de pirates in dis yar fashium."

Solomon's warning was sincere, and was spoken with the utmost earnestness; but Bart was quite inaccessible to sincerity and earnestness. He laughed at Solomon's fears, reminded him of his foolish behavior on former occasions, brought to his memory the time when he had fled from the braying of an ass, and the other occasion when he had fled from the hoot of an owl. But, though Solomon could not help owning that he had acted on those occasions with shameful cowardice and folly, yet the consciousness of this could not lessen in the slightest degree the superstitious terrors that now filled his breast; and so, as Bart found him incorrigible, he had to give up the effort to calm his mind.

That night all on board slept more soundly than they had for weeks. The Antelope was anchored in smooth water, in a secure and sheltered harbor, near a friendly land, and no care whatever was in the minds of the boys, or of the captain. Such perfect freedom from anxiety had not been their lot for a long time; and in proportion to this peace of mind was the profoundness of their sleep.

On the following day they cruised all about the bay, keeping ever on the lookout for the Island of the Buccaneers. But they soon found that the search was hopeless under the conditions which they had imposed upon themselves. To seek for what is unknown, and not ask for directions, is surely one of the most impracticable of tasks. The experience which they had thus far had was enough, and they found themselves compelled either to give up the search altogether, or else to break through the secrecy which they had imposed upon themselves.

VI.

*The Cruise around the Bay.—A quaint and curious Town.—
Sleepy Hollow.—A home-like Inn.—A genial and communicative
Landlord.—A delicate Manipulation.—Aspotogon and Deep
Cove.—Bart enters into an Argument.—The Landlord plunges
into the Subject of Captain Kidd.—A wonderful Revelation.—
The Treasure of the Seas at last.—The Island of golden Store.*

The cruise around Mahone Bay had thus proved useless, as might have been expected. The search after one island out of hundreds, where the appearance, and even the name, of that island were unknown to them, was certainly an extraordinary piece of folly. Had they allowed themselves to make direct inquiries, they could have found the island without any trouble. But this was the very thing which they were unwilling to do; partly, as has been said, from the fear of drawing attention to their proceedings, and of being interrupted or interfered with in some way; but partly, no doubt, because they found a much greater charm in movements which were thus surrounded by mystery. It was appropriate for the members of the great secret society of the B. O. W. C. to enter upon this new undertaking in secrecy.

But now this had to be given up, and they concluded to go ashore at the chief settlement of the bay, and make inquiries. In these inquiries they resolved still to maintain their secret as far as possible, and not to divulge it unless it was absolutely necessary; they determined to hint, rather than ask, and obtain information indirectly, rather than directly.

The chief settlement of Mahone Bay is the town of Chester, one of the greatest curiosities in America. It is not a settlement. It is a town. It is situated on a peninsula, with a harbor on its front and on its rear. This peninsula is all laid out in streets, which cross one another at right angles, with perfect regularity. At the point where the peninsula terminates, is a spacious place, intended to serve as a promenade; and here there is a narrow shoal running off to another piece of land, which is a peninsula or an island by turns, as the shoal is covered or uncovered by the water.

There is a wonderful quaintness and quiet in Chester. It is the Nova Scotian representative of Sleepy Hollow. The streets, which are so nicely laid out, are all covered with turf, and are as green as the town lots on either side. The houses are all old; the people are all quiet and leisurely, taking the world in the easiest manner possible. The very dogs, affected by the peace and calm around, seem unwilling to bark, except under the strongest possible provocation.

The scenery around this quaint little town may safely be classed among the most beautiful in the world. The wide bay, with its hundreds of islands, forms an almost unequalled place for yachting. Many of the islands have curious names, associated with some curious legend. The waters abound with myriads of shell fish, and sometimes have a marvellous transparency. The winding shore of the bay forms one of the loveliest of drives, and affords perpetual variety of scenery; and the climate in summer time is so genial, that it forms the perfection of a watering-place for those who have to fly from the heat of southern latitudes. And this will one day be the destiny of Chester, when the world knows it; when the rush of parched travellers takes place; when great hotels face its promenade, and the streets, once laid out with so bold a design, are lined with houses and shops. Such changes will one day take place; but whether Chester will be then so altogether lovely as it is now in its Sleepy Hollow epoch, is a matter about which there may well be doubt.

Such was the place, then, in which the boys found themselves; and they all agreed with one opinion, that Chester was, in every respect, worthy of standing here in this lovely bay, in the immediate vicinity of the mysterious Island of the Buccaneers; where lay stored up the treasure of the sea and the plunder of the Spanish Main.

On looking about the place, they came to an inn, which had such an air of comfort and tranquillity, and such a home-like appearance, that they determined to put up at it, and prosecute their investigations in a leisurely fashion. They arrived in time for dinner; and, if there had been any doubt in their minds as to the propriety of deserting the Antelope, it was dispelled at the appearance of the dinner which was served up. For there were salmon and green peas,—delicacies of which, like all good boys, they were particularly fond, and to which they had been strangers for a long time. There, too, were strawberries, the last of the season, with cream of the richest kind; and together with these were the mealiest of potatoes, the whitest of bread, the freshest of butter, and the most immaculate coffee. To all these things their late sea fare afforded a striking contrast, and Solomon's star declined sadly.

The landlord they found most good-natured, and most genial, like all the inhabitants of this favored spot. He was communicative about himself, proud of his town, proud of the scenery around, and yet not at all inquisitive as to the purposes of his guests. This seemed to them to be the very man whom they might interrogate without endangering their secret; for, while his communicativeness would lead him to tell everything that there was to be told, his lack of curiosity would prevent him from asking any unpleasant questions.

Accordingly, as soon as they could get a convenient chance, they button-holed the landlord, and began a series of questions of a very non-committal character, referring chiefly to the scenery of Mahone Bay, and the places most worthy of a visit. They did not make the remotest reference to the buccaneers or to Captain Kidd, but seemed to have their thoughts occupied with scenery only.

The landlord grew eloquent upon the theme of the scenery of Mahone Bay. He told them about the islands, and mentioned the number very particularly, insisting upon it that their number was exactly three hundred and sixty-five. He spoke of the drive along the shore, of a place called Gold River, where there was excellent fishing, and finally mentioned a place which he called Aspotogon. Upon this theme he grew more enthusiastic than ever. Aspotogon, he said, was the highest mountain on the Atlantic coast of Nova Scotia, and the approach to it afforded a view of the most remarkable scenery in the whole bay. This approach lay through a narrow inlet which ran to the base of the mountain, and was called Deep Cove. It was bordered by precipices, for a long way, on either side, and was a wild and romantic spot. It terminated in a circular basin, on one side of which was a deep declivity, by which they could find the shortest ascent to the summit of Aspotogon; and, in addition to this, they could find fishing and bathing to their hearts' content.

In all this, however, there was no mention made of any island like the one which they wished to find. He mentioned, indeed, the names of several islands, in a casual sort of way, but made no allusion to any legends of the buccaneers. The only reference which he made to treasure, was on the name of that fishing stream which he had described to them. This was Gold River; and the name excited their attention. Bart asked what the name had reference to; and the landlord replied, that it arose from the color of its water. This commonplace derivation of such a name disgusted and disappointed them all, for they hoped to hear of a different origin, and one more in accordance with their present purpose.

The landlord dwelt to a great extent on Aspotogon and Deep Cove, and finally offered to go there with them, if they felt inclined to make a visit to the place. Though the boys were still as eager as ever about the Island of the Buccaneers, yet they were by no means indifferent to the charms of a romantic place like this, nor at all disinclined to roam about the bay farther. The offer of the landlord was also an additional inducement, and they thought that in the intimacy of shipboard they might manage to get something more direct out of him, and learn from him all that there was to be learnt about any existing legends current among the people, such as the governor of Sable Island had mentioned. It was arranged, therefore, that they should go on the following day.

After dinner the boys started off in different directions. Bruce in a boat, Arthur along the shore, Tom and Phil over the hills, while Bart and Pat sauntered about the wharves, catching star-fish, sea-urchins, and jelly-fish, of which there were myriads. Towards evening they returned to the inn, and found the landlord seated on the steps. They seated themselves too, and gradually fell into a conversation.

"This bay must have been a great place in old times," said Bart, trying to feel his way as easily as possible towards the subject of the buccaneers.

The landlord shook his head with solemn emphasis.

"Tre—mendous!" he slowly ejaculated.

"Such a capital place for hiding from any ship that might be chasing!" said Bart; "so many islands! Why, if a ship once got in here, she could never be found."

"Best dodging-place in the world," said the landlord. "Lots of islands, lots of harbors, and deep water too, everywhere."

"The old French days must have been pretty exciting hereabouts," continued Bart, making a fresh advance. "The English and French used to have it hot and heavy; and I dare say this bay had its share of the fun."

"Of course, of course," said the landlord; "and before that too, long before; and worse goings on than fair, stand-up fights. There's been queer doings in these waters."

To these words the landlord gave emphasis by a significant shake of his head, which spoke unutterable things, and drove Bart and Pat wild with curiosity.

"What do you mean?" asked Bart.

The landlord looked at him solemnly for a few moments, and then asked,—

"Did you ever happen to hear of Captain Kidd?"

"Captain Kidd?" repeated Bart, in innocent wonder, "Captain Kidd? Hear of him? Of course I've heard of him. Everybody knows about him."

"Well, if that man's ghost don't haunt this bay, then I'm a nigger."

"Haunt this bay? What do you mean? What had Captain Kidd to do with this bay? He was hanged at London."

"He had a precious lot to do with this bay," said the landlord, positively. "Why, I don't see how that could be," said Bart, trying to get the landlord excited by contradiction. "I don't see how he ever could have been here. His story's a simple enough one; soon told. I've heard it often. How he went from New York to London well recommended, and got a commission from the British government to command a ship, for the purpose of putting down pirates in India and the East. But this didn't suit him quite; so he turned pirate himself. Most of his piracies took place in the East, though. It's true he returned to America, and made a great panic; but he was captured and sent to England, where he was tried and executed. That was in 1699. I remember the date very well. So I don't see how he could have done much about here."

Bart spoke very volubly, and seemed to have the Life of Captain Kidd at his tongue's end. The landlord listened very attentively. But Bart's words, instead of shaking his own convictions, only served, as Bart had hoped and intended, to strengthen and confirm them. As Bart spoke, he raised himself up out of the lounging attitude in which he had been sitting, looked full in Bart's face, and as he ceased,—

"Very well. Grant all that," said the landlord, with a comprehensive sweep of his hand, which seemed to concede every single statement that Bart had made, in the fullest and frankest manner. "Grant—all—that— every word of it. I don't doubt it at all—not me. Very well. Now mark me. Captain Kidd did really, and truly, and actually, flourish about here, in this here bay—for he's left behind him the most—un—mis—tak— able in—di—ca—tions. I've seen 'em myself, with my own eyes. I've handled 'em myself, and with my own hands. And besides, that there pirate must have been about over the coast of America a good deal more than you give him credit for, or he wouldn't have left a name behind, from one end of America to the other; and, at any rate, he must have been here, or else he wouldn't have left behind what he has left, and what I've seen with my own eyes."

"I didn't know," said Bart, "that he had left any traces of himself here. What are they? What kind of traces?"

"What kind of traces?" said the landlord. "Traces that beat everything in the way of traces that any pirate ever made. What do you say, for instance, to a pit so deep that nobody's ever been able to get to the bottom of it?"

"A pit? What sort of a pit?" asked Bart, full of excitement.

"What do you say to his filling that pit with oaken chests, crammed full of gold and silver ingots, and gold candlesticks, plundered from Catholic churches, and precious stones, such as diamonds, rubies, and emeralds—beyond all counting?"

"Gold! silver! precious stones!" repeated Bart, who was so overcome by this astounding information, that he could only utter these words.

"What do you say to his taking the prisoners that had dug his hole, and filled it, and killing them all, to keep his secret?"

"Killing his prisoners!"

"What do you say," continued the landlord, enjoying with keenest relish the evident excitement of Bart,—"what do you say to his contriving the most extraordinary plans ever heard of to prevent anybody ever getting at that treasure,—by making the hole, in the first place, far down

40 | JAMES DE MILLE

under the level of the sea,—by building a drain, so as to let in the sea water; and then, after killing the prisoners, filling up the hole to the very top? What do you say to all that?"

"Why, I never heard of this in all my life! How do you know it? Tell me, now. Tell me all about it. Where is the place? Is it here—in this bay?"

"Of course it is. I've said as much," replied the landlord.

"But you didn't mention it this morning."

"No, because you only wanted to hear about fine scenery. This place isn't particularly remarkable for that. It's a little island, not more than three miles from here, up that way to the right. It's called Oak Island, because Captain Kidd planted it with acorns, so as to know it when he came back. Well, since his day, the acorns have grown to be oaks—some of them pretty big—though being near the sea, they haven't grown so big as they would have done if they had been planted farther inland."

"Oak Island!" repeated Bart, in a tone which expressed the most profound interest,—"Oak Island!"

"That's the place," said the landlord. "I wonder you ain't heard of Oak Island before."

"Never," said Bart; "that is, I've heard the name mentioned; but never knew that Captain Kidd had anything to do with it."

"That's just what he had," said the landlord. "Everybody in these parts can tell you all about it. People have been full of it ever since Chester was settled. I've heard it all my life."

"But if there's money there, why don't they get it?" asked Bart.

"Because they can't!"

"Can't?"

"No, can't. Captain Kidd knowed what he was about, and he made his arrangements so that, from that day to this, nobody's ever been able to get down to the bottom of that money-hole, and, in my humble opinion, never will."

"Why not? I don't understand."

"Well," said the landlord, "it's a long story; but as I've got nothing to do just now, I don't mind telling you about it."

So saying, the landlord settled himself into an easy, lounging attitude, and began the story of Oak Island.

VII.

The wonderful Story of Oak Island.—The Circle in the Forest.—Digging for Gold.—Exciting Discoveries.—Far down in the Depths of the Earth.—The Treasure touched at last.—The Treasure snatched away.—A new Search, and its Results.—Boring through the Chest of Gold.—A Company.—A new Pit made.—The Drain.—New Efforts.—The Coffer Dam.—New Companies.—Captain Kidd too much for them.

"I believe" said the landlord, "there's always been a talk, among the people around here, that Captain Kidd used this place as a kind of head-quarters; and this idea seems to me to have come down from old settlers who might have been here in his own day,—French and others,—though Chester wasn't actually settled till long after his time. At any rate, there it was, and everybody used always to believe that Captain Kidd hid his money somewhere in this bay. Well, nothing very particular happened till some sixty years ago, when a man, on visiting Oak Island, just by chance saw something which seemed to him very curious.

"The island was overgrown with oaks and other trees intermixed. Now, right in the midst of these trees, he came to a queer-looking place. It was circular, and about fifteen feet in diameter. Trees grew all around it. Just on this circular spot, however, nothing grew at all. not even moss or ferns. It looked as if it had been cursed, or blasted. The trees were all around it—some oak and some maple; but among them was one,—pine or spruce, I don't know which,—and this one looked a good deal older than the others. One of the boughs of this old pine tree projected right over the blasted circular spot in a very singular fashion, and on this the man noticed something that looked like very queer growth for a pine tree. He climbed up, and found that it was a pulley, which was so rotten that it might have been hanging there a hundred years. It was fastened to the bough by a chain, and this was so rusty that it broke in his hands. This pulley and rusty chain the man removed and took with him.

"Of course, as you may imagine, he was a good deal struck by the appearance of things. He had always heard that Captain Kidd had once frequented Mahone Bay, and had buried treasure somewhere about; and here he had discovered this blasted spot with a pulley over it, in the very midst of the woods on a lonely island—a place that looked as though no one had ever been there but himself since that pulley was last used. Of course he asked himself what the meaning of all this was; and to him it seemed most likely that the circular space marked some pit in the ground, and that the pulley had been used to lower things down into this pit.

"Well, he went home, and didn't say anything about it to a living soul, except his son, a young man, whom he wanted to help him. He determined to examine deeper, and after talking it over with his son, he was more determined than ever. So the very next day they began their preparations, taking over picks, and spades, and ropes, and provisions, and everything that could be needed for their purpose.

"They went to work and dug away for a little distance, when they came to something hard. It was a stone hewn,—not very smooth,—a kind of sandstone, and on this they saw some marks that looked like strange letters. They were ignorant men, but they knew the alphabet, and they knew that this was no kind of English letters at all; but it seemed to them that they might be letters of some strange alphabet. They took this stone away, and it's been preserved ever since, and it's there yet on the island, built into the wall of a cottage there for safe keeping. I've seen it myself dozens of times. That's what I mean when I say I've seen the traces of Captain Kidd, for it's my solemn conviction that he cut that inscription on the stone in some foreign letters, or perhaps in some secret cipher.

"After taking out that stone, they went on digging harder than ever, and about two feet down they came to a sort of wooden flooring. The wood was in good preservation, and consisted of large logs, a dozen feet long, laid across side by side, and rough-hewed about six inches square. They thought that they had come to the money-hole now, for sure, and pulled up the logs quick enough, you'd better believe; but they didn't know what was before them. After taking up the beams, they found they had to dig deeper; and so they went on digging away deeper and deeper. It took a long time, for they had to stay up the earth as they dug down, to prevent it from falling in, and they soon found that the job was a bigger one than they had bargained for; but what they had already found excited them, and cheered them on day after day.

"Of course they couldn't do this all in one day. One day's work couldn't take them far into that hole, though they worked like beavers. Well, they dug on this way, and at last, about five or six feet farther down,—some say ten; but it don't make any difference,—they found another flooring just like the first, only the logs were smaller. These they took up, and then went on digging as before, day after day. They now found bits of things that looked favorable; they found cocoa husks, and West India grass, and bits of cane, all of which showed that the people who worked here must have had something to do with the West Indies and the Spanish Main. These things never grew in Nova Scotia. The had been brought here by the men that made the hole, and had got mixed up with the earth that they shovelled in. They also found shavings or chips made with tools. Well, about the same distance down that the second flooring had been from the first, they found a third flooring, which was just like the second.

"At this third flooring there was a fresh disappointment, just as there had been at the other two; but the very fact that there was this flooring encouraged them to go on, and so they continued to dig. After a time they came to another flooring, and continuing on, they came to another, and yet another; and at every place they had the same disappointment and encouragement. All the way they found the same signs, that the soil had once been turned up by people who had dealings with the Spanish Main, for the cocoa-nut husks and the West India grasses were mixed with the soil all the way. All the time they had to keep staying up the sides, and the deeper they went, the more careful they had to be, for the soil seemed loose and dangerous just here.

"Well, they worked this way for about three months, and at last had got ever so far down—I have heard some say that they got down as much as a hundred feet, and that would be about seventy feet below the level of the sea at low tide, for the island is only a small one, and doesn't rise more than twenty-five feet at the highest point. All the way down they had found the signs continuing, showing that diggers had been here before, and that the soil had been turned up. This it was that led them on to such a depth.

"Well, now it was down at this depth that they touched the treasure. It was evening, and quite dark down there. They had been digging all day, and were about to just knock off. The son, before going, took his crow-bar, and drove it with all his might into the ground. It was soft, loose, and gravelly just here, and the iron sank for about a foot into the soil, and struck something hard. Their attention was attracted by this at once, and they tried it again and again. Each time it struck something hard. It seemed like wood. At one or two places it seemed like metal. They tried this a good many times, until at length they became convinced that this was a wooden box with iron hoops or fastenings, and that this box contained the treasure for which they were searching. But by this time it was too late to do any more. To get at that chest would require a good day's work. To hoist it up would not be possible. They saw that they would have to break or cut into it as it lay, and empty it of its contents. They were also worn out with their long day's work, and in addition to this, they did not feel comfortable down in that particular place after dark. So, for all these reasons, they concluded to postpone the completion of their work till the following day. After all, there was no reason why they shouldn't. No one could come and take it. It would be there unmoved till they might want to remove it themselves. And so the long and the short of it is, they went up, and went off to sleep in the hut where they lived.

"That night they slept soundly, and waked a little later than usual on the following day. They at once rushed to the money-hole; they did this the moment they waked, without waiting for breakfast, or taking anything to eat. They both felt anxious, for everything was at stake, and the sleep of both, though sound, had been marked by unpleasant and harassing dreams.

"Well, they reached the place, and there an awful sight met them—a sight that meant ruination to their hopes, and to all the hard work that they'd put forth in that place. The hole was gone; the earth had all fallen in; the stays had all given way; and there was nothing there now but a basin-shaped hollow, and bits of board projecting. What was worse, it was all mixed with water, and so soft, that in attempting to walk into it, they sank up to their knees in the mud. And that was the end of this first digging after Kidd's treasure; for though they tried to dig again, they found it impossible on account of the water. It seemed to come straight from the sea, and they couldn't do anything at all. So they had to give up at last, and go home.

"Now, some people think that the staying wasn't strong enough, and the sides caved in on that account; others, again, talk about Kidd's ghost baffling these diggers; but, from what was discovered afterwards, I feel perfectly sure that they themselves somehow let in the water of the sea into the hole by a drain or channel underground that Kidd himself had made. I think those knocks on the chest with the crowbar loosened some stopper, and the water poured in at once. It was this rush of sea water that destroyed everything, and made the hole cave in altogether. As to the drain, that was a contrivance of Kidd's to prevent the treasure from being dug up by outsiders. He had it made underground from the shore of the island at low-water mark to the bottom of the money-hole. He himself, or any one in the secret, would know how to dig and get the treasure; but any one who didn't know the secret would be sure to do something that would let in the sea water. And that's just what these first diggers did.

"Well, after this nothing was done for a long time. These two, father and son, went home, and for a while they kept the whole business a secret; but after some years the old man died, and the son married, and so the whole story leaked out, till everybody knew all about it. Everybody went then to see the place, and the story soon got to be as well known as the alphabet all over the bay; and I won't swear but that some additions were made to the story as it passed from mouth to mouth, for that would only be natural, after all; but at any rate, that story lived, and people didn't forget the treasure on Oak Island. And so time passed, and the son died at last, and the grandson grew up, and this one thought that he would make a dash at the treasure. This was as much as forty years after the first digging. He went with a few friends, and they tried to dig, but couldn't. The money-hole remained as it had been left by the first diggers,—all sand; and gravel, and water,—more like a quicksand than anything else. They put a pump in it, and set it to work, but couldn't do anything that way. So they gave it up.

"Well, these operations got known everywhere, and the whole story came up again. A lot of men formed themselves into a company, the grandson was one of them. They bought the island, and resolved to go to work on a grand scale. They rigged a pump which was worked by a horse in a very peculiar fashion, and had a hoisting apparatus worked by another horse to lift up the dirt. They got a lot of wood on the place for stayings to the hole, and went to work. Before they began, they bored down for a hundred and twenty feet. On taking out the auger, they saw on the lowest part scraps of wood, then bright scrapings that looked like gold, then wood again. And this showed that the auger had gone clean through the chest, and had brought back signs of the chest itself, and of the treasure inside. This created the greatest excitement, and the company went to work as eagerly and as industriously as the original diggers. Well, they kept at it, and dug, and hoisted, and pumped for a whole summer; but it was no go. As fast as they pumped, the water poured in, and faster too; and in fact, they couldn't make the slightest impression on the water in the money-hole, do what they would. So they gave up.

"Well, after this, another company started. The new company bought out from the old all its rights, and started on a new plan. Many of the old company belonged to the new one, and these had learned by experience the impossibility of doing anything by digging in the money-hole itself. The new plan consisted in digging a new hole altogether. In the operations of the old company they had discovered that though the money-hole was all sand and gravel, yet all around it the soil was a hard blue clay, quite impervious to water, and very easy to work in. They thought by digging alongside the money-hole, as near as the clay would allow, they might go down to the same depth, and then tunnel along at the bottom till they reached the treasure chest. So they went to work about thirty feet away from the money-hole, digging in the clay. They had no trouble in digging. The soil was free from stones, firm clay, impervious to water, and they made first-rate progress to a certain extent. They got down about a hundred feet, and then ventured to tunnel towards the money-hole. They worked very carefully, for it was rather dangerous, as they were under the level of the sea, and were therefore exposed to a rush of water at any false movement that they might make. But in spite of all their care, they failed at last; for one day they went up to dinner, and on going back again, they found the new hole filled with water to within thirty feet or so of the top. It was a sore disappointment, and they could only console themselves by the thought that they had been so fortunate as to have left the hole at that particular time. They tried to pump out the water, and made some faint efforts to continue their work, but it was no use. The failure had been too great, and this attempt broke down.

"Well, they now concluded that there was a drain,—the same one I spoke of a while ago,—reaching from the shore of the island at low-water mark, or beneath it, down to the bottom of the money-hole, and that they had somehow broken into this drain, the waters of which had poured into the new hole, and flooded it. This discovery created fresh excitement; and as this company gave up, a new one was formed, which bought out all previous rights, and on the following summer proceeded to make a fresh attempt. Each one of these companies which had been bought out still retained, however, a claim on the profits that might be made; sometimes twenty per cent. and sometimes ten per cent. of the treasure. The new company, even if it had succeeded, could only have received about one fifth, or perhaps one fourth, of the treasure, the rest being all forfeited, or mortgaged, so to speak, to the old companies. Still the new company had many members who belonged to the old companies, and who still stuck to the enterprise through thick and thin, so that their undertaking, under such circumstances, is not so surprising, after all.

"This new company, using the experience and discoveries of the preceding ones, went on a new principle. The idea now was, that, first of all, the drain should be discovered, and the supply of water intercepted. If this were done, they would be able to get to the bottom of the original money-hole itself without any trouble. So they set to work, and explored the whole shore of the island. They found one place where at low tide there was a great bubbling in the water, and this they took for the place where the drain began. Here they built a coffer dam, and then tried to find the drain itself. On the shore they met with no success; so they dug pits at intervals along a line stretching from the coffer dam to the money-hole. The soil in all these places consisted of that same tenacious blue clay which I have already mentioned. I don't know how many of these were dug, but there were several, at any rate. Now, whenever they attempted to strike the drain, the water was invariably too much for them, and rushed in, giving them nothing to do but to fly as fast as they could. In other places they were afraid to venture too near the drain. The end of it was, that this last company was as unsuccessful as the others, though it had spent ten times as much as any of them."

VIII.

The Toilers of the Sea.—New Efforts to find the Plunder of the Spanish Main.—Modern Science versus Captain Kidd.—The Landlord's Faith.—Scoffers and Mockers at the Money-hole.—Objections considered.—The Timber Floorings.—The Stone, with its mysterious Inscription.—The Gravel pit, with its Surroundings of blue Clay.—The Drain from the Sea to the Money-hole.

"So you see," said the landlord, "how all these efforts to get at the treasure have failed; and it is not difficult to see the reason, either. For, you see, as I have already said, the money-hole has been all filled in with sand and gravel, and there is a drain, or channel, connecting with the sea, which lets in the sea water; so, the moment any one undertakes to touch the money-hole, he has to contend with the sea itself, and there hasn't, thus far, been force enough put forth there to do that. The money-hole is something peculiar. All around it the soil is this blue clay. No doubt the soil where this was first dug was blue clay also; but, after burying the treasure, Kidd, for his own crafty purposes, filled it up with this gravel. No doubt his idea was, that the sea water should affect it the more thoroughly, and make it like a great quicksand. The pumps they set up there did no more good than if they were so many toys.

"Well, the failure of the last company has been followed by a pause, partly on account of discouragement, but still more from the determination, on the part of a few, to begin again on a grand scale; on a scale, indeed, so grand, that it will take some time to make all the preparations. Some of the leaders in the previous undertakings are at the head of this new movement, and have already done very much towards putting it into life and action. This new plan is to get up a regular joint stock company, with a thousand shares, each worth a hundred dollars, or thereabouts. It will be a regular company; the shares will be sold in the market, and the stockholders will stand in the same relation to this business as they would to a coal mine, or any other ordinary undertaking. They'll have a president, a board of directors, and a superintendent of the mining works. It is proposed to employ a regular engineer to survey the ground, and design the best mode of going to work; to put up a steam engine of sufficient power to pump out the money-hole, and keep a large force of men at work, night and day, in separate detachments. The idea is, to do it up as fast as possible, and get at it once for all, or fail utterly.

"Now, this company is already started, and about a quarter of the stock has been taken up. I shouldn't be surprised to see them set to work next year, or the year after, at the farthest. The thing is bound to go on. Besides those who believe that the treasure is here, there are ever so many who wish to see the mystery cleared up, irrespective of any treasure. These men are going into the new company almost as extensively as those who believe in the money. Then, again, there are ever so many people about the country who have heard about it for the first time, and are taking shares just as they would buy tickets in a lottery; not because they expect to make anything, exactly, but because they are willing to run the risk, and take their chance.

"This sort of thing, of course, has a far different prospect from what the old companies had. It puts the whole plan on a different footing. It makes it, in fact, a thoroughly legitimate business, and sets on as sound a basis as if it was an iron or coal mining company. A real, practical engineer—a man who is a practical geologist also—could tell more about Oak Island in one walk round it, than the other workers found out in years. He could find out the real place where the sea water enters; whether there is one only, or more than one. When once that is found out, and stopped, the rest is easy. But, if they can't stop it, why, then, let the steam pump go to work, and I don't think the money-hole would be flooded much longer. Then, again, the plan of having two gangs to work night and day, so as to have no stoppage in the operations, will be a most important thing. And so, what with modern science, and steam, and continuous work of large gangs, even old Kidd himself'll find his match.

"The fact is, the gold is there—the treasure of Captain Kidd—brought here by him, and buried in that hole. I no more doubt that than I doubt my own existence. If that hole had never been touched, and people went to work now at the fresh ground, I believe the treasure would be got at. Why, the first diggers almost got it, though there were only two of them. The gold is there—there's not the slightest doubt of that—a treasure beyond all estimate—worth millions on millions, no doubt—gold and silver ingots—the plunder of Spanish cathedrals and Spanish galleons—diamonds and rubies—and all that. Millions? Why, it's equal in value to the revenue of a great nation. There it is; and all it wants is for people to go to work in the right way; not in a pettifogging, mean, peddling fashion, but in a large-handed, bold, vigorous way. That's the thing that'll fetch up the plunder of the Spanish Main! I've sometimes heard people say that there was once a great confederacy of pirates that made this bay their headquarters, and that Captain Kidd was the last and greatest of the brotherhood. Until his time the plunder had been kept in a safe place, but in a place where it could be got at; but that he, being the last of the brotherhood, determined to fix up some safer place, and so he arranged this place—the hole and the drain; and if that's so, we have here not merely the plunder of Captain Kidd himself, but of all the pirates, for no one knows how long a time—centuries, I dare say."

To all this extraordinary story the boys had listened with the deepest attention. The landlord's announcement of his own belief in it was to them very impressive, and his extravagant conclusion did not seem at all extravagant to them. It accorded perfectly with what they had heard from the governor of Sable Island. They were most profoundly impressed, and the treasure island seemed to them more attractive than ever. The landlord's mind seemed to be filled with a vision of inconceivable treasure, and by long familiarity with the thought, it seemed quite natural to him to speak so glibly about gold, and silver, and precious stones, and all the rest that went to make up the plunder of the Spanish Main.

Bart and Pat were not critical; none of the boys were. This remark has already been made in connection with the story of the governor of Sable Island. Had they been critical, they could have picked various holes in this narrative, and asked questions to which it would have been difficult for the landlord, or any other believer in Kidd's treasure, to give any sufficient answer. They might have asked how it was that the tradition about the early diggers had been so minute, and why it was that no competent scholar or archæologist had been found who might decipher the inscription on the stone. They might have asked how it was that the so-called "drain" had been discovered, and also how it was that Kidd's so-called "place" was known so accurately. But they were not at all critically inclined, and the questions which they did ask were of a totally different kind.

They did ask questions, of course; and the questions referred to the chief points in the landlord's story. They had much to ask about the first discovery, the size of the island, the appearance of the blasted circular spot, of the tree and the projecting bough; about the pulley and its chain; about the log floorings, their number, their distance apart, and their probable use in a money-hole; about the West Indian grass, the cocoa-nut husks, and the sugar-cane, which were the signs of some connection with the Spanish Main; about the shavings and chips of wood; about the gravelly soil, contrasting with the blue clay around it; about the eventful moment when the first diggers touched the money-box with the crowbar, and the destruction of their work during the night. They asked also, very minutely, about the stone with the inscription, its kind and its size, and why it should have been inserted into the chimney of a hut: about the drain, its size, and whether it was built of wood, or brick, or stone; and about the nature of the signs brought up by the auger when they bored through the money-box.

All these questions showed how close had been the attention with which they had listened. To every one of them, without exception, the landlord responded in the most unhesitating and the most comprehensive manner. It was evident that he had turned over every point in his mind that they now suggested; that he was familiar with every objection, and was armed and equipped at all points with facts and arguments to sustain his theory.

That there were plenty of objections to that theory became evident from the landlord's own very frequent allusions to them, and it seemed, by the way in which he spoke of them, as though he himself had often and often done battle with scornful or sceptical opponents.

"For my own part," said the landlord, "I don't think much of any of these objections. Objections are easy enough to make. You can make them to anything you like—or don't like. The truest things in the world meet with lots of unbelievers, who offer objections. Now, I know this whole story to be true, and I don't value the objections a rush.

"One objection, for instance, is, that the story of the first diggers has been exaggerated in every particular. In passing from month to month, they say, each one has added to it, and that all the little circumstances that I have mentioned have been either thrown in to make up a story, or colored so as to favor a belief in the money-hole. Now, as to that, all I can say is, that the two men always told a straight story, without any additions, and the younger one lived down to my time, and so could easily be referred to by any one. He always made the same statement.

"A great objection is, that two men could never have dug down so far, and stayed up the sides of the pit, as the story said they did. It has been asserted that they couldn't have dug down more than twenty or thirty feet, and that they probably got down that far when they came to the water, which prevented them from going any farther. To which I answer, not only that two men could have dug a hundred feet, but that they have done so, over and over, on the same ground, for in the holes made since, it isn't possible for more than two to work at the same time. The shafts are only about six feet long by three wide, and in that space there isn't room for more than two, of course.

"When I find men who don't believe in Kidd's treasure, and ask them what could have been there, they make various answers; but the favorite one is, that it was some sort of a signal-station. But, unfortunately, Oak Island is the last place about here that one could think of for such a purpose as that. Still, that is what they urge, and they say that the timber floorings were probably intended as a foundation. When I ask them why there were so many timber floorings, they quietly deny the fact. They say that there might have been one or two such floorings, to the depth of perhaps ten feet, or so, but won't believe any more. When I point to the testimony of the surviving one of the first diggers, they deny the value of it, and say that it is only the exaggeration of an old man, who has been telling the same tall story for years, till it has grown to its present dimensions. And when people choose to argue in that style, and reject the best sort of evidence that there can be, why, of course, there's an end of all discussion. They set out with a blind prejudice, deny plain facts, or explain them away in the most fanciful manner, and then turn round and ridicule those who believe in what is as plain as day."

The landlord was silent for a moment, overcome by a kind of mild indignation at the sceptic of whom he spoke, after which he proceeded.

"Then there's that stone with the mysterious inscription. It's been seen by hundreds. No one has ever been found yet who can make out what it means. As I said before, it is either some foreign language, or else, as is quite probable, it is some secret cipher, known only to Kidd himself—perhaps used by the great pirate confederacy. It shows, more than anything else, that this hole was dug by Captain Kidd, and that his treasure is there. Now, how do you suppose they get over that?"

And with this question the landlord looked earnestly and solemnly at the two boys.

The two boys couldn't imagine how anybody could get over it; though Bart could not help wondering a little how it came that, if the inscription could not be deciphered, the landlord should nevertheless know so well that it referred to Captain Kidd.

"I'll tell you," said the landlord, "the way they get over it. They have the impudence to say that it isn't an inscription at all. Actually, because no one can decipher it, they say it ain't an inscription! They say it's only some accidental scratches! Now, I allow," continued the landlord, "that the marks are rather faint, and irregular; but how any man can look at them, and say that they're not an inscription—how any man can look at them and say that they're accidental scratches—is a thing that makes me fairly dumb with amazement.

"Well, then there are other things, too," continued the landlord, "which they handle in the same manner. One of the strangest things about this whole story is the fact that the soil in the money-hole is different from that of the rest of the island, being sand and gravel; whereas the rest of the island, as I told you, is blue clay. It's just as if a hole was dug in the blue clay, and then filled in with sand and gravel brought from somewhere else. Well, how do you think they get over this?"

Again the landlord looked inquiringly at the two boys.

Again the two boys gave it up.

"Why," said the landlord, "they get over it in the usual fashion. They say it isn't a fact that the island is blue clay, but that there's streaks and patches of gravel all over it, and the two men hit upon a place where the soil was sandy and gravelly. That's the way they get over that point; and I'd like to ask any man if that's fair; if that's honest; if that's decent. Yet that's the way they talk—when they can go to the island, and see wherever fresh holes have been dug, the blue clay is turned up. But when I point out that, they say, 'O, that's because the holes are all dug on that one side of the island where the blue clay is.'

"Then, again, there's the drain," continued the landlord. "Now, if any one thing is an established fact, next to the buried money—it's Kidd's drain. It's been broken into time after time. It's flooded hole after hole. Yet, in the face of this, they say that there isn't any drain at all; that there's merely some loose soil on the island, or some subterranean passage, made by nature, through which the sea water passes, and that the bottom of the so-called money-hole has been connected with this. Some say, that as the island is small, the sea water trickles through the soil, in some places, all the way across. So, of course, these men, shutting their eyes obstinately to hard facts, laugh at the very idea of a drain. And that's the sort of objections that we have to meet!" concluded the landlord, with a snort of contempt.

"Is any one working on Oak Island now?" asked Bart, after a pause.

"Well, no, not just now. There isn't a soul on the island. Since the last company gave up, no one has touched the works—except, occasionally, some visitors. Everything is standing there—the pumps, the hoisting tackle, and all that. You'll see the holes all about; and the money-hole can easily be known, for it is a hollow in the ground, shaped like a bowl, close by the largest pump, with a deep hole beside it, full of water; for, unfortunately, they struck the drain too soon, and of course the water rushed upon them."

At this point the landlord recollected some business that he had to attend to, and rising to his feet, he slowly sauntered away.

IX.

Bart and Pat take a Walk.—A Conversation.—Pat makes a Suggestion.—Bart adopts it.—A Tunnel to the Treasure of the Sea.—A Plot kept secret from the others.—Plans for Aspotogon.— Keeping their own Counsel.—Bart and Pat set forth.—Stealing a Boat.—The Search for the Treasure Island.—The Intelligent Native.—A new Way of getting at the Treasure.—Blood and Thunder!—Once more on the Way.—The Pirates' Isle!

The landlord's story had produced a very profound impression upon the minds of the boys, and the reiterated emphasis which he placed upon the treasure supposed to be buried there did not fail to kindle their imaginations to a wonderful degree. But together with this excitement, and astonishment at the magnitude of the supposed treasure, there were also other feelings, which latter tended to repel them as much as the former tended to attract them. These feelings consisted of discouragement and disappointment, at learning the insuperable difficulties that lay in the way, and at hearing the story of repeated failures. Efforts had been made, as they now knew, far greater than any which were possible to their feeble arms; and in every case the money-diggers, whether digging in person or by deputy, had failed utterly and miserably, each one only learning of some new difficulty which necessitated still more arduous toils.

As the landlord strolled off, Bart and Pat moved away also up the hill towards the back part of the town; and here they sat on a secluded grassy slope, looking down into the back bay, whose blue waters lay at their feet.

"Sure an it's a great thing entirely, so it is," said Pat, "an that's all about it."

"I hadn't any idea," said Bart, "that people knew so much about it. I didn't imagine that anybody had tried to dig there."

"Sure an it's natural enough for them to do that same, if they thought there was money in it."

"Of course it was, an that's the very thing we haven't been taking into account."

"Faith, an that same's true for you, thin; niver a bit did we take it into account. Haven't we been making a wonderful secret of it, when all the wurruld knows it like A, B, C."

"Yes, and what's worse, at this very moment they are sending out agents in all directions, all over the province, I dare say, to try to get people to take stock in the new mining company. Why, every body must know all about Oak Island. I don't see how we never heard of it before."

"Deed, thin, an I think they must have kept it all to thimselves here in Chester, so I do, or else we'd have heard some talk about it at school, so we would; an if there's any talk about it now through the country, it's something new entirely, so it is, and is the doin of this new company, sure."

"I don't see what we can do," said Bart, in a dejected tone; "we can't do a single thing."

"Sure, thin," said Pat, "but it's meself that's been thinkin different; an I don't know now but what the chances for us are better thin they were before."

"Chances for us better? What in the world do you mean by that?" asked Bart, in surprise.

"Sure an it's plain enough. Ye see that treasure was a hundred feet an more under ground, an so it was clane beyond anything that we could do. But these companies have been a workin, an a diggin, an a pumpin, an a borin holes all about, an we've got that much of the work done."

"Yes, but what good'll that do us? These holes weren't any good to the companies. They couldn't get to the money-hole, after all."

"Yis, but sure an may be they didn't go to work the right way."

"O, I dare say they did all that could be done; and I don't see how anybody could do any more, except they get a steam engine, the way they're going to do."

"O, sure an that's all very well; but still, whin the holes are already bored, the hardest of the work's done; an a handy boy might be more use than a stame ingin, so he might. Sure an I'd like to see meself at the bottom of one of thim pits that's nearest to the money-hole. I'd make a grab for the trisure, so I would."

"Pooh, nonsense! What could you do?"

"Sure I'd make a dash for it. There's nothin like tryin. Nothin venture, nothin have. I've got a notion that a body might make a bit of a tunnel in under there, an git at the money-box. At any rate it's worth tryin for, so it is."

"A tunnel!" exclaimed Bart. "I never thought of that. Do you really think that you could do it?"

"Why not?" said Pat. "Sure I've seen it done. All ye've got to do is to lave an archway, an there it is. It'll howld till doomsday. A tunnel is it? Sure I'd like to see meself down there with a bit of a pick, an I'd soon have the tunnel. An besides, it's only blue clay I'd have to work in."

"So it is," said Bart, in great excitement. "He said blue clay. It's only in the money-hole where the sand and gravel are."

"An blue clay," said Pat, "to my mind, is as aisy cuttin as chalk or chaise. It's like cuttin into butther, so it is. Why, there's nothin in the wide wurruld to hender you an me from goin down there an tunnelin through the blue clay from the nearest pit straight into the money-hole."

"But what can we do about the water rushing in?" asked Bart.

"Sure an we can only try," said Pat. "If we can't kape the water out, we'll give up. But we may work along so as to kape clear of the water."

"But can we do that?" asked Bart.

"Do it?" said Pat. "Sure an what's to hender us?"

"The other workmen couldn't, you know," said Bart.

"I don't know it," said Pat, "an you don't, either. How do we know that they ever tried? They dug the pits to try and stop the drain; that's what they tried to do. But we're a goin to try to tunnel into the money-hole; an there's all the difference in the wurruld between the two, so there is. Besides, there's no harrum in tryin. If we can't do it we can come back, an no harrum done."

"Shall we tell the other fellows?" said Bart, after a thoughtful pause.

"Sorra a one of them," said Pat. "Tell them, is it? Not me. What for? Sure only two can work in a hole at a time, an that's me an you; an what do we want of any more? We'll tell them after we've got the trisure; and thin we'll all go halves all around, so we will; only we'll have the glory of gettin it, an no harrum done to anybody."

"Well, it isn't a bad idea," said Bart, thoughtfully. "The other fellows needn't know. They haven't heard the story, and perhaps wont hear it; at any rate, not before to-morrow; and it's a crazy sort of an undertaking, and mayn't amount to anything; so, as you say, Pat, it may be best for us to start off, us two, on our own hooks, and investigate. My idea is, for us to get off there in a quiet way, land on Oak Island, and look around to see if any of the holes are suitable."

"Shuitable!" said Pat. "Sure they'll all shuit, so they will, if they ain't full of water. All we want is, a impty pit, within aisy an accessible distance of the money-hole for us to tunnel."

"Well, that's what we'll have to find out first. But when can we go?"

"To-morrow morning," said Pat, "airly."

"But we're going to Aspotogon," said Bart.

"Sure an we may slip off an let the others go by themselves. We'll go to Oak Island at four in the morrnin, an'll be back by nine or tin—about the time when they're startin. If they wait for us, all right; we may go with them there or not, just as it shuits us; that depinds on the prospects at Oak Island. But if they don't wait for us it won't make any difference in the wurruld, so it won't."

After some further conversation, the two boys resolved to carry out this proposal. They thought they could easily leave the hotel on the following morning, at the earliest light, and then go off to explore Oak Island by themselves. The others would not probably start for Aspotogon before nine or ten. If they found Oak Island affording no prospect of success in their plan, they could easily return to Chester, in time to start for Aspotogon with the others; while if, on the other hand, they did see any chance to make Pat's tunnel, they could remain there and go to work. The others would probably think they had gone fishing, and set off without them.

The proposal of Pat was a wild and impracticable one, but to Bart it seemed easy enough. The thing that had influenced him most was the idea of a "tunnel," of which Pat spoke so knowingly. Without having any very distinct conception of the difficulties in the way of a "tunnel," he allowed himself to be fascinated by the very mention of it, and so flung himself headlong into the scheme.

Their determination to keep this plan a secret from the others, did not, of course, arise out of any desire to forestall them, or to seize for themselves the treasure which they supposed to be on the island. It was rather the design of achieving some exploit which should astonish their friends. It was glory, not covetousness, that animated them.

In this frame of mind, then, and with this purpose, they returned to the inn. Nothing was said about Oak Island. The landlord himself did not refer to it. Perhaps he had talked enough about it for one day, and was tired of it; or perhaps he was merely husbanding his resources, so as to tell it with full effect on the following day to those of the party who had not yet heard it; for when a man has a good story, and meets with a perfectly fresh crowd of hearers, he naturally feels unwilling to throw the story away, and prefers to tell it under the best possible circumstances. That evening they talked chiefly about the expedition to Aspotogon. Bruce, Arthur, Tom, and Phil did the talking. Bart and Pat were comparatively silent. The first four said nothing, however, about the buccaneers, for they, like the landlord, were reserving this subject for the following day. They also had all conceived the idea that Aspotogon was the very place where the treasure of the buccaneers might be buried; and this, of course, threw additional attractions around the proposed trip. The name seemed suitable to such a deed. It was sonorous and impressive; and to them it seemed to suggest all sorts of possible crimes and tragedies. Deep Cove, also, was a name not without its significance; and they fancied in this place they might find the hiding-place of the old pirates of which the governor of Sable Island had spoken.

Before retiring, they decided that they would not start till nine o'clock, which hour would be most convenient for all, especially the landlord, who protested against getting out of bed at any unusually early hour. With this understanding they all retired.

But Bart and Pat were awake and up before the dawn. Dressing themselves hastily, they quitted the house as noiselessly as possible, and went off to the promenade or square, at the end of the town. Here a number of boats were drawn up on the beach. At that early hour it was impossible to find any owner; nor did Bart or Pat feel inclined to stand on any ceremony. They selected the best of them, and thought that on their return they might apologize to the owner, whoever, he might turn out to be, and pay him for the use of the boat.

The question now was, how to find Oak Island. That the island was somewhere in the bay on this side of Chester they knew from what the landlord had told them, but which particular one it might be among the hundreds of the bay they could not imagine. The knowledge that it was covered with oaks, was the only guide they had; and with this they set forth, hoping to find the object of their search. There was a sail in the boat, and a pair of oars, and a gentle breeze was blowing; so they hoisted the sail, and slipped at a very good pace over the water. On their way they passed several islands. One of these had farm-houses on it; another had no houses at all; but still they saw nothing of those oak trees, and frames, and pumps, and other engines which marked Oak Island.

They kept on, however, sailing past some islands, and around others, until more than an hour had passed, and they both concluded that it would be far better to go ashore somewhere and ask directions. They saw a house not far away on the main land, and at once sailed in this direction. The wind still continued very moderate, and though neither Bart nor Pat knew much about navigating a boat, they managed to get along in this breeze without any trouble whatever.

On landing, Pat remained in the boat, while Bart went to the house just mentioned. On his way he crossed the high road which here runs along the shore, winding beautifully around every curve and inlet as it encircles the bay. Bart had some difficulty in rousing the people, for it was yet very early in the morning, and they were all sound asleep. At last, however, he heard sounds of movement inside, and then a man appeared, half dressed, and rubbing his eyes.

"Good morning," said Bart, pleasantly.

"Morn'n," said the man, with a yawn.

"Can you tell me where I can find Oak Island?"

"Oak Island?" repeated the man, stretching himself with another yawn and looking at Bart,—"Oak Island?"

"Yes," said Bart; "Oak Island."

"Why, you ain't a tryin to walk there, surely!" said the man, in some surprise.

"O, no," said Bart; "that's my boat just down there."

"O," said the man. "Wal, Oak Island's jest over there;" and he pointed up the bay farther, in a direction which Bart had not taken at all. "You go straight up about two miles from here, an you'll hit it. You can't mistake it. It's a little island with some oak trees and some stagins."

"There's no one there now, I suppose," said Bart.

"No," said the man, "not jest now. They've knocked off,—the last batch did,—and there ain't likely to be no more till the next lot of fools turns up that's got more money than brains."

From which remark Bart gathered that the man was an unbeliever.

"You don't seem to believe in Kidd's treasure," said he.

"Wal," said the man, "I ain't goin to say that; but I'll tell you what I don't believe in. I don't believe in people a throwin of their money away into the airth an into the sea when they might be doin better with it. Yes, a throwin of it away, tryin to get at a money-box that's out of the power of man to touch. Yes, sir; flesh and blood won't never lay hands on Kidd's treasure—leastways not unless there's a sacrifice made."

"A sacrifice!" repeated Bart, in amazement.

"Yes," said the man. "It's an old sayin hereabouts, as to the fact as that that thar treasure bein buried there with the sacrifice of human life, is laid under a cuss, and the cuss can't ever be lifted, nor the money-box either, till some of the diggers kills a man. That's the old sayin; an mind you, it'll have to come to that. Blood must be shed!"

The man uttered these last words in a deep tone, that suggested all sorts of superstitious horrors; and from the tenor of these last remarks, Bart perceived that this man, far from being an unbeliever, as he had at first supposed, was one of the firmest possible believers, and surrounded his belief with the accompaniments of the darkest superstition. To Bart this only served to intensify the interest which he already felt in Oak Island; for he saw that the people of the neighborhood were the firmest believers in the existence of the treasure.

A few more questions followed, referring chiefly to the appearance of the island; and having at length gathered all the information that he wanted, Bart returned to the boat, and once more the two boys proceeded on their way. The place towards which the man had pointed was straight before them, and every little while grew more and more plainly defined against the line of land beyond, until at length they could see that it was an island. Nearer and nearer they drew, and gradually they saw the oak trees, which differed from the trees of the other islands. The trees stood apart more like a grove planted by man than a forest of nature's planting. Other signs soon appeared; a rough hut, some stagings in different places, of peculiar construction, and here and there mounds of earth. There could be no doubt about it. This was the place which they sought. This was the home of the buccaneers; the haunt of Captain Kidd; the place where lay buried far down in the earth, and far beneath the sea; the plunder of the Spanish Main!

X.

The Isle of the Pirates.—The Oaks and the Mounds.—A Survey.—The flooded Pits.—The empty Pit.—The Staying.— The Money-hole.—The Hut and its Contents.—The Stone with the Inscription.—Preparations for a Descent.—The Rope and the Beam.—Pat's Plan with the Pickaxe.— Bart goes down.—All right.—Come along.—Pat goes down.—Terrific Result.—The Sword of Damocles.

The bows of the boat grated on the pebbled beach, and Bart and Pat stepped ashore. On landing, their first thought was to secure the boat. This was not a difficult task. Close by them was a tree, growing near the beach, and all that they had to do was to draw the boat up for a short distance, and fasten a line around the tree. After this, they stood by the boat for a little while, and looked at the island upon which they had landed.

It was small, not over a quarter of a mile across, and rose gently from the sea to a height of not more than thirty feet. Oak trees, planted at considerable intervals, grew over the surface, none of them being of any very great size. Under these there was, in some places, a thick turf, which looked as though the ground had once been cultivated, and had run out, while in other places it was rough, and rose in those mossy mounds or cradles which characterize soil that has been cleared, but has never been subject to cultivation.

As they stood here and looked at the scene before them, they saw, not very far away, a mound of earth. They had seen this from the boat as they approached, and had at once thought that it might be the very ground removed from the earth in forming one of the numerous pits. In digging these pits the earth would be raised, and thrown on one side.

"Sure that's what I towld ye," said Pat. "Ye know there must be a deep hole from the height of it."

"Yes," said Bart. "There must be a hole there. Come, let's have a look at it."

With these words the two started forward, and walked towards the heap of earth. As they came up, they noticed that the soil consisted of clay of a dull bluish tinge, like pale slate, and they recognized at once the bluish clay of which the landlord had spoken. The heap of earth was of considerable dimensions. They both walked up it, and on reaching the top, they saw on the other side an opening in the ground. Hurrying down towards it, they recognized in it at once one of those pits made by some one of the companies digging here. The mouth of it was about six feet long and four feet wide. The sides were stayed up by planks. They could not see far down, however, for the pit contained water, which came to within a dozen feet of the surface. How deep the pit was they could not see; but they at once conjectured that this was one of those pits mentioned by the landlord, where the diggers in search of the "drain" had broken into it, and had thus been compelled to fly from the waters that poured in upon them. This pit was flooded (as the landlord had said) from "Kidd's drain."

After examining this pit, they proceeded farther, and saw another mound not far away. It was just like this, of about the same dimensions, and consisting of the same bluish clay. To this they directed their steps, knowing now that another pit might be expected here, and in this expectation they were not disappointed. There was a pit here of precisely the same appearance as the one which they had just examined, stayed up in the same way around the sides by stout planks, and of about the same size. Like the other, it was also full of water. Here too, then, as they thought, the diggers had broken into the "drain," and had flooded the pit. The occurrence of these two pits, both full of water, showed them, in a very striking and very significant manner, the difficulties that those encountered who sought to penetrate to the hidden treasure.

But the boys were curious to see some pit that might not be full of water, so as to see with their own eyes the depth of these excavations. The landlord had mentioned a hundred feet. Such a depth as that, they knew, exceeded the height of an ordinary church spire, and they both wondered whether it would be possible for them to descend. They, therefore, turned away from this pit after a slight examination, and looked around for others.

Several mounds appeared not very far away, and they at once went off to the nearest of these. Here, then, was a pit which was also flooded. The sight of this third pit, full of water, made them fear that this was the condition of all of them, and their discouragement was consequently great; however, they had not yet examined all, and two or three other mounds yet remained to be visited. They went on, therefore, to the next; and here, on reaching the pit which adjoined it, they found, to their great delight, that it was dry.

Dry and deep. The hundred feet which the landlord had spoken of seemed to be a moderate estimate for this pit. Its length and width at the mouth were the same as those of the others; and the staying of the sides with stout planks was the same. On looking down, they could see no bottom. Bart took a stone and dropped it, and the time which was taken up in the fall to the bottom seemed to fully warrant the estimate above mentioned. But such a pit as this did not appear to offer much chance of descending into it. None of the pulleys or windlasses which must once have been used here to lower the workmen, or hoist up the earth, now remained. The planks used as staying were over an inch apart, and these offered occasional spaces which might possibly be used as a foothold. Still, to climb down here without some sort of a rope was not to be thought of, and though Bart and Pat were both excellent climbers, they both saw at once that this was a task beyond their powers. And they had not brought a rope with them.

On looking around once more, they saw at no very great distance a staging, which at once reminded them of the directions given them by the man on the shore, and also of the words of the landlord. This staging they had also noticed as they approached the island in the boat. They now set out for this, and reached it in a short time. This staging was about the highest point on the island, and was in the midst of an immense collection of mounds of earth, and sand, and blue clay. As they stood here, they could see several pits around them; but their attention was at once arrested by one place close by the staging. It was a hollow in the earth, shaped like a bowl, about twenty feet in diameter, and perhaps the same depth. At once the landlord's description of the present appearance of the "money-hole" flashed across their memories.

This, then, must be the place,—this bowl-shaped hollow. There could be no doubt about it. This must be the spot chosen by the buccaneers for that pit in which they were to hide their treasure. Here beneath,— far beneath,—lay concealed the plunder of the Spanish Main. Here was that blasted circular spot, with the blighted tree, and the decayed pulley, which had revealed the secret to the first diggers. Here those two had worked who had so nearly reached the treasure, and this bowl-shaped cavity showed them what appeared to the eyes of those first diggers, when, after they had just touched the treasure, they went forth on the following morning to see their labor destroyed, and all their toil wasted.

Around this were the signs of other labors, and the unmistakable traces of all the toilers, who in succession had labored here. Some pits had caved in, like the original "money-hole." Others had filled with water. The sand, gravel, and clay, that had been drawn up out of these various excavations, covered a large space. Close by a pit, which lay nearest to the "money-hole," rose the staging which had attracted them. On examining this, its purpose was at once evident. It was erected so as to allow of the working of pumps by horse-power. The circle was there which the horses traversed, and all the machinery was in perfect order. They understood the purpose of this machine at once from the landlord's story. It had been intended to reach the bottom of the "money-hole" by a new pit, and this pit was to be kept dry by pumping. The pit must evidently be the one which immediately adjoined the "money-hole." But how completely this plan had failed, was now evident to them from this pit itself, which, like the others that they had first seen, was full of water. This pit had proved of no avail against "Kidd's drain." Horse-power had been weak against the tides of the sea. Here was the melancholy result— a failure complete and utter; a pit flooded; engines useless; costly works deserted. Would the attempt ever be made again? or if so, would steam succeed when pitted against the waters of the ocean?

They went down into the bowl-shaped cavity which marked the "money-hole,"—they did so cautiously, for they had vague fears of quicksand. But their fears were idle. The ground seemed as hard and as solid as on any other part of the island. They stood there, and stamped, and jumped, but the firm soil yielded not. They could scarcely believe that this was the very central point affected by the waters of the sea. And yet this must be so, for this was the point to which the "drain" had been directed, and far down the waters guarded the treasure from the hand of man.

After remaining here for a time, they emerged from the cavity, and their attention was next attracted by a hut not far away. To this they directed their steps. They found the door wide open, and entered. Inside they saw two rooms divided by a board partition, with a chimney rising in the middle. This had been the place where the workmen lived, for signs of these occupants were still visible around. The two rooms were filled with spades, and chains, and boxes, and a miscellaneous collection of articles that had probably been used by the last excavators, and had been left here in anticipation of further use. Among these they saw a quantity of ropes in coils of different sizes; and they saw at once that if they wished to go down into any one of the pits, a way of descending was now supplied.

The chimney at once suggested to their minds the remarks of the landlord about the stone with the inscription. To the boys that stone seemed the most important part of the whole story, and offered a more direct evidence as to its truth than anything else. They wished to see it, and judge for themselves. They accordingly examined the chimney on every side, but, to their very great disappointment, could not see anything of the kind. At length Bart found a place in the chimney from which a portion seemed to have been detached, and he at once declared that this must have been the place where the stone was, and that it had probably been taken away, so as to be made use of for the purpose of affecting the public mind, and inducing people to take stock in the new company.

The sight of the ropes at once awakened within them a desire to put in practice their intention of descending into one of the pits. It did not seem to them to be dangerous. Bart was as active as a cat in climbing, especially when he had anything to do with ropes; while Pat, though not equal to him in this respect, was still quite able to do any ordinary work of the kind. One of the pits, as they had seen, was dry, but it was a little too far away. They wished to find one which was rather nearer the "money-hole," where there might be some chance of putting into practice Pat's idea about the tunnel. No thought of danger entered into their minds, no dread of the treacherous waters which had broken through into the other holes, and flooded them. They prepared to put their scheme into execution as calmly as if it was no more than climbing a tree.

But first they must seek a pit nearer the "money-hole;" and with this intention they went back to that central spot, where they examined the pits in its neighborhood. To their great joy they soon found one. It was on the side opposite to that where the staging had been erected, and was quite dry. This they knew by dropping stones down, and listening to the sound made when they struck. All of them fell with a dull thud, and without any splashing noise, such as would have been produced had water been there.

This at once decided them in favor of the pit just mentioned; and the next thing was, how to arrange the rope so as to make the descent. One could not lower the other; and if such a thing had been possible, neither one would have been willing to stay up. There was therefore nothing for them to do but to adopt the simple plan of climbing down by means of a rope secured to the top. First of all they had to select the rope. This they did without much delay. Among the various coils in the hut, one seemed suitable from size and quality. It had been used, like all the others; it seemed perfectly strong enough; and it was also sufficiently soft and smooth to the hands. This coil was therefore selected and brought to the place. A stone was quickly attached to one end, and was thrown down. The rope fell all the way to the bottom without being more than half expended. The rest of the coil lay at the edge of the pit.

And now how were they to secure this, so as to descend? Something was needed which might bear their weight. At first they thought of tying the upper part of the rope to one of the planks which formed the staying of the sides of the pit; but this did not seem strong enough. They then went off to hunt up something. In the house there was a crowbar, which was strong enough, yet not long enough, to satisfy them. But outside of the house there was a large beam, fully twelve feet long and eight inches thick. This seemed to be the very thing. It was apparently sound and strong, and, as far as they could see, was quite able to support ten times the weight to which it would be subjected. This beam therefore was chosen without the slightest hesitation, and Bart and Pat, taking it up in their arms, carried it to the mouth of the pit; then they laid it across, and tied the rope about it as securely as possible.

All now seemed perfectly safe, and nothing remained but to make the descent. Bart went first. The planks used for staying around the sides of the pit were far enough apart to offer here and there interstices in which the feet might be inserted, though in many of these places the earth bulged through so as to prevent a foothold. They thus afforded assistance; and Bart, as he began his descent, availed himself of it. As he went down, Pat watched him anxiously from above. Before his head had disappeared, he said,—

"O, by the way, Pat! throw down that pickaxe."

For Pat had brought a pickaxe from the hut, in order to make his tunnel; and it was now lying on the ground, close by.

"Sure, but I was goin to wait till you got down."

"What! and throw it on my head! No, thank you."

"Sure an I niver thought of that at all at all," said Pat; "and it's lucky for you that you thought of it just now."

With these words Pat dropped the pickaxe into the pit, and it fell with a dull thud far down at the bottom.

Bart now continued his descent, and Pat watched him all the way. At length a voice came up from far below,—

"All right! Come along!"

Upon this Pat descended, and went down cautiously and carefully, clinging with feet and hands to the rope and to the sides of the pit. He was not so dexterous as Bart, and once or twice he lost his foothold on the side of the pit, and slid for several feet, the rope cutting his hands; but still he kept on, for Bart was waiting for him, and encouraging him.

At length, when about thirty feet from the bottom, where Bart was standing, he found a place where he could stick his foot, and waited for a moment to look down through the darkness. He could see nothing. As he looked, his foot slipped from the place, and he fell with a jerk, the rope sliding painfully through his chafed hands. At that very instant it seemed to him that the rope itself was falling. From above there came a dull creaking sound, and from below a cry of horror burst from Bart. At that instant, Pat's feet touched the bottom of the pit.

Bart grasped his arm convulsively, and pointed upward.

"The beam! the beam!" he almost screamed. "It's broke. O, what shall we do!"

Pat looked up; and there, clearly defined against the sky, he saw the beam around which the rope was fastened, no longer lying straight across the mouth of the pit, but sagging down in the middle at a sharp angle. It had been rotten in the middle. It had cracked at that last jerk occasioned by his fall from his foothold; and it now hung broken midway, still cling-ing together by a few fibres, but suspended there above them, like the sword of Damocles, as if by a single hair, and threatening every instant to fall and crush them.

The rope and the beam had both been rotten, and the jerk which had been given when Pat lost his foothold had cracked the one and broken the other. There, about thirty feet above them, hung the end of the rope where it had parted. The rest of it was still in Pat's hands.

XI.

*The missing Ones.—What has become of them?—Theories
about Bart and Pat.—The Decision.—A new Disappointment,
and a very serious one.—A bad Substitute.—The Voyage to
Aspotogon.—The mysterious Cove.—A romantic Spot.—
Picturesque Scenery.—Speculations about the Buccaneers.—
The very Place.—The Knoll.—New Themes.—The Mound over
the Treasure of the Seas.—Plans to get at said Treasure.—A
most unpleasant Discovery.—Their Plans knocked in the
Head.—New Plans, by which to avoid all Difficulties.*

The other boys rose that morning at the usual hour, and descended
leisurely to breakfast. The absence of Bart and Pat was noticed and com-
mented on. It was supposed, however, that they had gone off somewhere
to get up an appetite for breakfast, and that they would be along before
the meal was over. Time passed, and the breakfast was ended; but still
no signs appeared of the absentees. It was now nearly time to start, and
they all strolled down to the wharf where the Antelope was, thinking that
the two boys might possibly be there. On reaching the place they looked
around, but saw no signs of them. Captain Corbet had not seen them, nor
had Solomon. Everything was ready, and it was only a few minutes of
the time.

"It's queer where those fellows can have gone to," said Bruce.

"They've gone on a walk, of course," said Arthur; "and I dare say
they've gone farther than they intended."

"O, they'll be along soon," said Phil; and won't they be half starved?
Methinks!"

"It's a strange thing," said Tom, "that they should have slipped off in
this way. No one knows anything about them. No one at the inn saw them
go out. They must have got up precious early."

"Well, they're both rather early risers," said Arthur; "and they may
have gone off fishing."

"I dare say they have," said Bruce. "Bart is crazy about fishing, and if
he has got one solitary bite, he'll give up the expedition to Aspotogon."

"And Pat's as bad, every bit," said Phil. "Depend upon it, those two
have gone out to catch fish for breakfast, and won't be back till somewhere about evening."

"For my part," said Tom, "I shouldn't wonder if they've both backed
out deliberately."

"Backed out?"

"Yes. I don't believe they cared about going to Aspotogon."

"Pooh! nonsense! What makes you think that?"

"Why, last evening I noticed that they didn't say a single word. Both of those fellows were as mum as mice, and all the rest of us were in full cry about the expedition. Depend upon it, they didn't want to go, and have backed out. They didn't want to say anything about it, for fear we'd tease them to come, but quietly dropped off, leaving us to go without them. O, that's the way, beyond a doubt."

"Now that you mention it, Tom," said Phil, "I do remember that they didn't say anything last night, neither of them."

"Neither did they," said Arthur.

"Fact," said Bruce; "it looks very much as if they had talked the matter over, and concluded to back out in this quiet way; and I don't know but what they have concocted some scheme of their own."

"O, some fishing scheme, of course. Bart was crazy about it, you know, and he's persuaded Pat to go with him."

"Well, in that case we needn't wait."

"O, we may as well hang on till ten—in case they should turn up after all."

Such was the opinion, then, to which the other boys came, about the disappearance of Bart and Pat. It was a perfectly natural one under the circumstances. Bart and Pat were distinguished above all things for their fondness for fishing; their silence during the conversation of the preceding evening really made it seem as though they had no desire to go to Aspotogon, but had some plan of their own. This plan seemed to the boys to be undoubtedly a fishing expedition. There was, therefore, not the slightest feeling of uneasiness in the mind of any of them, nor did even Captain Corbet, who had listened to the conversation, imagine that there was any cause for alarm. To have imagined danger to them in such a place as this, on dry ground, in a civilized country, was out of the question. Notwithstanding this conviction, they thought it possible, however, that the two might yet return in time, and therefore they decided to wait for them till ten.

The conversation about Bart and Pat was suddenly interrupted by the appearance of the landlord, who brought them another disappointment. He told them that important business had most unexpectedly required him to go up the country for twenty miles or so, and that he should not be able to accompany them. He expressed the greatest possible regret, and the boys expressed still more. They at once offered to postpone their expedition till the following day; but the landlord was not certain whether he should be back by that time or not, and advised them to go without him. He said a friend of his would go, who knew the whole country, and could tell them all that they wanted to know about it.

Great was the disappointment of the boys at this unexpected occurrence. They had particularly wished to have the landlord's company, for reasons already stated. He was so genial, so communicative, and so destitute of inquisitiveness, that he seemed the very man whom they might be able to pump to their hearts' content, without making their purpose apparent to him. One great charm of the expedition lay in their belief that Aspotogon and Deep Cove had been the haunts of the buccaneers, and that the landlord would show them the traditionary place where the treasure had been deposited. They did not think that another man could supply his place; and when, shortly after, the landlord brought his friend along, they were sure of it. For the friend, whose name the landlord gave as Turnbull, was a heavy, dull-looking man, and the last in the world whom they would have chosen in the landlord's place. However, there was no help for it. It was useless to postpone it, and, consequently, at ten o'clock the Antelope started on her voyage.

On emerging from the little harbor of Chester into the bay, the scene that presented itself was beautiful in the extreme. Much of it was familiar to their eyes, owing to their previous cruise about the bay on the first day of their arrival; but they now saw it under a somewhat different aspect. On one side arose an island, bare of trees, and covered with grass, of no great size, but conspicuous from its position. In its neighborhood were other islands, some all wooded from the shore to the summit, others showing green meadows peeping forth from encircling foliage. Before them spread the shores of Tancook, all green with verdure, dotted with white houses, and showing, here and there, the darker hue of forest trees, amid the green, grassy meadows. Beyond this, and far out to sea, was Ironbound, which, from this distance, looked dark and repellent. It was more wooded than the other islands, and did not seem popular as a dwelling-place. Naturally so, for at that distance out, it was exposed to the storms and the fogs of the ocean, while those islands within the bay were in the possession of a far more genial soil and climate. On the left, the coast-line ran on beyond a neighboring point, till it terminated in a distant headland; and here, on that line of coast, several miles this side of the headland, the land arose to a wooded eminence, which was no other than the very place which they were seeking—Aspotogon.

The boys were disappointed, for they had expected something much higher. It did not seem to them to be more than a very ordinary hill, nor did it rise very high above the level of the surrounding land. Still, they were willing to be pleased, and therefore tried to think that it might really be much higher than it seemed.

The line of coast ran on, showing cleared fields along the shore, which, farther back, were succeeded by wooded slopes. In this line of shore there did not appear the slightest opening, nor could they imagine how it was possible for a schooner to reach the base of Aspotogon. That there was a passage, however, they were again and again assured by Turnbull, who, though not at all inclined to give any information, was yet capable of answering direct questions, and telling the names of places. The existence of a cove, or strait, in such a place, where there seemed nothing but an unbroken line of coast, gave additional strength to that fancy in which the boys had already been indulging, and made them think that this place, so completely hidden, must be, above all others, the place once chosen as a secure retreat by the buccaneers. This feeling gained strength as they went on. The distance was not far. The wind was fair. The Antelope did her best, and so they gradually drew nearer and nearer. Still, no sign appeared of any opening, nor could they make out any place where an opening might be likely to be found. At last Turnbull remarked that this was the place, and that the Antelope would have to anchor here, as it would be inconvenient, in this wind, to get out of Deep Cove if they were to enter it in the schooner. Down went the Antelope's anchor, and the boat was hauled up alongside.

They were not more than a quarter of a mile from the shore. Deep Cove was there,—for so Turnbull said,—and they were about to visit it, yet there was still no more appearance of any opening than before. The shore seemed to run on without any break, and the boys sought in vain to find some place into which a boat might go; but the boat was ready, and this mystery was soon to be solved.

They drew very near to the shore before the long-sought-for opening appeared. The opening was at such an angle that it could not be detected from the direction in which they had approached, and the curve made by the cove was of such a kind that it was difficult to detect it from any direction. On entering it they saw that it was deep and spacious, with the shore on one side covered with forest trees, and on the other side cleared. Rowing on a little farther, the cove curved, and the cleared land was left behind. Now a scene of grandeur appeared. The cove ran between lofty heights, which bordered it, now with precipitous rocky cliffs, now with steep slopes, heavily, wooded. After rowing a few hundred yards, it seemed as though they were shut out from all the world. Behind and before there was a circle of hills, and they seemed to be rather upon the bosom of some sequestered lake than upon an inlet of the sea close by the waters of the stormy Atlantic.

They still moved on, and as they advanced, the scenery retained the same general features, possessing an air of wild and romantic grandeur of the most striking description. At length they came to a place where the cove widened into a smooth basin, surrounded by an amphitheatre of hills. The water was as smooth as glass, and as black as ink. This, they were informed, was the head of the cove; and straight in front of them was the base of Aspotogon, which was bathed by these waters. The boat approached a grassy knoll close by this, and the boys all got out.

Here, then, the mystery was solved, for they had come up by this passage-way to Aspotogon itself. Close beside them there was a steep declivity, bare of trees just here, and covered with stones. Far up trees began, and hid the summit of the hill.

The picturesque beauty of this place, the deep, black water, the high, encircling hills, the sombre, primeval forests, the utter seclusion, all produced a profound impression upon the minds of the boys, who always were alive to the beauties of nature, and who here had something in addition to natural beauty. For their thoughts turned at once to that which had been for days the supreme subject in their minds—the treasure of the buccaneers. Was not this the haunt of the pirates spoken of by the governor of Sable Island. They all felt sure that it must be. No better place than this could be found in all the world. Here was a hiding-place without a parallel. Here a vessel might pass from the outer seas into absolute seclusion, and find a haven safe from all storms, shut in by high hills. Here, too, was a place to bury their treasure, if such was their desire; and, if the governor of Sable Island had spoken the truth, the place best fitted to receive the pirate's deposit must be the very knoll on which they were standing.

Here it was, on this spot, that they regretted most deeply the absence of the landlord. It was this knoll, above all things, that seemed to them to contain the plunder of the Spanish Main, and they felt sure that, if the landlord had been here, he would have told them all about it, and confirmed their suspicions. But he was not here, and his substitute Turnbull was of no use whatever. He either could or would tell them nothing. He would only answer in monosyllables, and the boys, after a fruitless effort to draw him out on the subject of Deep Cove and its local traditions, gave up the task in despair. They could only console themselves by the thought that they could pump the landlord on their return to Chester, and then, if their suspicions were confirmed, they could visit the place again, and dig for the buried treasure.

And what a glorious place it was to dig, if this indeed was the place which they supposed it to be! How completely shut out it was from all observation. Here they might dig to their hearts' content, and nobody would know it. Perhaps the treasure was not very far down. The knoll rose not more than ten feet or so above the sea. Some of them, indeed, thought that the whole knoll was the work of the pirates, and was neither more nor less than the mound of earth with which they had covered up their treasure. This view was even more charming than the other, and they went about it on every side, examining it all over, and scrutinizing it most carefully.

Suddenly Tom made a discovery of a very unpleasant character. As he wandered about, he found himself, all at once, upon a regular carriage road. It was not a first-class road by any means, but it was a road for wheeled vehicles, and, from its appearance, was evidently in constant use. The sight of this created at once a deep disappointment, in which all the others shared as soon as they saw it. They found that the seclusion of the place was broken up. To dig for gold here, by the side of a public road, would be a difficult matter, and a very different thing from what they had at first supposed. So completely had their minds been impressed by the apparent seclusion of Deep Cove, that they had forgotten all about the houses and settlements which they had seen, only a short time before, on the outer coast. Yet these settlements were only a little distance away, and this was, no doubt, the road that joined them together, which had to make the circuit of Deep Cove, in order to effect a connection.

The boys now seated themselves apart, out of hearing of Turnbull, in order to discuss the situation.

"There can't be any doubt," said Tom, "that this is the mound made by the pirates to cover up their treasure. They didn't dig a hole, but covered up the treasure by piling earth over it."

"That's about it," said Phil; "and what's more, I don't believe that we'll have to go very far down, either."

"I wonder if any one has ever tried it," said Arthur.

"I don't believe it," said Tom. "There isn't the slightest mark on the place."

"But wouldn't people have tried it, if it is really the place?"

"Perhaps they don't know the actual place; and we may be the first who ever suspected this mound. It isn't impossible."

"No; it may be that the people here are too dull; or it may be just a happy guess of ours, which has never occurred to any one else."

"And this miserable road here," said Tom, dolefully, "is going to spoil all."

"I wonder if we couldn't manage to dig, in spite of the road."

"How?"

"Why, we might stick up the sail of the Antelope, and make a big tent, and pretend to be fishing, or roughing it."

"Well, there may be something in that."

"Something! Of course there's everything in that. I call it a good idea, and the only way we can go about it."

"But wouldn't we be bothered with visitors?"

"No; certainly not; or, at any rate, they couldn't get in."

"They'd see the earth thrown up."

"O, we wouldn't throw up much. I don't believe we'd have to dig far, and we could put up both sails, so as to cover up everything. Some of us could watch, to give notice to the diggers to knock off in case any one passed by."

"Well, it's not a bad idea; and it's the only thing we can do. So it's worth trying."

"Yes; but there's one thing first."

"What's that?"

"Why, we'll have to talk with the landlord, and see if we can find out from him what the probabilities are about this place being really the resort of the old buccaneers."

XII.

The Ascent of Aspotogon.—Slippery Slopes.—Treacherous Stones.—Tangled Thickets.—A great Disappointment.— Disgust of the Party.—A refreshing Bath.—Exploring a Cave.—Where are the Buccaneers?—In the Water.—An Alarm.—A terrible Monster.—Fright and Flight.—Sauve qui peut!—The Monster in Pursuit.—The Agonies of Death.—Bruce ashore.—He turns to give Help.—The others safe.—Tom yet in Danger.—The abhorrent Sight.

The boys at length had exhausted all their powers of examination, speculation, and conversation, and began to look about for something to do. It was not yet the appropriate time to dig into what they now all called the "mound," though that would have been the most agreeable thing in the world in their present frame of mind; so they had to think of some other form of active exercise. Phil suggested that they should climb Aspotogon, and the suggestion was at once welcomed. Here they were at its base. They had come to visit it, and they could not be said to have done it, unless they should also reach its summit. So no sooner was the suggestion made than they all prepared to put it in execution.

The place which they chose for the ascent was that open spot already mentioned. Other places were overgrown with a thick forest, with underbrush, and fallen trees. The ascent was somewhat difficult. The slope was steep, and was covered with loose stones that slid at every step. At first, one went behind the other, but after a few paces they found that this could only be done at the imminent risk of their precious limbs, for the stones dislodged by the foremost climber invariably rolled down upon the one following. They therefore avoided going behind any other of the party, and climbed up abreast. At length the slope of sliding stones was traversed, and they reached a place which was covered with the primeval forest. Here the ascent was, if possible, even more toilsome. There was a thick underbrush through which they had to force their way by a process which made their undeniably shabby clothes even more shabby; the ground was very irregular, now sinking into holes, again rising into low mounds; while at intervals they would encounter some fallen tree, over which they had to climb, or else crawl beneath it. Such were the difficulties in the way of their ascent.

These, however, were all happily surmounted, and the whole party at last stood on the summit of Aspotogon. Here a deep disappointment awaited them. They had taken for granted that they would be rewarded by an extensive view. They hoped to overlook the whole of Mahone Bay, to count its three hundred and sixty-five islands, to see the windings of Deep Cove, and speculate upon the operations of the buccaneers. But instead of this they saw—nothing. For the summit of the hill was all overgrown with trees, which shut out the whole view. Such a reward for so much toil excited the deepest disgust.

"And this is Aspotogon!" cried Bruce. "Why, it's a complete sham."

"Talk of this place in comparison with Blomidon!" said Arthur. "Why, it's sacrilege. This place is only a thicket."

"What nonsense to call it a mountain!" said Tom. "I don't believe it's over a couple of hundred feet or so. I know it's ten times harder to go up Blomidon."

"Aspotogon's a humbug," said Phil. "What do they mean by saying it's the highest land in Nova Scotia? It's the most ridiculous nonsense I ever heard in my life. Besides, as to Blomidon—why, the view from that is the finest in America. And what is there here? A parcel of scrubby trees!"

Such being the sentiments of the climbers, it is no wonder that they did not linger long on the summit. There was nothing to keep them there; so they soon descended. The way down, however, was even worse than the way up, especially when they reached the loose stones. For here the stones slid from under their feet at every step, and it was almost impossible to stand upright. Tom and Phil both went down, and a score of big stones rolled about them, and over them, bruising and scratching them; while before them a whole cartload of cobble stones and granite boulders went bounding down towards the cove. The boys tried it a little way, and then took to the trees, where they completed the descent.

On reaching the knoll once more, they all felt tired and hot. Phil proposed a bath, and the proposal was most agreeable to all. In a few moments their clothes were off and they were all in the water.

The water was pleasantly warm. They had not had a bathe for some time, and here it seemed the perfection of bathing. There was no surf; the water was as smooth as glass, and gave the quiet of a lake with the salt water of the sea. Phil was the best swimmer of them all, and struck out boldly to cross the cove. The others followed. On reaching the middle, Phil turned off in another direction, to a point on the shore where he saw a curious rock that looked like a cave.

"Boys," he cried, "there's a cave; let's go and see it."

He swam on, and the others followed. They soon reached the place, and climbed up over the rough rock, to see what they supposed to be the cave. To their disappointment, it was not a cave at all, but only a slight recess of no depth in particular.

"I thought we might find some traces of the buccaneers," said Phil, in a tone of vexation. "We're not in luck to-day."

"O, yes, we are," said Tom, cheerfully. "The discovery of that mound is a good deal."

"Yes; but then there's that public road," said Bruce.

"O, we'll work it yet. Only wait till we get our tent up."

Once more the boys plunged in the water, and played, and sported, and dived, and floated, and swam this way and that way; now on their backs, and again in their natural positions. At length they began to feel tired, and directed their course towards the shore.

Tom was last, swimming along leisurely enough, and thinking about the mound and its hidden treasure,—as were all the other boys,—when suddenly he became aware of a movement in the water behind him, as of some living thing swimming. It was not any of the boys. They were all ahead; and it could not be Turnbull. It was not a man at all.

In an instant a terrible thought came to him, that sent a pang of dreadful anguish through his inmost soul.

A shark!

That was the thought that flashed into Tom's mind.

Hastily and fearfully he turned his head, dreading the worst. One glance was enough. That glance froze his very life-blood with utter horror.

There, not more than six or eight yards away, he saw a black muzzle on the surface of the water, pointing straight towards himself,—a muzzle narrow, and black, and horrible. Tom had never seen a shark; but he had read of them, and had seen pictures of them. One look was enough to convince him that this was a shark, who had scented them from afar, perhaps from the outer sea, and was now about to seize his prey.

His brain whirled, and all the scene for an instant swam before his eyes. A half dozen yards! Could he hope to escape? Impossible! Yet, out of utter despair, there came to him the strength of a giant. He struck out with frantic and frenzied vehemence, shouting and screaming to the other boys,—

"A shark! a shark! a sha-a-a-a-a-a-ark!!!"

The other boys heard his yells. They looked around and saw all—the ghastly face and staring eyes of Tom, with the horror of his expression, and beyond—the black muzzle. At that sight, there seized them all a terror equal to that of Tom. In any other position they would have sprung to his help. But what help was possible here? None. They were naked. They were unarmed. They were in the water. Helpless thus, and despairing, there was nothing which any one of them could do, but to swim blindly on. It was an instinct of self-preservation that animated them all. They fled as they would have fled from an earthquake, or a roaring torrent—blindly—in frantic haste.

Not one word more was uttered. Not a sound was heard except the plashing noise of their movements through the water, and the heavy pantings of the exhausted swimmers. Still, though exhausted, not one of them dared to slacken his efforts. Not one of them dared to look around. In Tom's mind there was the chilling horror of the monster behind, and a curdling dread of that moment when he would be seized. In the minds of the others there was an equal horror of expectation, as they listened to hear the yell from Tom, which might announce that all was over.

Thus they hurried on.

Tom, in his anguish, thought of something that he had once read of about sharks. He had read that the shark is cowardly, and is kept off by splashing in the water—at least for a time; just as a wild beast is deterred by a fire, or a horse is scared by a log at the road-side. At this thought he grasped. It was his only hope. As he swam, he plashed in the water, with all his force, with arms and legs, making it boil and foam all around him. This retarded his progress somewhat; but at any rate, it seemed to prolong his safety, for the monster did not seem inclined to draw nearer.

The moments passed on. They were not far from land,—yet, O, how far that distance seemed to each despairing swimmer! Upon their distance what issues depended! O, that they had thought of the danger in time, or had seen it a little while before!

The moments passed on—moments terrible, full of sickening anguish, of horror intolerable! How long those moments seemed! To Tom each moment was prolonged to the duration of an age, and an age of hideous expectation—expectation of a doom so frightful, so abhorrent, that every nerve tingled, and every fibre of his body quivered. And there, through the noise of the splashings made by his own efforts, he could plainly distinguish the movements of the monster behind. It did not seem nearer, but it was near enough to seize him at any moment. Why did the monster delay? Was it his splashings which deterred it? Tom hoped so, and thrust the water aside with greater energy.

And now he could hear the movement of the monster a little towards his right. It seemed to him that his pursuer was about to close with him, to attack him from another quarter. He remembered reading somewhere that sharks swim around their prey before seizing it. This movement, he thought, was for that purpose. Every moment he expected to see the dread form of that pursuer appearing between him and Phil, who was nearest. But he dared not look to assure himself. There was too much horror in the awful sight. He dared not turn his head to look behind; he dared not turn his eyes even to one side. He could only keep them fixed, with a wide stare, upon vacancy, straight before him.

The moments passed on,—the awful moments, each of which threatens death, when the delay of the impending doom fills the soul with awful suspense; still the monster hesitated to seize his prey. Still Tom's ears rang with the noise of his pursuer. Still the other boys, as though their tongues were frozen into silence, hurried to the shore. Still they waited, expecting every instant to hear the terrible shriek which should announce the awful doom of Tom. But the doom was still delayed, and still Tom waited, and still the others listened. So they all hastened, till each one's heart seemed almost ready to burst, through the frenzied energy of his efforts, and the intensity of his emotions. And there, behind them all,—a little on Tom's right,—the black muzzle advanced over the surface of the water.

In that desperate struggle, when they made such frantic efforts to reach the shore, Bruce happened to be first. The shore to which they were swimming was that which happened to be nearest; not the grassy knoll before mentioned, but a beach covered with gravel, which was intermixed with larger stones. Bushes grew close down to this beach, and beyond these was that road which had so disgusted the boys.

At this place Bruce first arrived. His feet touched bottom. No sooner did he feel the solid ground under his feet, than all his panic left him, all his courage returned, and his presence of mind. Tom's expected death-yell had not yet burst upon his ear; not yet had his shriek announced the grasp of the monster. There might yet be time to save. In an instant he had thought of what he should do. Plunging through the water, and bounding forward, he soon reached the beach; and then, stooping down, he hastily gathered several large stones. Then he turned, and rushing back a few steps, stood with uplifted arm, taking aim, and preparing to hurl these stones at the monster. At that very moment Arthur reached the place, and turned to look back, standing close by Bruce. Phil was now only a few yards away, swimming in, with horror yet stamped upon his face. Beyond him was Tom, swimming, kicking, plunging, rolling, dashing the water in all directions, and making as much commotion as would have satisfied an ordinary whale. As Tom thus swam on, his despairing glance caught sight of the forms of Bruce and Arthur. There they stood, up to their waists in water—Bruce with uplifted arm, holding an enormous stone, which he was about to throw—while in his other hand were several more stones. Arthur stood by his side.

Tom devoured them with his eyes; and he struggled on, wondering, yet scarcely daring to hope—wondering whether the stone which Bruce was preparing to throw would drive back the monster. To him it seemed that Bruce was delaying for an unaccountable time. Why did he stand idle, when every moment was so precious? Why did he delay to throw? Why did he not do something? Why did he stand there as if rooted to the spot doing nothing? Was there some new horror? Were the monster's jaws already opened to seize his prey?

Tom would have cried to Bruce to throw, but he could not speak. Not a sound could he utter. The thought came to him that Bruce was afraid to throw, for fear that the stone might strike him instead of the shark. What matter? Far better to throw, and run the risk. This he would have said, but he could not in that paralysis of horror.

Suddenly a frown came over Bruce's face—which frown as suddenly faded away, and was succeeded by a blank look, accompanied by an indescribable expression. The same changes passed over Arthur's face. Tom saw it all, in his despair, and was bewildered. What was this? Were they deserting him? Would they give him up? Impossible!

Yet it seemed as if they would. For suddenly Bruce's uplifted arm descended, and the stones all dropped into the water. The blank look upon his face was succeeded by one of astonishment, which faded away into various expressions, which successively indicated all the varying shades of vexation, shame, and sheepishness. Arthur's face was equally eloquent. Had not Tom's feelings so preoccupied him, he might have found a study in those two faces; but as it was, he was not in a position to think of such a thing; for these looks and gestures only served to inspire him with greater alarm.

"They can do nothing," he thought; and the thought brought to his soul a bitterness as of death.

At this moment Phil's feet touched bottom. He rushed up to Bruce and Arthur, and turned, as they had turned, to look back.

And at the same moment the abhorrent sight appeared to Tom—of the black muzzle shooting through the water close by his right shoulder. Involuntarily he shrunk aside, with the thought that his last hour had come.

XIII.

A Roar of Laughter from Bruce.—End of this tremendous Adventure.—Reticence of the whole Party on the Subject.—No one can taunt the other.—Departure from the Haunt of the Buccaneers.—The Antelope expands her white Wings, but in vain.—The Precautions of the venerable Corbet against dead Calms.—All labor at the Sweeps.—The Solace of Toil.—What Vessel are you gliding in?—Taking to the Boat.—Tumbling into Bed.

Suddenly a roar of laughter burst from Bruce.

"It's a dog! It's a dog!" he cried.—"Tom's shark's turned out to be a dog!"

And saying this, he burst into another roar of laughter. The laughter proved contagious. Arthur and Phil both joined in. Their recent horror had been so great that this sudden and unexpected turn affected them in a comical way, and the reaction was in proportion to their former panic fear. So their laughter was loud, boisterous, and unrestrained.

At the very moment when this cry had burst forth from Bruce, together with the peals of laughter, Tom had shrunk back in horror from the black muzzle that appeared on his right. But as he did so, and at the very moment of this horror in which his eyes were fixed on the monster, this monster became plainly revealed, and he saw it as it was.

He saw, what Bruce and the others now saw—a dog! a dog whose long, sharp muzzle and forehead were above the water, as also part of his back and his tail. He was a hound of some kind. Where he had come from, or where he was going to, or why he had appeared among them, they were, of course, unable to conjecture. Their whole recent terror had thus been the result of pure fancy in Tom's case, and in the case of the others the result of Tom's first shriek of alarm. In the case of all of them, however, the whole trouble was owing to the belief, of which they were not yet able to divest themselves, that this cove was some very sequestered spot. So convinced had they been of this, that even the sight of a public road had not altogether disabused them. They had been determined to find here the haunt of the buccaneers, and were unwilling to think that it might be a common resort, or even a regular thoroughfare. And therefore, when Tom had first caught sight of this black muzzle appearing above the surface of the water, he had been incapable of thinking about anything except a shark; and the horror that this thought created within him had been communicated to the others by his cries. Tom was the real cause of the whole mistake, and no one felt this more keenly than Tom himself; yet the others were all too much ashamed of their own recent terrors to twit or taunt him with his unfounded alarm.

The dog now swam alongside of Tom, and a little ahead of him, turning once or twice, and showing his face—not the cruel face of a monster of the deep, but the mild, humane, civilized, and benevolent countenance of a hound of the highest respectability; a face the sight of which made Tom feel renewed shame at his foolish and baseless fears.

The other boys walked up to the beach, and Tom soon joined them. The hound joined them also. He was a very friendly dog, and shook himself so violently that they all received a shower-bath from him. They patted him, and petted him, and stroked him; and these friendly advances of theirs were received in the politest possible manner by the well-bred hound, who finally planted himself on his haunches in the attitude known to dogs as "begging," which so affected the boys, that they would have given him some biscuit if their coats had not unfortunately been elsewhere. But the dog had evidently his own business to attend to, for after a short delay he took his leave, and trotted up the road. This sudden and unexpected turn which had been given to what had, at one time, seemed like the most terrible of tragedies, rapidly restored their strength and spirits, in spite of the tremendous sensations which they had but recently experienced, and the exertions which they had put forth. They now prepared to return to the place where they had left their clothes; and since the fear of sharks had departed, they took to the water again, and soon reached the knoll. Here they clothed themselves, and prepared to return to the schooner.

On reaching the Antelope, they were all sensible of the most extreme fatigue and prostration. The exertions which they had made in the ascent and descent of Aspotogon, and more especially in their efforts to escape the imaginary shark, were the cause of this in part; but a greater cause existed in the intense excitement and terror to which they had been subject. They were fortunate, however, in having such a place of refuge as the hold of the Antelope, for there they found awaiting them a dinner, prepared by Solomon, in which that famous cook had surpassed himself, and had turned out the rarest specimens of the culinary art. Their exertions had sharpened their appetites, and the long time that had elapsed since breakfast made this dinner seem like a banquet. It acted upon them all like a charm. Their physical natures were refreshed, and their moral natures also. Strength came to their bodies, and at the same time to their minds.

The affair of the shark was not mentioned. Under other circumstances, Bruce, and Arthur, and Phil might have taunted Tom with his absurd mistake; but as it was, they were all too much ashamed of their own fears, and of their own part in the affair. The consequence was, that all, with one consent, allowed the matter to drop, and made no reference to it whatever.

After dinner they went upon deck, and found all sail set, and the Antelope on her way back to Chester. But there was no wind whatever; it was a dead calm, and consequently the return to Chester was not likely to be accomplished very speedily. There was, from time to time, a faint puff of wind, it is true, which served, perhaps, to prevent the calm from being so dead as it might have been; yet, after all, their motion was so slight, and their progress so slow, that after two hours they had not put much more than a mile between themselves and the shore.

It was about four o'clock when they returned from Deep Cove to the Antelope. By six o'clock they had not made more than this one mile. The boys were now anxious to get back to Chester for various reasons. First, they wanted to have a good night's rest at the inn. Secondly, they wanted to see the landlord, and ask him all about Deep Cove. Thirdly, they wanted to see Bart and Pat, and tell them about their wonderful discovery of the "Mound," and their theory about the buried treasure. But the failure of the wind made it seem impossible for them to get back to Chester that night, and there was some talk of anchoring. To this, however, the boys would not listen, and they urged Captain Corbet to keep on and take advantage of any slight puffs of wind that might arise from time to time. Against this request Captain Corbet had no objections to offer, and so it was that the Antelope still moved on.

The Antelope therefore still held her sails expanded to catch any breath of wind that might arise, while the boys lounged along the taffrail, looking impatiently around. At another time they would not have failed to admire the beauty of the scene—the blue sea washing the long line of shore, and surrounding the numerous isles; but on the present occasion, they were too impatient and too tired to be affected by it. Time thus passed, and at length the sun went down in the western sky in a blaze of glory. By that time the boys found themselves approaching an island, which was about three miles from Aspotogon, and which thus indicated to them the distance which they had gone since leaving Deep Cove. Less than three miles in four hours had been their rate of progress.

The sun thus set, and the moon had now come out, throwing a gentler glow upon the scene, and lighting it up with wonderful beauty. The edges of the hills, and the outlines of the islands seemed all tipped with silver. On one side appeared Aspotogon, and Ironbound, and Tancook, rising out of the dark, shadowy water; while on the other side the islands shone in the lustre of the moon, and there, too, a broad pathway of radiant light lay outspread upon the surface of the water, reaching from the schooner to the horizon, where a low coast bounded the scene. Never had Mahone Bay appeared clothed in greater loveliness.

Captain Corbet had learned a very useful lesson during this last voyage of the Antelope, and that was to have some means on board by which he would not drift so helplessly. The long drifts which had borne him hither and thither over the Gulf of St. Lawrence, and over the ocean, had left a deep impression; and accordingly he had taken advantage of this visit to Chester to procure a pair of long sweeps, which may be described as oars of the largest size. On the present occasion, the sweeps were brought into requisition, one of them being worked by Turnbull, Bruce, and Phil, while the other was taken in hand by Wade, Arthur, and Tom. The venerable Corbet stood at the helm and steered, while Solomon stood at the bows, gazing pensively into space, and, as Tom declared, attitudinizing for a figure-head.

The sweeps were moved with very long, slow strokes. The two parties who managed them at first made an effort to work them in time, but at length gave this up, and each made their stroke at random, without reference to the others. Whether the Antelope made any progress or not, was not for a long time perceptible; but still the boys all felt as though they were doing something, and the lapse of time certainly seemed to bring them nearer to the island which they had been so long approaching.

The exercise was a pleasant one, and in order to cheer their spirits, they burst forth into songs. One was volunteered by Tom.

> *What vessel are you gliding in?*
> *\Pray tell to me its name;*
> *Our vessel is the Antelope,*
> *And Corbet is my name,*
> *And Corbet is my name,*
> *And Corbet is my name;*
> *Our vessel is the Antelope,*
> *And Corbet is my name.*

At this Captain Corbet's venerable face was all suffused with sudden smiles.

"Why railly," said he, "railly now, dew tell. Why, ef you ain't ben an done it agin. Only think, more himes about me. Why, it doos beat all. How upon airth dew you ever manage to fix em up that way? It doos—beat—my—grandmother!"

Other songs followed, till almost everything was made use of that they had ever heard—the Canadian Boat Song, the Maltese Boat Song, and others of a kindred character, including "Hail to the Chief," and "March!

March! Ettrick, and Teviotdale." In this way the time was beguiled, and their toil at the long sweeps lightened.

Around them the whole scene glowed in the moonlight. The silver islands set in silver seas, clothed in soft lustre, lay reflected in the smooth water. Overhead the moon hung in a cloudless sky, and lightened up all things with its soft and mellow radiance. They could see also by the change in their position, which they noticed from time to time, that they were actually making some progress with their sweeps, and the discovery, when it was made, encouraged them not a little.

So at it they all went again, more vigorously than ever, and sang new songs, some of which were of a kind never before heard in these waters. One in particular, which was sung to a remarkable fugue tune, was called Ode to Disappointment.

> *I never had a piece of bread*
> *Particularly wide,*
> *Partic-kik-kik-kik-kik-cu-lar-ly wide,*
> *But fell upon the dusty floor,*
> *All on the buttered side.*
> *All on the but—*
> *All on the but—*
> *All on the but—*
> *All on the but—*
> *All on the but-tut-tut-tut-tut-tut-tered side.*
> *And always thus, from childhood's hour,*
> *This luck on me has fell.*
> *This luck-kuk-kuk-kuk-kuk on me has fell.*
> *There always comes a soaking shower,*
> *When I've no umberell,*
> *When I've no umb—*
> *When I've no umb—*
> *When I've no umb—*
> *When I've no umb—*
> *When I've no umb-bum-bum-bum-bum-bum-bum-be-rell!*

This spirited ode was the arrangement of Phil, who prided himself hugely upon it. He did not claim it as original, but as having been "arranged" and "adapted" to its present tune.

"Well, boys," said Bruce at length, "I dare say we are making some progress; but it strikes me that it hardly pays."

"No," said Tom. "At this rate it'll take us till to-morrow morning to make another mile."

"I don't object to rowing all night," said Phil, "but I do object to row without getting the benefit of it."

"I move," said Arthur, "that we vote the sweeps a humbug."

"I second that motion," said Phil.

"Gentlemen," said Bruce, "it's being moved and seconded, that the sweeps are a humbug. Those of that mind will please manifest it by saying Ay."

"Ay!" rang forth from Arthur, Tom, and Phil.

"Contrary minds, Nay."

No response.

"It's a vote," said Bruce. And now, gentlemen, we may as well consider what's to be done next."

"O, well," said Phil, as he and the other boys left the sweeps which Turnbull and Wade, however, still kept working. "I suppose there's nothing left to do but to turn in."

"It can't be helped," said Arthur.

"We'll have to make the best of it," said Tom.

"I say, boys," said Bruce, "why can't we take the boat and row to Chester?"

"A good idea," cried Arthur. "Capital. I only wish we'd done it before."

"Captain," said Tom, "we're going to take the boat."

"Hadn't you better wait a little," said the anxious Corbet, who was evidently not pleased with the proposal.

"O there's no use; we want to get to Chester to-night. You'll get along before morning. How many miles is it from here?" he asked, turning to Turnbull.

"Four," said that taciturn individual.

"Four miles. Well, boys, what do you say?"

"I'm agreed," said Bruce.

"And I," said Arthur.

"Anything's better than this," said Phil; "so I agree to the boat."

With this agreement they all turned to the boat, and got in. A few brief directions were given by Turnbull, and the boys pulled away. First Bruce and Arthur pulled, then Tom and Phil. Taking turns in this way, they had the satisfaction of seeing themselves making good progress, and at length reached the wharf at Chester.

It was about three o'clock in the morning. They knocked up the people at the inn, and hurried up to their rooms. They were so utterly worn out, and so sleepy, that they did not think of asking about Bart and Pat, but tumbled into bed, and in a few moments were all sound asleep.

XIV.

Bart and Pat.—Terrible Situation.—The first Horror, and its Effects.—An Attempt to climb.—Another Attempt to scale the Corners.—Trying the Sides.—Too wide by far.—Pat wants to tie a Rope to Nothing.—The Pickaxe.—New Attempts at Climbing.— New Disappointments.—Pat's Fertility of Invention.—A new Suggestion.—A dangerous Experiment.—Running the Risk.— Tugging at the Logs.—The obstinate Fabric.—Baffled and beaten.

There, side by side, stood the two boys, at the bottom of that deep pit, into which they had descended; and, standing there, they looked with unutterable feelings at the opening far above them, across which was suspended the treacherous beam. At first there was a thrill of expectation, in both of them, that the beam was even then breaking, and at any instant might fall and crush them. It had sagged down so far, and the fracture was so complete, that the end might come in another moment. Thus they stood, and looked up in silence, and with hearts that throbbed fast and painfully. Neither of them spoke a word. It was as much as they could do to breathe.

A terrible position it was, and how terrible they knew only too well. One hundred feet below the ground, and seventy feet below the level of the sea—such was the depth of that pit. It was so long and so narrow that the bottom was quite dark. As they stood with their eyes thus fixed on the threatening beam, they noticed that the sky beyond it had changed in its color from blue to black, and two or three stars were faintly visible. It was like the sky of night, and not like that of day. That little piece of sky thus indicated to them the change in their fate, and seemed to frown upon them from above.

In their minds there was one prevailing sense of mute horror and awful expectation; yet, together with this, a thousand other thoughts flashed through them—thoughts of friends, thoughts of home, wild speculations as to the possibility of escape; and with these they noticed also that black piece of sky, with its faintly-twinkling stars. But between them and it, between the upper world which that sky spoke of and themselves, there intervened that broken beam stretching across like a bar, to shut them in forever.

Now, gradually, the first horror passed. It was too intense a feeling to endure. The delay of their fate made them calmer, and brought back presence of mind; for the beam moved no more—it fell not—perhaps it might remain as it was, threatening them, but doing no more than that.

This respite from their doom thus, brought them back to themselves, and made them search eagerly the sides of the pit as they looked up.

"I wonder if we can't climb it, thin," said Pat.

"I'm afraid not," said Bart, in a dejected tone.

"Sure an there's no harrum in given it a thrial," said Pat; and, as he said so, he laid his hands upon the staying around the hole. Scarce had he done this, than he was aware of a difference between the staying here, and that which was higher up. Bart, also, who had done as Pat had done, and tried to find some way of climbing, noticed the same thing.

Had the staying below been like that above, the question of their escape would very soon have been settled by such practised climbers as these two; but, unfortunately, there was a very important difference. Above, the staying had been made of stout planks and deals, and these were far enough apart to have served for grasping by both hands and feet. They would thus have afforded an actual ladder. Below, however, it was very different. The staying of the sides of the pit was made, not of planks, which could be grasped by the hands, but of round logs, which the hands could not hold, though the feet could insert themselves well enough in the interstices. These logs rested closely one upon the other, nor was there any way by which the hands could pass between them or around them so as to grasp them. This, then, was the discovery that Bart and Pat made the moment that they tried their hands at climbing; and thus the first plan of escape which had suggested itself was baffled most completely.

"If we only had the planks!" sighed Bart: "but these round logs give no chance."

Pat made no reply.

Bart then tried to climb at the corner, for here there would be more advantage to the feet, since the sides, being at right angles, would afford an easier foothold. But, though it was easier for the feet, it gave no greater help to the hands than before. Still, there were the round logs; nor was there at the angle formed by the sides any spaces sufficient to receive the hand and afford a hold.

"If we cud only get up as far as the rope," said Pat, "it might give us a help, so it might."

"What! when that beam is hanging there? Why, if you touched that rope the beam would come down."

"Sure an I forgot that for the moment, so I did," said Pat, dejectedly.

"Strange we didn't notice that the beam was rotten," said Bart, mournfully. "It looked sound enough."

"It looked as sound as a nut, so it did; and how it managed to howld on till I jarked it bates me intirely, so it does."

"It must have been sagging down and cracking all the time. The only wonder is, that it didn't give way when we were higher up. If it had, there'd have been an end of us."

"Sure 'n you niver spoke a truer word in your life, so you didn't; an, be the same token, it's a good sign, so it is, an a fine thing intirely, that we're down here now at this blissid minute, wid our bones not broke to smithereens. Sure but it makes me fairly shiver whin I think of you an me, one after the other, hangin away up there from that bit of rotten stick that was broken all the time."

"If this wasn't quite so wide," said Bart, "we might stretch our legs across, and get up that way. I've seen men go down into wells as easy as you please, just by stretching their legs across."

"Sure an meself it is that's seen that same," said Pat, briskly; "an I wondher whether, afther all, our legs mightn't be long enough to do it."

"O, no," said Bart; "it's too wide altogether."

"Sure an we might then; an there's nothin like tryin."

With these words Pat set himself to try, and Bart did the same. They tried by stretching their legs as far as possible on each side to secure a foothold, and thus ascend. Had the pit been narrower, or had their legs been longer, they could have done it; but, as it was, they found it quite impossible. "They could, indeed, touch the beams on either side if they stretched their legs as far apart as possible; but, having accomplished this, they could do no more. They could not raise their feet higher to the log above. So rigid were their legs when thus spread apart, that they could not raise them. At length they were compelled to desist from these efforts.

"It's too wide intirely, so it is," said Pat, dolefully. "An whativer was the use of makin the hole so wide is beyond me. It wasn't any use at all at all, so it wasn't; an there you have it."

"The fault's in our legs as much as in the pit," said Bart. "If we were five years older we might do it."

"Sure I always thought I cud climb betther thin any man till this blissid momint," said Pat.

"I only wish I was a man for about five minutes," said Bart, fervently.

"Two minutes'd jist do it, so it wad," said Pat.

"Yes," said Bart.

"An these logs don't go all the way up. If we cud only get up to the planks we'd be all right."

"I didn't notice particularly," said Bart, "but it seems to me that the plank staying reaches nearly halfway down."

"Full that, ivery inch of it, so it does," said Pat.

"If we could only get up as far as that!" exclaimed Bart.

"Faith, I have it," said Pat, suddenly.

"What?" asked Bart, with some excitement.

"I have it," repeated Pat. "It's a rope we want."

"A rope!" exclaimed Bart.

"Yis, a bit of a rope; ony we haven't got one long enough."

"Why, what good would a rope be to us here?" asked Bart, in a puzzle to know what in the world Pat had got into his head.

"Sure, I have it. Can't we twist a rope an make this longer?"

"I don't know what you're after," said Bart, impatiently. "What do you mean?"

"Sure an we can tear up our coats an shirts, an make a rope that way; ony," he added, thoughtfully, "it mightn't be long enough, so it mightn't."

"Nonsense," said Bart; "you're crazy. What do we want of a rope?"

"Sure, to climb with.

"How? Where would you fasten it?"

"Fasten it, is it?" said Pat, in a dubious tone; "sure that same I niver thought of at all at all. I forgot all about it, so I did."

"Well, we'll have to do something," said Bart. "We can't stand still here and die."

"There's the bit of a pick here," said Pat. "Sure an we ought to be able to do somethin with the pick, so we ought."

And with these words he stooped and lifted up the pickaxe which he had thrown in before they went down, and which, in the anguish and excitement which they had thus far felt, had been altogether forgotten.

"We ought to do something with that," said Bart.

"It won't do any good to more thin one of us," said Pat, sadly, "for only one of us can use it at a time."

"Nonsense," said Bart; "if one of us can only climb up, can't he help the other?"

"Sure an so he can," said Pat; "an I niver thought of that, so I didn't."

"I wonder if we can climb with that?" said Bart.

"Sure an we can try," said Pat; "an we ought to do somethin, so we ought."

With these words, he thrust the pick between two timbers, a few feet above his head, and then clutching it, he raised himself up to a level with the pick, in the easiest way possible. Hanging there for a moment, with his hands grasping the pick, and his feet stuck tight between the logs, he tried to raise himself higher. To do this, it was necessary to hold himself there, while removing the pick, and raising it to the logs farther up. But here was the fatal and insuperable difficulty; and this brought them exactly back to where they were before. Do what he would, his hands could not grasp the round logs with sufficient firmness to maintain a hold. After a few efforts he gave it up, and jumped down.

Bart then tried, making his attempt at the corner of the pit, where the angle of the two sides favored him more. Striking the pick in between two logs, as high up as he could reach, he raised himself up as Pat had done, and then tried to lift himself higher. He found a place which he could grasp, and clinging to this with a convulsive effort, he raised the pick to the logs farther up, and succeeded in thrusting it into a new place. Then he drew himself up higher, and once more searched about for a place to grasp. But now no place could be found. In vain he tried to thrust his fingers between the logs; in vain he sought to grasp the round surface. It was a thing that could not be done. After a long but fruitless effort, Bart was compelled to give up. Yet he was not satisfied. He tried the other three corners of the pit in succession. In all of them his efforts met with the same result—failure, utter and hopeless.

At length he flung down the pick, and stood panting.

"Deed, thin, an I'm glad to see you back, so I am," said Pat.

"Glad!" said Bart.

"Yis, glad I am; that same's what I mane. I'd rather have you fail down here, than half way up. You niver cud go all the way; an if you had to turrun back when half way up, it's a sore head I'd have watchin you; an you cud niver expict to git back here again without broken bones."

"If we only had one other pickaxe," said Bart, "I could do it."

"Of coorse you cud; an if we had dizens of other thing, you cud do it, so you cud, an so cud I; but there's the throuble, an that's what we've got to contind against, so it is."

"We'll have to do something," said Bart, gloomily and desperately.

"Sure an that's thrue for you, so it is, an you niver spoke a thruer word in yer life, so you didn't," said Pat; "an be the same token, it's with this pick, so it is, that we've got to work,—for it's the only thing we've got at all at all."

"What can we do," said Bart, in the same gloomy tone, "if we can't climb?"

"Sure an there's lots more, so there is," said Pat, who on this occasion showed a wonderful fertility of invention. "I've ben a thinkin," he added, "that we might dig away these logs with the pick."

"What good would that do?" asked Bart.

"Sure an we might dig thim out one by one, an pile thim up as we dug thim, an so we might make a pile of logs high enough to reach to the top."

Bart was silent for a few moments. The suggestion was certainly of some value.

"I wonder whether we mightn't shake that log down on us, by pounding away down here?"

"Sure an it's the only thing," said Pat. "We've got to run some risk, of coorse; an I don't think that our blows would be felt so high up. Besides, we needn't sthrike very hard."

"Well," said Bart, "it's the only thing we can do."

Upon this, Pat inserted the point of the pick between the logs near him, and tried to pry the lower one out at one end. But the stubborn log resisted his efforts. It had been too firmly fixed in its place to yield to such a slight force as that which he could bring. Bart lent his efforts, and the two exerted themselves with their utmost strength, but altogether in vain.

"If we cud ony git out one log," said Pat, "it wud be aisy workin out the others, so it wud; but this one seems a tough customer, so it does."

"There ought to be some log about here," said Bart, "weaker than others."

"Sure an that's thrue for you," said Pat, "an so we'll jist thry thim all one afther another, ivery one of them. We've got lots of time, so we have."

"See, here's a smaller one," said Bart.

Pat struck the point of the pick where Bart pointed, and once more the two boys exerted themselves to pry out the log. But though this one was somewhat smaller than the other, it was quite as firmly fixed, and the utmost efforts of both of them failed to move it, even in the slightest degree, from its bed.

"Sure an there's no danger of this pit iver cavin in," said Pat, as he desisted from his efforts. "They made this pit strong enough to howld a iliphant, so they did—the worse for us."

"Well," said Bart, "we'll have to try every log that's within reach."

"Sure an we ought to find some weak spot if we do, so we ought," said Pat.

Bart now inserted the pick between the logs just above the last one.

"This is jist what we intinded to do whin we come down," said Pat; "for weren't we goin to thry to git to the money-hole?"

Bart said nothing.

The two boys now tugged away as before. But the result was the same, for this log was as firmly fixed, as tough, and as obdurate as the others.

"Sure an it's hard, so it is, that the very log we trusted our lives to should turrun out to be rotten, an all these logs here should be as sound an as strong as steel an iron, ivery mother's son of thim. If we cud only find a rotten one, an pull it out of its place, we'd be able to git at the others aisy, and haul out all the rist of thim."

The boys now tried other logs, one after the other; but from all of them they met with the very same stubborn resistance. They had all been placed here evidently by men who worked conscientiously; and were determined to leave no weak spot exposed to the pressure of the earth. And, as was natural, that which had withstood so well the pressure of the surrounding soil, was easily able to withstand the puny efforts of a couple of boys.

XV.

Pat and the Pick.—A dangerous Plan.—Undermining the very Foundation.—A terrible Risk.—Something like an Earthquake.—A Way opened.—They make an Ascent.—A sudden Stop.—The projecting Log.—The Pickaxe.—Who shall go down?—A new Descent.—The Watch of Bart.—Alarm.—A Call.—Silence.—Terror.—An Answer.—Fearful Intelligence.—The very worst.—The Drain.—The rising Waters.—The Pit flooded.—The impending Doom.

In this way they went over all the logs, and at length reached the lowest layer of all. At this point, Pat's superior dexterity with the pick enabled him to invent and to put in practice a plan which could not have been used before, or with any of the logs except these lowest ones. For beneath these was the earth, and Pat's plan was the natural and simple one of digging this earth away, and so undermining the log that lay there. Pat worked nimbly and thoroughly, and as he loosened the soil, Bart scraped it away with his hands. Pat dug down to the depth of a foot all along, and then thrust the pick far in, scooping out the earth that lay on the other side of the log. In this way they succeeded in removing the earth that kept the log in its place, and at length they were able to detach it, and draw it forth.

The removal of this one log served to make the removal of the others possible. By diligent efforts the four logs which composed the lower tier were detached. The side logs were too long for the pit, and therefore had to be placed erect, and leaned against the side. The end logs could lie down easily. The second tier then followed and was removed more easily than the first. Then the third tier was detached, and the fourth. In each case the logs of the side had to be stood erect, while the end logs were laid on the ground at the bottom.

A serious difficulty now appeared before the boys, and one, too, for which they had not been prepared. The length of the side logs was a very embarrassing circumstance. They were too long to be placed at the bottom, and had to be stood up. But this took up space, and infringed very seriously upon the narrow area in which their operations were carried on. In passing from one side to remove the logs on the other, they had to lift these backward and forward so as to get them out of the way—a work which was most exhaustive, and at the same time hindered them in their proper efforts. Still they kept on, until at length about eight tiers of logs had been removed, and the longer ones filled up so much space, that it was quite impossible to do any more. They still worked away at those which were within reach, and managed to remove a dozen logs more; but after this they could do nothing, for the bottom of the pit was completely filled, and the staying was now a compact mass from which nothing further could be detached until the logs were removed which were covered up by those piled against it.

Bart and Pat were now compelled to desist for a time, and as they felt quite exhausted, they raised themselves to the top of the pile of upright logs, and there sat down. Scarcely had they done this, when they were aware of a trembling all around, like an earthquake. In horror they sprang to their feet. The sides seemed to be moving; the logs separated, and descended, and through the crevices there protruded sand and clay. It was as though the whole mass of the casing was falling in. In an instant they knew what it was. In their thoughtlessness they had taken away the foundations of this structure, and it was all falling in. An involuntary cry of terror burst from both. They shrank together, clinging to the pile on which they stood, and awaited their last hour.

But once again there was a respite. The movement ceased. The worst seemed to be over, at least for the present. Yet the result of this one movement was fearful as far as it went. All the logs of the casing seemed severed and distorted, and had apparently descended as far as they had dug away the foundations. Seeing this, another frightful thought came— the broken beam above. They looked up fearfully. As yet, however, the danger impending hesitated to strike, for there, across the mouth of the hole, they saw the broken beam defined against the sky. It did not appear to have moved; nor was there that appearance of irregularity about the upper casing of the pit which now marked the lower. It seemed to them as though the slighter staying of plank had been put in the upper part of the pit, because it was clay, and needed but little protection; but down below, where the soil was looser, stout logs had been required. As they looked up, they saw that all this lower casing of logs had fallen.

No sooner had they discovered this than they saw also something which inspired them with hope. Not only had the lower staying of logs thus descended, but it had also lost its cohesion, and the logs all seemed to be separated by spaces of more or less width, while many of them protruded into the pit as though thrust in by the pressure of the earth. Now they recognized at a glance the tremendous risk that they had run while removing the lowest logs; but at the same glance they perceived that the immediate danger had passed, and that they were now at least less helpless than before. For now, at last, there need be no difficulty about climbing. Now the spaces between the logs were wide enough for them to find something which they might grasp with their hands, and for some distance up, at any rate, they could see what seemed like a ladder, up which they might climb in search of escape from this fearful place.

No sooner had they made this discovery than they at once caught at this prospect which thus had so unexpectedly opened before them, and began to climb. The task was not very difficult. Each one took a corner of the pit where the meeting of the two walls favored the ascent, and for some time they continued to mount without much difficulty.

"Sure but I'm afraid this is too good to last," said Pat.

Bart made no reply. That very fear was in his own mind. In that suspense he could say nothing. At last they had mounted as high as the place where the rope had broken. The end hung here suspended most tantalizingly. O, what joy it would have been for them had it been the rope alone which had thus broken,—if the beam had only continued sound; but now that rope was useless, and they dared not touch it for fear lest even a touch might bring down upon their heads the beam that hung there impending over them. Fortunately they were able to ascend yet higher, for still above them the log casing had been started asunder, and still they found themselves able to grasp places of support. The staying had certainly undergone a universal disintegration, and nothing but its great compactness had prevented it from falling in ruin over their heads, and burying them alive. It was with amazement and consternation that they recognized their work, and these feelings would have overwhelmed them had they not found the result, after all, so fortunate for themselves. The risk had passed away. For the present, at least, they were receiving the benefit.

The fear which Pat had expressed, and which Bart had felt without expressing, that the ascent was too good a thing to last, was at length proved to be only too well founded. After they had climbed some distance farther, they found their ascent brought to an abrupt termination. For here there was a kind of separation between the lower casing and the upper; a log bulged forward about a foot, and above this there was a gap in the casing about two feet in height which showed the earth behind, a kind of clay, and in this there was a cavity caused by the falling of the casing. Above this the casing had held firm, but unfortunately they had not reached the planks. They were the same round logs which rose above them, and which would be as difficult to scale from this point as they had proved from below.

Upon this ledge, formed by the bulging logs, they clambered, and seated themselves, dejected at the termination of their ascent, yet relieved slightly by the chance which was now afforded of some rest and breathing space. Here they sat, and looked up.

"Sure an it's hard, so it is," said Pat, "to find an ind to it just here, whin, if we'd only been able to climb twinty or thirty feet further, we'd have got to the planks, an been all safe."

"Yes," said Bart, looking up, "there are the planks; and they're not more than thirty feet above us at the farthest."

"An yit they're as much out of our raich as though they were a hundred, so they are."

"I'd rather have the thirty feet, at any rate," said Bart. "Come now; can't we manage to get farther up."

"Nivir a farther," said Pat. "We've got to the ind of our journey."

"Come now," said Bart. "See here, Pat. You spoke of a tunnel once. In fact we came down here with the pickaxe on purpose to make a tunnel to the money-hole. Well, we're after something more precious than money—life itself. Can't we tunnel up to life?"

"Tunnel, is it?" cried Pat, in great excitement. "Of coorse we can. Ye've jist hit it, so you have. It's what we'll do. We will thin."

"The soil here seems like clay; and if we cut up behind this casing, it'll be comparatively safe," said Bart. "We need only cut up to the planks."

"Sure an we'll have to cut up to the top."

"O, no! When we get to the planks, we can break through, and climb them like a ladder to the top. Once up to the planks, and we're safe."

"Break through the plankin is it? Sure enough; right are you; that's what we'll do, so it is."

"And so that makes only thirty feet to cut away. It'll be hard work cutting upwards; but you and I ought to manage it, Pat, when our lives are at stake."

"Manage it? Of coorse; why not? Only we haven't got that bit of a pick with us, so we haven't, for we left it down below; an sorra one of me knows what's become of it. It may be buried under the roons of the fallin logs."

At this Bart looked at Pat with something like consternation.

"Well," said he at length, "we'll have to go down again—one of us; we must have that pickaxe. I'll go."

"Sure an you won't," said Pat; "meself's the one that's goin to go."

"No, you shan't. Poh! Don't be absurd."

"Sure I'm bound to go; and so don't you go too. There's not the laste nicissity in life for both of us to go."

"O, well, then," said Bart, "we'll have to toss up for it. That's all."

And saying this, he took out a piece of money, and said to Pat—

"Head or Tail?"

"Tail," said Pat.

Bart tossed. Pat lost. It was Pat's business therefore to go down.

"Sure an it's aisy climbin," said Pat, "an the pick'll be a help whin I returrun."

With these words he departed.

Seated on the log, Bart looked down, watching Pat's descent. They had climbed about half way up the pit, and Pat had about fifty feet to go down. Looking down, it was dark, and Pat at length disappeared from view. Bart could only hear him as he moved about. At length there was a deep stillness.

Bart grew alarmed.

"Pat!" he called.

No answer came.

"Pat!" he called again.

Still no answer.

"Pat!" he called, as loud as he could, for he was now thoroughly frightened. As he called, he put his feet over, and prepared to descend.

"I'm here," Pat's voice came up. "Don't come down. I'm coming up."

These words filled Bart with a feeling of immense relief. He now heard Pat moving again, and at length saw him ascending. Nearer he came, and nearer. But Bart noticed that he did not have the pickaxe. He feared by this that it had been buried beneath the fallen logs. If so, their situation was as desperate as ever. But he said not a word.

Pat at length reached the place where Bart was, and flung himself down, panting heavily. Bart watched him in silence.

"The pickaxe is buried," said he at length, "I suppose."

"Worse," said Pat, with something like a groan.

"Worse?" repeated Bart in dismay.

"Yis, worse," said Pat. "The water's comin in. There's six feet of it, an more too. The hole's flooded, an fillin up."

At this awful intelligence Bart sat petrified with horror, and said not one word.

"It's the diggin away at the casin," said Pat, dolefully, "an the cuttin away of the earth, that's done the business, so it is. I can onderstand it all easy enough. Sure this pit's close by the money-hole, an the bottom of it's close by the drain that they towld us of. An them that made this hole didn't dare to go one inch further. An that's the very thing, so it is, that we've done. We've cut, and dug, and broke through into the drain. What's worse, all the casin an all the earth's broke and fallen down. An there's no knowin the mischief we've done. Any how, we've broke through to the "drain"—bad luck to it; and the water's jist now a powerin in fast enough. Sure it's got to the top of them logs that we stood upon end—the long ones; and they're more'n six feet long, an it's risin ivery minit, so it is, an it's comin up, an it'll soon be up to this place, so it will. An sure it's lost an done for we are intirely, an there you have it."

After this dreadful intelligence, not a word was spoken for a long time. Pat had said his say, and had nothing to add to it. Bart had heard it, and had nothing to say. He was dumb. They were helpless. They could go no farther. Here they were on this log, half way up the pit, but unable to ascend any further, and with the prospect before them of swift and inevitable destruction.

They had worked long and diligently. Not one mouthful had they eaten since morning; but in their deep anxiety, they had felt no hunger. They had labored as those only can labor who are struggling for life. And this was the end. But all this time they had not been conscious of the passage of the hours; yet those hours had been flying by none the less. Time had been passing during their long labor at the logs below—how much time they had never suspected.

The first indication which they had of this lapse of time was the discovery which they now made of a gradually increasing gloom. At first they attributed this to the gathering of clouds over the sky above; but after a time the gloom increased to an extent which made itself apparent even to their despairing minds. And what was it? Could it be twilight? Could it be evening? Was it possible that the day had passed away? Long indeed had the time seemed; yet, even in spite of this, they felt an additional shock at this discovery. Yet it was true. It was evening. The day was done. They two had passed the day in this pit. This was night that was now coming swiftly on.

They remained motionless and silent. Nothing could be done; and the thoughts of each were too deep for utterance. Words were useless now. In the mind of each there was an awful expectation of a doom that was coming upon them—inevitable, swift, terrible! They could only await it in dumb despair.

Night was coming, adding by its darkness to the horror of their situation. Death in daylight is bad enough, but in the dark how much worse! And the fate that threatened them appeared wherever they might turn their eyes—above, in the shape of that broken beam which yet in the twilight appeared defined in a shadowy form against the dim sky; around, in this treacherous casing, which, being undermined, might at any moment fall, like the lower portion, and crush them; beneath, most awfully, and most surely, are those dark, stealthy, secret waters which had come in from the "drain" upon them as though to punish their rashness, and make them pay for it with their lives. In the midst of all these fears they remembered the superstitious words of the man whom they had questioned, "Flesh and blood will never lay hands on that treasure, unless there's a sacrifice made—the sacrifice of human life!" Such was the declaration of the man on the shore, and this declaration now made itself remembered. The sacrifice of life. What life? Was it theirs? Were they, then, the destined victims? Awful thought! Yet how else could it be? Yes, that declaration was a prophecy, and that prophecy was being fulfilled in them. But O, how hard it was to die thus! so young! in such a way! to die when no friends were near! and where their fate would never, never be known to those friends.

XVI.

Waking from a sound Sleep.—The Missing Ones.—An earnest Debate.—Various Theories.—Fishing versus Sailing.— Afloat or Ashore.—Emotion of the venerable Corbet.—His solemn Declaration.—The Antelope or the Whaler.—Stick to the Antelope.—A new Arrival.—The Landlord's View of the Case.—New Doubts and Perplexities.—"Afloat or Ashore" again.—The Landlord's View of the Sailing Theory, and his Decision in Favor of the Fishing Hypothesis.— The Lost Ones must be camping out for the Night.

The boys at the inn slept soundly, and did not wake until after their usual time. On going down to breakfast, they looked about for Bart and Pat. At first they thought that their two friends had already taken their breakfast, and gone out; but an incidental remark of the landlady made known to them the fact that they had not been back to the inn at all. This intelligence they received with serious faces, and looks of surprise and uneasiness.

"I wonder what can be the meaning of it," said Bruce.

"It's queer," said Arthur.

"They were very mysterious about going, in the first place," said Tom. "I don't see what sense there was in making such a secret about it. They must have gone some distance."

"Perhaps they didn't think we'd be back so soon," said Phil, "and have planned their own affair, whatever it is, to last as long as ours."

"O, they must have known," said Bruce, "that we'd be back to-day. Aspotogon is only a few miles. In fact we ought to have been back yesterday, in time for tea, by rights."

"Where in the world could they have gone to?" said Arthur.

"O, fishing, of course," said Tom.

"But they ought to have been back last night."

"O, they've found some first-rate sport."

"After all," said Phil, "there wasn't any actual reason for them to come back. None of us are in any hurry."

"Yes; but they may have got into some scrape," said Bruce. "Such a thing is not inconceivable. It strikes me that several members of this party have already got into scrapes now and then; and so I'm rather inclined to think that the turn has come round to Bart and Pat."

"What I'm inclined to think," said Arthur, "is, that they've gone off in a boat for a sail before breakfast, and have come to grief somehow."

"Well, if they tried a sail-boat, they were pretty sure of that," said Tom.

"Yes," said Phil; "neither Bart nor Pat know anything more about sailing a boat than a cow does."

"At any rate," said Bruce, "they can't have fallen into any very serious danger."

"Why not?"

"There hasn't been any wind worth speaking of."

"Neither there has."

"But there was some wind yesterday morning," said Arthur. "It carried us to Aspotogon very well."

"Pooh! Such a wind as that wouldn't do anything. A child might have sailed a boat."

"O, I don't know. That wind might have caught them off some island, and capsized them."

"I don't believe that wind could have capsized even a paper boat," said Phil; "but still I'm inclined to think, after all, that they've met with some sort of an accident in a boat."

"I don't believe it," said Tom. "They couldn't meet with any kind of accident. My opinion is, that they went off fishing, kept at it all day, got too far away to think of coming back last night, and so very naturally put up at some farm-house, where they have by this time eaten a good, rattling breakfast, and are on their way back, walking like the very mischief."

"The most natural thing in the world too," said Bruce. "I quite agree with Tom. It's just what any other two of us fellows would have done. In the first place, they backed out of the Aspotogon expedition very quietly, so as not to make a fuss, then they went off, and, as Tom says, got too far to come back; though whether they've had such a tremendous adventure as ours at Deep Cove with the shark is a matter that has yet to be decided."

This first allusion to the shark was received by all the party with a solemn smile.

"Well," said Arthur, "I believe they've taken to a boat. Perhaps they've gone cruising about."

"But they couldn't have been capsized."

"No."

"Then how do you account for their absence?"

"Easily enough," said Phil. "I believe they've gone visiting some of the islands, and somehow they've lost their sail, or their oars, or else they've been careless about fastening the boat, and she's drifted away. And so I dare say that at this very moment they are on some desert island in this bay, within a mile or so of this town, looking out for help; but if they are, they must be pretty hungry by this time, for it isn't every island that can furnish such a bill of fare as Ile Haute gave to Tom."

"A perfectly natural explanation," said Arthur. "Those two fellows are both so abominably careless, that, if they did go ashore on any island, they'd be almost certain to leave the boat loose on the beach, to float away wherever it liked. I believe, as Phil says, that they're on some island not far away."

"I don't," said Bruce. "I believe that they went fishing."

"Well, what are we to do about it? Oughtn't we to hunt them up?" said Phil.

"I don't see the use," said Tom. "They'll be along by dinner time."

"Well, for my part," said Arthur, "I can't sit here and leave them to their fate. I believe they are in a fix, and consequently I intend to go off to hunt them up."

"So will I," said Phil.

"Well, of course, if you go, I'll go too," said Bruce.

"So will I," said Tom; "though I don't believe there's the slightest necessity. Bart and Pat'll turn up somewhere about noon, and find us gone. They'll then go off in search of us. Well, it'll amount to the same thing in the end, and so, perhaps, it's the best way there can be of filling up the time."

"I wonder if the Antelope's got back," said Bruce.

"I don't know."

"Suppose we go down and talk it over with Captain Corbet."

"All right."

With these words the boys rose from the breakfast table, and went down to the wharf. As they approached they saw the Antelope lying there at her former berth; for she had arrived about an hour before, and had come here.

"Wal, boys," said he, as he saw them, "here we air once more, jined together as before; though whether you did well in a desertin of the ship in mid-ocean is a pint that I don't intend to decide. You might as well have turned into your old quarters aboard, an slep calm an comfortable, instead of rowin six or eight mile by night. However, you don't none o' you look any the wuss for it, an so we'll let bygones be bygones. Ony I'm pleased, likewise relieved, to see you here, instead of havin to larn that you're among the missin, an probably roamin the seas in a open boat. An where, may I ask, air Bart and Pat?"

The answer to this question plunged the good Corbet from the comfort in which he had settled himself, down into the depths of anxiety and worriment.

"What! Not back yit?" he said. "You don't say so. Is this railly so?"

"Yes."

"What! all yesterday, an all last night?"

"Yes."

"An no word of partin—and no directions as to where they went, an when they'd return?"

"Not a word."

"An nobody seen them go?"

"No."

"An nobody's seen anythin of them at all?"

"No, nothing."

"An you don't even know whether they're in danger or safety?"

"No."

"Nor even whether they're on land or water?"

"No."

Captain Corbet shook his head slowly and sadly, and turned away with the profoundest dejection and melancholy depicted upon his venerable yet expressive features.

"Tom and I think they've gone off fishing," continued Bruce, who had told the tale of woe; "but Arthur and Phil are afraid that they've gone off in a boat, and have met with some accident. They're determined to go off to hunt them up, and we've concluded to go too, as we don't care about staying behind doing nothing; though, at the same time, we don't believe they've come to any harm, and we think they'll be coming after us. We thought we'd let you know; and perhaps we'd better put off in the Antelope, unless you think a small boat would be better."

"O, yes," said Arthur, "let's go in a small boat. The Antelope won't do. There'll be another calm, and we'll have to stand still and do nothing."

"We could get one of these whalers," said Phil, pointing to a number of boats at the wharf.

These boats were sharp at each end, and were therefore called "whalers" on account of their shape, and not because they were ever used, or ever intended to be used, against whales. They were large and capacious and well ballasted; while, at the same time, they were not too large to be rowed, in case of calms or head winds.

"O, bother the whalers," said Tom; "let's stick to the Antelope, whatever we do. Whenever we leave the Antelope, we're sure to come to grief. Besides, I don't like to have to stuff myself into a little open boat. I like to move about, and walk up and down, and change my position."

"So do I, for that matter," said Phil; "but then, you know, we may be caught in a calm, as we were last night."

"O, there's lots of wind now."

"But it mightn't last."

"Then, if it don't, we can take to the boat."

"What, our little row-boat?"

"Yes; why not?"

"Why, we can't go any distance in her; she's too small."

"O, let's get a whaler," said Arthur, "and then we'll be ready for wind or calm."

"Well," said Bruce, "if I thought that Bart and Pat were really out anywhere in the bay, I'd say, take a whaler; but as I consider this expedition a wild-goose chase, I go in for comfort, and vote for the Antelope."

"Well, we won't do anything; that's all; and if they are in danger, we'll be sorry for it."

"O, I'll run the risk."

"We're a tie," said Phil. "Let's give Captain Corbet the casting vote. Come, captain, what do yon say about it? Do you think they're on land or water? and do you advise a whaler or the Antelope?"

"Me?" said Captain Corbet, mournfully. "Me? Wal, for my part, I've come to believe the wust. I believe them two air at this moment on some lone rock of the deep, gazin in despair upon the waste of water, and lookin wildly in all directions for help. And so it ever hath been, and ever shall be. Amen. For my part, I'm free to say, that I never see, nor never hear tell of, nor never even dreamt of the likes of you. If you get out of my sight for one moment, you're sure to be engaged in reskin your lives about nothin. An I'll give up. If Providence restores them two, I hereby declar solemn, that it's my fixed intention to start right straight off for hum; never to stop at one single place, nor even to go near any land, till I touch the wharf at Grand Pré. What this here's goin to end in beats me; and this last business doos beat my grandmother. As for you, I advise you to stick to the Antelope, and sail under the old flag. Them's my sentiments."

This advice of Captain Corbet was accepted as his decision, and so it was resolved to set off in the Antelope, and cruise round the bay. Such a search was, of course, not very promising; but Arthur and Phil had a vague idea that in the course of the cruise they would see the two missing ones making signals of distress from some lonely island, and that thus they might be rescued. As for Captain Corbet, he still remained melancholy, though not at all despairing; for though he insisted that the boys were in some danger, he yet believed that they would be rescued from it.

In the midst of this conversation, they were interrupted by the appearance of the landlord. He had just returned from that journey up the country, which had prevented him from accompanying them to Aspotogon on the previous day. He had learned at the inn the state of affairs, and had at once come down to the wharf. The boys, on the other hand, knowing that he had been up the country, thought it possible that he might have seen or heard something of their missing friends; and therefore, no sooner had he made his appearance, than they all hurried to meet him, and poured upon him a whole torrent of questions.

The landlord's answer was a complete defeat of all their hopes. He had seen nothing of Bart and Pat, and had heard nothing of them. He had known nothing of their departure, and nothing of their absence, until a few moments before, on his arrival home. He himself had to question them to find out the facts of the case.

Of the facts of the case, however, they themselves were, unfortunately, quite ignorant. They had nothing to communicate but fancies, conjectures, and speculations, more or less plausible, such as they had just been discussing. To these the landlord listened with the profoundest attention and the deepest gravity, and then considered them all in succession.

"I can't say," said he, at length, "that I see any danger for them in any way. Praps they've gone in a boat, an praps they've gone fishing. If they've gone in a boat, why, there hasn't been wind enough to capsize a walnut-shell. An as to getting on an island, I don't see how their boat could drift away, unless they made it go, and actually shoved it off on purpose. You must remember that this bay ain't like the Bay of Fundy. There ain't any tides or currents here worth mentioning. The tide only rises and falls six or seven feet, and the currents are so trifling that they ain't worth considering. If these boys have got on an island and been left there, it's a puzzle to me how on earth they managed it. Then, again, there are boats and schooners passing backward and forward almost all the time, and if they had got ashore anywhere, they'd have been got off by this time. So it's my opinion that they haven't gone off in a boat, but that they've gone fishing. If they've gone fishing, it's the most likely thing in the world for them to go off a good bit, and not be able to get back the same day. The only trouble about this is,—that they wouldn't be likely to go away on foot; and if they got a wagon, they'd be most likely to take it from the hotel; but that's just what they haven't done. So there's a fresh puzzle on top of the others."

"O, I think they'd be just as likely to walk as not."

"Well, then, there's another puzzle. Where could they go? They never made any inquiries. We had a long talk the night before last, but not a word was said about fishing. If they'd been intending to go fishing, they'd have asked; wouldn't they? Of course they would. That stands to reason."

"O, I dare say they got up early, and a sudden notion took them, and they started off without having any particular place in view."

"Well, that's not unlikely," said the landlord; "and if they did, why, all I've got to say is, they'd have a precious long walk of it, for there isn't any really decent fishing within less than nine or ten miles; and so, if they walked that, and then went up stream, why, by the time they'd finished, they'd have walked ten miles more; and so, all together, they'd make a precious good day's work of it,—work enough, in fact, to make them rather indifferent about hurrying back here—especially when they'd have to do it on foot."

"I suppose they'd find houses to stop at."

"O, yes, there are houses enough; but it depends on what direction they went. In some places, they'd have to camp out for the night."

"Well, they understand that well enough," said Tom. "Bart and Pat can put up as neat a camp as any two fellows going."

XVII.

A new Arrival.—The "long-shore Man."—A strange and startling Tale.—Fears once more awakened.—The Stranger's superstitious Dread.—The Boat found, but the Boys gone.—The Landlord's Statement.—Fears confirmed and increased.— Off to the Rescue.—Oak Island.—The empty Boat.—Where are the Boys?—The flooded Pits.—No Signs of the Missing Ones.—The grisly Theory of Roach.—Kidd and his Gang.

The remarks of the landlord served to weaken the belief of Arthur and Phil in their theory of the boat, and they began to doubt the expediency of setting off in the Antelope. The easy way also in which the landlord met the difficulties of the case, and accounted for everything, had a very great effect in diminishing, if not in destroying, the anxiety which they had begun to feel. They had nothing to offer in reply, and they naturally gave up their proposal. They began to think that the absentees might make their appearance at any moment, and that under the circumstances it would be very unwise to start off on a long, uncertain, and unprofitable cruise in the Antelope. And thus it was that the whole party came to the conclusion to remain where they were, and wait for Bart and Pat.

With this intention they all went back to the inn. On arriving there, they found a man who had just come to the house, and was waiting to find the landlord. He looked like one of those half farmers, half fishers, who live about Mahone Bay; and the boys would not have paid any attention to him, had they not been startled by his first words.

"It's about a couple o' lads," said he, "jest like them there. I'm afraid there's somethin gone wrong with 'em."

At the mention of "a couple o' lads jest like them there," all the boys started, and gathered round the stranger with eager and anxious curiosity.

"Ye see," continued the man, "it was yesterday morn'n,—an them two come a knockin at my door about sunrise, or not much arter, and asked the way to Oak Island."

"Oak Island!" repeated the landlord, in a strange voice. The other boys noticed his tone, but as they knew nothing whatever of the character of Oak Island, they were of course unable to understand the cause of it, or the meaning of those words.

"It seems they was a huntin up the way there," continued the man. "They had a boat with them."

"A boat?" said the landlord; "a sail-boat, or row-boat?"

"A sail-boat," said the man. "They were strangers—that was evident; and they wanted to find Oak Island. Wal, I showed them the island, for it can be seen plain enough from my door. My name's Roach, an I live on the shore up there. So we had some talk about the treasure, an they asked me if I believed. An I says, 'Yes, I do.' For at first they thought I didn't believe. But I did, an I do. And I says to them, says I, 'Flesh an blood won't never lay hands on that thar treasure till there's a sacrifice of human life took place.' That's what I says, in so many words. Wal, some more words followed, an then them two went on an steered to the island.

"Wal, I don't know how it was, but I kep a thinkin about them two all day long. At last I fell a wonderin why they didn't come back. There wasn't no sign of any boat a comin back from that island. They was on it, I knowed; an why they staid on it I couldn't make out. It began to bother me. An all the time I couldn't help thinkin of what I told em, an the words kep a ringin in my ears as to how that there's got to be a sacrifice of human life before the treasure's riz out of the hole whar the pirates buried it. An I couldn't get them words out o' my head. An what's more, I got a thinkin that them two lads was kine o' connected with them words,—jest as if it was a sort o' prophecy like, that I'd gone an spoke,—not knowin, an not intendin it, you know, but givin a prophecy all the same,—as is generally the case, you know; for often it happens that them that prophesies hain't got no intention of so doin, an hain't got no reel idee of the meanin of what they're sayin. An that was jest the case with me, an it was only afterwards that these thoughts come.

"Wal, all day long I was in this state, an felt dreadful anxious, an more an more so as the day went by. It was yesterday. An I see no signs of that thar boat a comin back. An when evenin come I begun to feel pooty skeart, an I'd a gone off then but darsn't, for fear of the ghosts of them old pirates that prowl around on the island arter dark. I didn't close my eyes all last night, or sleep a wink, for thinkin o' them two lads. It seemed to me that I'd been kine o' to blame—though whar the blame was, no one can say, for I was as innocent of blame as a babe unborn. But so it was, an I couldn't sleep. Wal, this morn'n I was up before dawn, an into my boat, an off for the island. I got thar about sunrise.

"Wal, I landed thar, on Oak Island, an the fust thing I see was that thar identical boat that the boys had—the very one. I couldn't mistake it; an it lay hauled up on the beach, an tied thar. But thar wasn't any sign of any boys anywhars. I called, an shouted, but no answer come. Wal, then I walked up some distance, an looked all around everywhars. 'Tain't much of an island in size; so I soon walked all round it; but I didn't see nothin of them thar lads. I looked at one or two of them pits that's ben dug thar, but didn't see anythin but water. I kep a screamin an a shoutin all the time, but thar wasn't any answer at all. Thar was the boat on the beach,—but whar was the boys? I couldn't see em, I couldn't find em; and though I called for em, they didn't answer.

"Wal, I went back to the beach, an then I stood an tried to think what I'd best do. Somethin had happened. I knowed that the best thing to do was to make haste an try to let the friends of them lads know how things was. I knowed that they was strangers in these parts, an that they'd come from Chester. I thought I'd find out about em here at the inn, an that the best an quickest way would be to come right straight off to this place, an see if I couldn't larn somethin about em, or find some friends o' thairs that'd come with me back again, an find out, for sure an sartin, what it was that had happened. An what troubled me most all the time, and troubles me now, is them very words that I said to em as to how that it was necessary that thar must be a sacrifice of human life. For I'm kine o' feared that it's turned out true, an that them's the very ones that was destined to be that sacrifice. They've got into some trouble, I know—but how it was I don't know, an whether it was in the day time, or at night. This is what I want to find out."

"What did the boys look like?" asked the landlord, as the man ceased.

"Wal, jest sech lookin lads as these—not overly well dressed, in fact a leetle mite shabby; but one of them was a gentleman's son,—no doubt o' that; an the other was a bright-lookin lad enough."

"It's Bart and Pat. There's no doubt of that," said Bruce.

"And what sort of a boat was it?"

"O, an ordinary Chester boat, with a sail, as I said."

"Is the boat on the beach of Oak Island yet?"

"Course it is. I left it where it was. But air them thar boys a stoppin here? Do you know them?"

"Yes," said the landlord, in a husky voice; and he stood in silence for a few moments, with his eyes cast down.

Upon the boys this information had produced an effect which was at once distressing and puzzling. It was distressing, from the fact that this stranger more than hinted at some possible evil befalling their two companions; and his gloomy allusions to his prophecy about the "sacrifice of human life," together with the expression of his own anxiety, produced a corresponding effect upon all of them. But it was also puzzling, for they could not imagine what there was on this Oak Island to attract Bart and Pat; or, if there was any attraction in it, how Bart and Pat had found it out. Various expressions made use of, however, such as his allusions to "pirates" and "treasure," served to make them suspect that this Oak Island might be the very place, in search of which they had come to Chester, the place indicated by the story of the governor of Sable Island;

that somehow Bart and Pat had made this discovery, and had remained behind, while they went to Aspotogon for the express purpose of finding out the place for themselves.

In this suspicion they were right, and it was confirmed by the landlord.

"I see it," he exclaimed, suddenly. "I have it."

"What?" asked Bruce.

"Why, I know now why they didn't go with you."

"Why?"

"Why, because they wanted to go to Oak Island."

"Oak Island? But what is there in Oak Island?"

"Enough to attract any one. I told them about it the evening of the day you came—all about the pirates, and how Kidd buried his treasure there, and how it was found out, and the different attempts made to raise it. It's too long a story now. You can hear it some other time. But I told it to them, and they've gone wild with excitement to visit the island themselves. That's it. Yes, that's it. But I didn't think they'd clear out this way. What made them do it? They made a great secret of it. What was the use of that? And now what in the world has become of them?"

"They went to that thar island," said Roach, "an they've never left it."

"Are you sure you went all over it?"

"Sure? Of course."

"And the boat was on the beach?"

"Yes; an it's thar yet. An if them lads belong to this here party, then my advice is, you'd better hurry off an find out what's become o' them. I'm dreadful anxious still, an want to know the wust. An I'm afeard that if we find out anything, it'll be the very wust."

To this disheartening remark there was no reply made. The boys all felt the same. Arthur and Phil, who had at first felt anxious about the absentees, now felt a worse anxiety; while Bruce and Tom, who had explained away their absence, now knew not what to say or to think. Although the evident superstition of the man Roach lessened somewhat the value of his testimony, still they could not conceal from themselves the fact, that there were grave reasons for alarm,—such as the boat on the shore, and the failure of his cries to reach the ears of the boys. Where could they be, that in a circuit of the island, this visitor had not been able to see them, or to make his cries heard? What could have happened to them? What sort of dangers could have presented themselves? The dangers which had been suggested by the superstitious fancy of Roach had no terrors in their eyes, and no weight in their minds,—at least in broad day. But there might be other dangers, of a material kind, of which they knew nothing. What did he mean by those "pits" full of water? What pits? They could not guess at this, for they had not heard the landlord's story, and Oak Island was all an unknown ground to them.

Such, then, were the questions and the fears which were started by the anxiety of the boys; and the more they thought over these things, the more that anxiety increased.

But one thing, of course, now remained to be done, and that was, to hasten, as fast as possible, to the place where Bart and Pat had gone, and search for themselves after their lost companions. The landlord at once began his preparations. The Antelope was not to be thought of. By taking her, time would be lost; for it was necessary to start from the back bay, which was very much nearer to Oak Island. Roach had landed on that side, and his boat, a roomy whaler, was at their disposal. They therefore at once decided to embark in her, and go by that way in search of the lost ones.

They set forth at once, the landlord accompanying them. It was not thought necessary to send word to Captain Corbet, as he would not be able to do anything, and might only embarrass their movements by an untimely fussiness, or by an anxious determination to accompany them in Roach's boat. A walk of a few minutes brought them to the back bay, where the boat was lying. It was soon afloat, and the party embarked. Then the sail was hoisted, and as the wind was fair and fresh, they moved rapidly through the water, heading for Oak Island. On the way the landlord informed them that he had told to Bart and Pat the story of Oak Island, and gave them a kind of summary of the same story. From this the boys were able to understand why it was that their absent companions had not accompanied them, though they were still at a loss to know why it was that they had made such a secret of their plan, and what their purpose had been in thus setting out by themselves. They could only conclude that Bart and Pat wished to have the whole glory of making some discovery by themselves, with which they should astonish their companions; and if there was any hope left in their minds, it was that they had purposely secreted themselves from Roach, so as not to be disturbed in their investigations. And this hope, though it was a faint one, served to sustain them to some extent.

In a short time they reached Oak Island, where they landed at the very place which had been chosen by Bart and Pat for their landing. Here the first thing that they noticed was the boat which their friends had brought, and which lay as they had left it. It was with melancholy forebodings that they looked upon it, wondering what had been the fate of those who had brought it here. But there was no time to waste in useless regrets or idle fears. There was a very serious business before them—the search after their lost companions.

They went up from the beach upon the island just as Pat and Bart had gone, and noticed the same things. They came to the mound of bluish clay, and saw the pit close by filled with water. They examined this narrowly, as though they feared to find their friends here. Then they went on further. Another mound, marking the presence of another pit. They now began to understand the full meaning of these "pits" to which Roach had alluded. It was with a feeling of great relief that they saw no signs here of their lost friends. From this they went on farther to a third pit.

"I can't imagine," said the landlord, "how any harm could have happened. Two sensible boys like these couldn't have fallen into any trouble here. They wouldn't feel inclined to jump into a flooded pit and drown themselves. As to this pit, it is dry; and I don't think they would go down into it. Why should they? They wouldn't jump down, for they were not yet quite tired of life, and there's nothing here to show that they lowered themselves down."

Roach solemnly shook his head.

"'Tain't that," said he; "'tain't that. It's the sperits—the ghosts of the old pirates, that allers haunts this island. No man dare live on it, except when they come in companies. One or two, men or boys, air at their mussy. 'Tain't no or'nary uthly dume that's come over them thar lads. It's Kidd an his gang that's ben an done for them."

XVIII.

A Place of Peril.—The Descent of the Darkness.—Dreadful Expectation.—The Sound from the nether Abyss.—The rising Waters.—Higher and higher.—A Gleam of Hope.—The Beams intermixed.—Borne upward on the Waters.—The last Chance.—A final Struggle.—Pat up to the Surface.—Dropping a Line to a Friend.—The midnight Sky, and the moonlit Sea.—The lone Hut.—The Explorers.—Despondency.—A last Resort.— Sleepers awake.—Wild and frantic Joy.—The Voice of the Landlord.—The Joint Stock Company, and the Steam Engine.

The coming of darkness gave a new horror to those which already surrounded Bart and Pat far down in the pit. This made them perceive how long they had already been down, and threw a new difficulty in the way of escape. But that way of escape seemed already to be effectually closed when Pat brought back his terrible intelligence from the bottom of the pit. They had formed a new plan, which had given them hope; but now the only way of carrying out that plan into execution was snatched from them by the advance of the waters. There was nothing for them to do. To climb up the log casing was impossible, and to dig through the clay was equally so without some strong, sharp instrument, like the pickaxe.

Nothing was visible down below, and up above it grew steadily darker. Whether the water below was rising higher in the pit or not they were unable to find out from actual sight, but they had a full conviction that it was steadily advancing higher and higher towards them, and that with its advance it was also unsettling or sapping away altogether the sides of the pit. Awful were the moments, and terrible the forebodings. The darkness intensified every fear, and made the actual dangers by which they were surrounded still more formidable.

Overhead they could see the shadowy form of the broken beam still hanging, and still threatening to fall at any moment. The rope fastened to it had broken below the point where they were seated, and was within reach of their hands; but it was of no use. Had the beam above been strong, they could have easily saved themselves in this way; but the beam being broken, they dared not touch the rope. The terror of the broken beam was, however, lost sight of in the presence of that greater terror advancing from below, minute by minute—the terror of that water into whose mysterious sources they had penetrated; whose secret fountain they had broken up, and which now, like some formidable monster too rashly challenged, was advancing step by step, in irresistible power, to take vengeance upon these reckless intruders. That soil beneath had shown its looseness by tumbling down in the removal of the lower logs; the tenacious upper clay did not exist there; and it seemed to them that the rising water, by permeating all the soil, might at any moment cause all the pit to fall together in one heap of undistinguishable ruin. In that case, they would be overwhelmed beyond the possibility of escape, and snatched from the world to destruction, without leaving behind them the faintest vestige, or the slightest token of their awful fate.

At such a moment nothing was said. Nothing could be said. They sat there then in silence, listening with sharpened senses for any sound that might tell of the approach of the water. For a long time, however, they heard nothing except the quick throbbing of their own hearts, until, at last, there gradually came up a dull sound, which slowly resolved itself into something like thumping and grinding.

They listened now with intense excitement and agitation to these sounds.

What were they?

There was only one meaning which they were able to give to them. It seemed as if these sounds must indicate the breaking up of the lower casing of logs that lined the pit—the first notice sent them of that break-up which was inevitable. Every sound seemed to tell of some new log severed from its place by the pressure of the surrounding soil, which, now saturated with water, and transformed to a sort of ooze, streamed through the crannies, and destroyed the staying of the pit. At this thought the expectation of the end grew stronger, their awful doom seemed more immediate, and every nerve tingled, and every fibre of their being thrilled with a sense of horror.

They sat with their legs hanging over, and their hands grasping the log beneath as firmly as they could. It was while they were in this position that Bart felt something strike his foot. At that touch his first impulse made him shrink back in terror, and jerk both feet into the air. The same moment Pat felt the same, and evinced the same repugnance by a similar gesture. A moment's thought, however, served to show Bart what it might be; so, reaching his feet down as far as he could in order to test it, he found that his suspicions were correct, and that the water had risen to that point. What had touched his foot was a log that had floated on the top of the rising water.

But there were more than one log, and this was the discovery that Bart made; and these logs were a dense mass that filled the pit, and were carried up by the water in this way. They had loosened many logs at the bottom, and had stood the long ones upright, while the shorter ones lay lengthwise. It was in about this same position that the mass of logs now floated up, and reached the place where they could be touched.

In a moment a joyful cry escaped Bart.

"What's the matter?" cried Pat.

"We're safe! we're safe!" cried Bart.

These were the first words that had been spoken since Pat first announced the entrance of the water.

"Safe, is it?" said Pat. "I'd like to know how, so I would."

"Why, these logs; only feel with your feet, Pat. They're all floating up. I never thought of that. Only feel how compact and solid they are. They'll bear our weight, and we can float up with them."

Pat for a moment made no remark, but reached out his feet, and felt as far as he could. Then a cry of joy burst from him.

"Huroo!" he cried. "By the powers! but it's safe we are. Sure it's as solid as a flure, so it is. It's a raft that we have, and it'll float us as high as it goes."

"Yes, if it don't cave in first."

"Cave in, is it? O, sure but it won't be likely to cave in up here at all at all."

"We'd better lie along at full length."

"An what'll we do that for?"

"O, so as to get the advantage of the floating power of all the logs. If we stand on one or two they'll sink down at once."

"Sure an that's so. It's right you are, so it is. We'll lie down at full lingth; an O, don't I wish we could take a bit of a nap!"

"No, don't think of that, Pat; we've got lots to do yet."

"Nappin? me nappin? Sure it's only funnin I wor."

"At any rate, we need only to float up to the plank casing. Then we'll be all right. And it seems to be coming up pretty fast. It's risen a foot already, since we first felt it."

"So it has, sure."

"We'd better be getting ready. I'll drop off first, and roll over to the other side, and hold on to as many as I can, and then you come along after me."

"Wait a bit, sure, till it gits a few inches higher. It'll be up fast enough, sure."

"O, yes, of course."

The boys now waited in silence for a little while longer. The water rose steadily, bearing up the mass of logs on their surface. At length, slowly and cautiously, Bart allowed himself to pass upon the logs, and to his immense delight, found that they supported his weight.

"Hurrah, Pat!" said he. "They're as solid as a rock. Come along."

In a few moments Pat was by his side.

"I had no idea," said Bart, "that they would be so solid."

"Nor me ayther," said Pat.

"I tell you what it is. The logs were stood upright, and as they floated up from the ground, they were turned in all directions, and got so mixed up, that each one supported the other, and the short logs have got mixed up with the long ones; and so it's just like a regular raft, and they bear us as well as if they'd all been laid crosswise on purpose."

"Thrue for you," said Pat; "an if it's so solid, I don't see why we mightn't stand up."

"O, we'd better not. This is the safest way. We might jar them, or shake them by putting too much weight on one spot."

"Well, it's best not to be in too big a hurry," said Pat, "an let well enough alone."

The boys now relapsed into silence, and watched anxiously their progress. By feeling the logs on the sides of the pit, they could perceive that they were rising at a rate that was very satisfactory. Inch after inch slipped away from their fingers; log after log on the sides was covered by the rising water. And at intervals, as they looked up to measure their distance from the top, they could see that it was steadily diminishing.

Yet the hope which had arisen within them did not blind them to the danger that still surrounded them. Still there was the danger of the broken log. The rope hung down, and never ceased to remind them, as they rose, that there was this above them, for the rope coiled itself over them, and they feared to make the slightest movement, lest they might give it a pull. Another danger was the chance that the pit might cave in, from having its foundations more and more sapped by the water. This danger had been delayed for long, but the longer the time was, the greater the danger grew. But most of all they feared lest the supply of water might cease before they reached the plank casing. If these waters came from the level of the sea, they would not rise in the pit higher than that level; and whether that would bring them as high as the plank casing, they could not tell. Their chief hope arose from the landlords statement that the island was not more than thirty feet above the water, and if this was so, they knew that they might get to within thirty feet of the top. And the plank casing came down about as far as that.

And so, full of hope and fear, which thus alternated, they floated up, rising higher and higher every minute, and feeling most carefully all the while in order to note the progress which they made. At length the progress grew somewhat slower, and hope began to grow faint; still, as it did actually continue, they struggled against despondency, and looked upward.

Their progress now grew slower. It seemed as though the force which pressed the waters on was being gradually exhausted. Was this because that water came from some internal reservoir, or because they had now reached a point almost at the level of the sea? They were not high enough yet, and they were not rising fast enough for their impatience.

Bart now stood up and felt. They were near to the lowest part of the plank casing, yet not near enough. Would they ever get nearer? At the rate at which they were now rising, they could scarcely hope to rise more than one other foot at the farthest. And the plank casing was four feet, at least, above his head—quite out of his reach. What then? Must they lie down here and perish almost within reach of safety? For a few moments it seemed so.

But it was only for a few moments. Suddenly the problem was solved.

"Pat," cried Bart, "I'll stand here. You climb up till you get your feet on my shoulders. You can reach the planking then."

"But how'll you git up yourself?" asked Pat, anxiously.

"Why, when you git up, you can throw me that rope, of course," said Bart.

"Sure enough. Och, but it's the fool I am, sure, not to think of that."

No more words were spoken. Pat did as Bart told him, climbing till his feet rested on Bart's shoulders. The lowest line of planks was within reach. Here he found a place to grasp with his hands, the logs below affording sufficient foothold. He found no difficulty. It was almost like going up a ladder now, and in a few moments he was at the top.

But all danger was not yet over. He dared not touch the broken log, and could not detach the rope without doing so. As the log was, it seemed to be hanging by a few fibres, and the slightest touch might send it down. But there were plenty of ropes at the hut, and he at once hurried away to procure one. He brought back one which was quite new, and therefore strong enough; and also a crowbar. Driving the crowbar into the ground, he bound the rope to it, and flung the end down to Bart, who had been waiting patiently in the mean time. Pat now held the crowbar to steady it, and Bart, seizing the rope, raised himself up. A slight effort was sufficient to bring him up to within reach of the plank casing, and for the rest of the way it was easy enough.

At last! There they stood, those two, who had of late been in such deep and dark despair. They stood there, drawing deep breaths of that glad upper air, and looked around. The moon shone from on high, throwing its lustre over the scene, and pouring upon the sea a silver flood. Joy and gratitude overwhelmed them, and with one common impulse they fell upon their knees, and gave thanks to that Merciful One who had drawn them up "out of a horrible pit," and restored them to the light of life.

But their excitement and their labor had utterly exhausted them in mind and body. They were terribly fatigued. To row back to Chester was impossible. They therefore went off at once to the little hut, and here, flinging themselves upon the floor, they soon sank into a profound slumber. Meanwhile the boys, with the landlord, and Roach, had searched about the island, until the minds of all were filled with the deepest anxiety. The hut still remained, and into this, not expecting to find anything, yet still anxious to search everywhere, they all went. There was an outer room full of ropes and tools, passing through which they came to an inner room.

Out of a profound slumber Bart and Pat were abruptly roused, and opened their eyes to find themselves surrounded by their four companions, perfectly frantic with excitement and joy, together with two strangers, the landlord and the man who had shown them the way, which two exhibited a most profound emotion. After their first bewilderment, Bart and Pat found it easy to guess at the meaning of this scene, and the memories which they had of their terrible adventure fully justified in their eyes the wild joy of their friends. It was a comfort to them to perceive that they had thus been promptly followed, for they saw that had they not been able to get out of the hole, they would have been rescued by these loving hands before all was lost.

Long explanations were deferred for the present. Bart and Pat were in a state of starvation, and their friends had forgotten to bring any food. But Chester was not far away. The wind was fair, and before very long they were all seated at the inn table, where the two lost ones satisfied their ravenous appetites, and the other boys made a second breakfast, which was more satisfactory than the first had been.

After which Bart and Pat told the whole story minutely, answering every question.

The wonder, the anxiety, and the horror that were manifested by the hearers during this narrative need not be described here. Roach insisted that it was all the doings of Kidd, and maintained that life must yet be sacrificed, before the malign spirits would be appeased, and surrender the treasure. The landlord, on the contrary, rightly viewed it as utter recklessness on the part of the boys. The previous diggers had several times broken into what he called the "drain," and the boys had done the same thing, and so he declared all would do, till they should organize the new company, and set up a steam-engine.

And here it may be as well to state that the new joint stock company was afterwards organized, and the steam engine set up, and a regular series of engineering experiments carried out. Coffer dams were constructed on the shore, and ever so many new pits were dug in many different places. In spite of all, however, the new company was a total failure; the waters of the sea proved stronger than their puny arms; and the place known as the original money-hole was never reached. Scientific men laughed at the theory of Kidd's treasure, and the drain, as all moonshine, and said that the company might as well try to dig pits in a quicksand; but the stockholders clung to their faith even after they had failed, and to this day talk about the "treasure," the "money-hole," the "chest," and the "drain," as though they were all solid and well-established facts.

XIX.

The Tale unfolded to Solomon and to Captain Corbet.—How they took it.—A New Departure.—A Bee-line for Home.— An Obstacle.—An old Enemy.—All at Sea, literally and figuratively.—Terrible Calamity.—Striking a Rock.—Perilous Position.—Taking to the Pumps.—Preparing for the Worst.

Two of the party in the Antelope had neither heard of the peril of Bart and Pat, nor known of their escape from it; and to these it was that the information of these things came last of all, yet not with the least profound effect. To Solomon the theory of the man Roach seemed unanswerable, and the very mention of it made his eyes roll about till nothing was visible except two revolving white disks on an ebon ground. His fingers clasped one another nervously, and his jaw fell and remained hanging, as though the owner of it had no further use for it, or had lost all control of it. From Solomon's former actions on different occasions, he had given indications of a nature that was not untinged with superstition, and a fancy that was ready to kindle and flame up with all those visions of the supernatural which seem so congenial to the negro mind.

"O, de sakes alive!" he exclaimed. "An under neaf de groun—an back agin safe! What! down below dar to dat ar place! Clar, if it don't make dis yer ole man go nigh stracted to think of. On dat ar island, down in dat ar hole, dar's a hull slew of ghosts an hobblegobblums ob de wustest sort ob pirates an murderers all lyin in wait, wid de ole boy himself, an a watchin ober de treasure. How ebber youns managed to git out ob de clutches ob dem dar hobblegobblums beats me—does so. Clar, if I ain't mos 'fraid to think ob it. Darsn't—no how. Ef I'd ben down dar, I'd gon mad wid fright. But dar couldn't be any danger ob me ebber goin down—no, sah! You may bet high on dat ar. Not for all de treasure dat Cap'n Kidd ebber buried."

Captain Corbet heard the harrowing story with a face full of sickening suspense and terrible anxiety. In his gentle and affectionate nature he seemed to suffer all that the boys had suffered. He made no remark whatever, and after it was all told, he remained in silence for some time, looking, in an abstracted way, at vacancy. The others respected his evident emotion, and stood regarding him in solemn silence.

At length he raised his venerable head, and surveyed Bart and Pat with an impressive gaze; after which he looked at each of the other boys.

"Well, well, well!" he said, slowly, and with emphasis; "had I a knowed—had I a thought—had I a s'posed—had I a dreampt of the posseebility of this, I'd never a ventoored into any harbure till I cud anchor opposite my natyve hum. An I might have expected it—tew. I know how it allus was, an might have expected how it allus was a goin for to be. But this here does clap the climax. And whuffore? What upon airth possessed you to ventoor down under ground on a broken rope, hangin from a rotten beam? Why, it won't bar a thinkin on. It's wuss than anythin that's happened among all that long an eventfuel serious of misfort'ns an clamties that's ben a befallin of us ever sence we fust assembled together on board this here schewner.

"And now what am I a goin to do? Do? Me? Why, I'll tell you what I'm a goin to do. I'm a goin to take up a bee-line for hum, an never enter another harbure—no, not so much as look at one, till I get to the wharf at Grand Pré. This responsibility is tew, tew kerushin. I ain't a stick, an I ain't a stun, an I can't abear it. A human heart beats in this aged boosum, an it's ben wrung on-common. I don't want to get another squinge. No—not me. An so I intend this day to hist anchor, an spread my sail to catch the gale. An, them that wants to go hum by land air at liberty so to do—an peace an joy go with em; but them as wishes to stand by the ship'll be welcome to the aged Corbet, an make his path of life all the brighter for their presence. An, so sayin, I'll kinclewd."

The conclusion, thus announced, was one which the boys were not unwilling to accept. There was nothing more here which they particularly cared to see. After the adventure of Bart and Pat, the treasure of the seas and the plunder of the Spanish Main lost that dazzling and alluring charm which hitherto had been found in those sounding words. The fact that it was so inaccessible was of itself sufficient to quell their ardor; but, more than this, they were affected by the information of past attempts to get at the treasure, and especially by the present efforts at forming a joint stock company. This at once vulgarized the whole affair. It put it into the hands of every one. It made it a matter of shares and shafts, engineers and steam-engines. With such things as these the boys felt they had nothing to do, and in them they took no interest whatever. Then, finally, the adventure of Bart and Pat had so exhausted the possibilities of Mahone Bay, that they could hope for nothing which could surpass it.

The consequence was, that, not long after the happy return of Bart and Pat, the Antelope once more set sail. The wind was fair, and the ship was ready. The landlord and Roach watched them as they moved away, and waved their hats after them as they passed down the harbor. And so the Antelope went away, leaving behind her, in its resting-place, undisturbed, the treasure of the sea.

All that day the wind continued fair from the north-west, and all the night following. The Antelope made a good run, and it was hoped that now they might reach their destination without any further trouble; but, on the following day, they found that these hopes were premature, and that trials yet awaited them; for, on going to the deck, they saw, all around, and above, and beneath, their old enemy—the enemy that they detested—the fog.

Yes, the fog was upon them—like some stealthy, vigilant, inexorable foe, who, finding them thus setting forth on their last voyage for home, now advanced upon them from all sides, to assail them for the last time. Bruce saw this first, and groaned. Arthur groaned likewise. So did Tom and Phil. And so did Bart and Pat. As for Solomon, he took no notice of it whatever, but devoted himself, as usual, to his pots and pans, while Captain Corbet had far too philosophical a soul, and far too much experience of such a situation, to be disturbed in the slightest degree by so commonplace a matter.

"I don't like this," said Bruce, after a long and most unhappy silence, which told more eloquently than words their opinions as to this last mischance. "I didn't expect it."

"We might have expected it," said Arthur, "judging from the past. We've had enough of it to make it seem natural. Still, I didn't expect it, I must say, any more than you did."

"For my part," said Phil, "I had forgotten all about it, and thought that the Atlantic Ocean would be like Mahone Bay."

"I wish we had left the Antelope," said Tom, "and gone off by land, as Captain Corbet advised, either to Grand Pré, or anywhere else."

"O, sure an it'll blow over, so it will," said Pat.

"Not it."

"Sure an it's best to be afther lookin on the bright side."

"There isn't any bright side to the fog that I could ever see," said Tom.

"Well," said Bart, "we'll have to do as we've done before—grin and bear it."

"But it's a great deal harder to grin now than it used to be," said Phil, plaintively; "and I can't bear it at all."

"O, well, Captain Corbet'll work his way along. He understands fog, at any rate."

"Well, I don't altogether think so," said Bruce. "After losing himself so utterly a few days ago, and fetching up at Sable Island, I rather begin to doubt his power to understand fog."

"O, well, that was in a strange place."

"Well, this is a strange place."

"Not quite. We are getting well on towards the Bay of Fundy."

"Well, we're not there yet. As yet, we're in the Atlantic Ocean. Now, Captain Corbet got lost once before in this same place,—the Atlantic Ocean,—and it's my fixed belief that he'll do it again."

"O, we know where the coast of Nova Scotia is now, and we're all right. I'm determined to look on the bright side."

"Well, and I'm determined to be prepared for the worst."

The event showed that this fog did not have a bright side, and that it was wiser, in these circumstances, to be prepared for the worst. That day passed, and the fog still held on. The wind that brought the fog was strong, steady, and sustained, showing neither violence nor irresolution, but blowing in a way that promised to last long after their stock of patience was exhausted. It was a sou'-wester, the wind of fog and storm.

After another day had passed, Captain Corbet's face assumed an expression, the meaning of which was but too well known to all the boys through sad experience. That meaning was, that he was puzzled, that he was uncertain, hesitating, and not decided where to go. And the boys discussed this among themselves, and perceived that once again their good, their venerable, their modest, but, after all, somewhat incapable commander had again lost his way.

"Ye see," said he to Bruce, who mentioned this to him in a mild way,—"ye see thar's ben so much tackin backard an forard that I kine o' got out o' the knack of it, an thar's a kink or two in my cal'lations. Ef we hadn't got to allus beat up agin this sou'-wester, we'd manage to keep a better course; but, as it is, we ain't got no course in pa'ticular, wuth mentionin. An then thar's them tides, an currents, an all that; an what with them, an tackin, an the fog, why, it's got to be precious hard navigatin."

"But why don't you keep well in to the Nova Scotia shore?"

"Wal, that thar's the very identical thing I'm a drivin at, an I dar say, if the fog was to lift, you'd see it quite handy over thar."

"But where are we now?"

"Wal, as nigh as I can cal'clate, we've about got to the end of Nova Scotia; an I've a mind to take a long tack to the nothe-west, next turn, an hain't got no reasonable doubt but what we'll keep on till we fetch up in old Fundy."

All this was rather disheartening to the boys. They saw that Captain Corbet did not even profess to have any exact knowledge of his position, and, judging from the past, they did not believe that he had any. Still, the change of course which he announced was something, and it seemed to afford some slight material for hope.

At length the Antelope came round on her next tack, and, taking a north-west course, she kept it for some time. At first the captain was rather watchful; but, after three or four hours, his vigilance began to relax, and at length he ventured to announce to the boys that they must be in the Bay of Fundy.

"An when I'm here, in this Bay o' Fundy, boys, mind you," said he, with something of exultation in his tone,—"when I'm here, why, I'm to hum. These waters was the place whar I sported in boyhood's days. Here I matoored into a man. Here I've held commoon with the ragin biller, an rode on the kerest of the toomultus ocean. You can't disturb me when I'm in old Fundy. It's my hum. Fog an tide hev ben my companions from childhood, an the Bay of Fundy recognizes in the aged Corbet her—"

But what he was going to say was never said, for the word was taken out of his mouth, and exchanged for the interjection,—

"Hallo!"

The Antelope had come to a sudden stop. The shock was strong enough to knock Captain Corbet on his knees, and huddle all the boys together in a startled and struggling crowd.

In an instant Corbet was on his feet, and rushed forward to see what was the matter. The boys followed. The helm was left to take care of itself, and the sails snapped and fluttered in the wind. All was confusion.

"Why, I do believe," said the captain, "I do railly believe she's struck! Dear me! Wal, I never! This—doos—beat—my—grandmother!"

This allusion to his grandmother, under such circumstances, far from reassuring the boys, only excited their alarm the more, and made them think that their revered commander had lost his senses.

"Boys," cried Bruce, "the Antelope's struck, and is sinking. We'll have to take to the boat. I'll fill a keg of water. The rest of you gather a supply of biscuit for a week, and one of you bring the compass."

"O, no; don't trouble yourselves," said Captain Corbet. "It's—it's— not—the slightest consekence. Don't—don't—hurry."

But these and other words were lost on the boys, who, now in the full conviction that the Antelope was sinking, hurried to do as Bruce had told them.

But Tom and Pat held back. Pat rushed to the mainmast, and busied himself with some ropes; and Tom went to the pump, and, after taking a peep into the hold, began pumping.

After a minute or so he called out,—

"I say, boys, there's no hurry. There's no water in her."

These words made the others desist from their preparations. Seeing Tom pumping, it struck them all that this was better than taking to the boat; so they all hurried to his help. As yet, however, there was nothing to be done.

"O, thar's no danger in p'tic'lar," said Captain Corbet. "She's struck a sand-bank, paps, or, paps, a reef, somewhars. An now I wonder whar it can be."

To this remark, which showed his utter ignorance of the situation, the boys had no reply to make. Bruce, however, tied an iron belaying-pin to a rope, and began sounding for bottom. At the stern he found three fathoms, at the bows only three feet. He took a boat-hook, and, plunging it down into the water at the bows, found that it was smooth sand, and the bows were resting upon it. This gave some comfort, for he hoped that they might yet escape.

But the wind was strong, and the waves made the Antelope roll and work about in her sandy bed after a most unpleasant fashion. If this continued long, the boys knew that the schooner would be lost, for she could not resist such a strain as this. Still, they turned their thoughts now rather to the task of saving her, if possible, than taking to the boat; and so, lowering the sails, so as to lessen the effect of the wind upon her, they set to work, some with the sweeps rowing, and others with the boat-hook pushing, and thus they tried to get her off the sand-bank.

"It's about the best thing we can do," said Captain Corbet, in a patronizing tone; "an we'll do it yet. An I dare say the tide'll lift us."

This mention of the tide cheered the boys. If the tide was rising, they could hope; if not, it would be bad for them. A little calculation showed them that it could not be falling, but must be rising, and this discovery made them work with renewed energy.

At length they had the satisfaction of finding that their efforts were successful. The water at the bows deepened; the schooner moved. She was afloat! Quickly the sails were hoisted, and the Antelope, catching the wind, came round, and once more sought the deep water.

XX.

Once more upon the Waters.—Terrible Discovery.—A Foot of Water in the Hold.—To the Pumps.—A desperate Struggle.—The Evening Meal.—Captain Corbet gazes on Vacancy.—A laborious Night.—New Toils.—Exhaustion.— Fighting with the rising Waters.—Discouragement.— The Leak gains on them.—The End approaching.

But though the Antelope was once more in deep water, their troubles were not yet over, for others soon arose almost as grave as the one from which they had just escaped. First of all, the uncertainty of Captain Corbet as to his position had evidently returned. He had that expression of concern, bewilderment, and confusion which shows a puzzled mind. He said nothing, but, after about a quarter of an hour's run, brought the Antelope about, and went on another tack. And now the wind, which all day had been rather fresh, began to lessen more and more, until after about a couple of hours it had almost died away.

All this time Solomon had been on deck. He had come up when the Antelope struck, and had worked away with the rest in their efforts in getting her off. Afterwards he had remained, out of a natural feeling of curiosity, to see whether any more rocks or sand-banks were to be encountered. This danger, however, now seemed to have passed away, and Solomon became mindful of the duties of a cook. He therefore went below to prepare the evening's repast.

Scarcely had he done so, than he bounded up again out of the hold upon deck. His eyes were staring, his jaw dropped, and if his black face could have shown anything like pallor, it would have done so at that moment.

"Da-da-da-dars—a—leak. Da-da-dars a foot of water down below!" he gasped.

At this astounding and alarming intelligence the boys rushed down into the hold. Solomon's information was right. Over the floor there was as much as six inches of water, and everything that lay there was saturated.

At once the whole truth flashed upon them. The Antelope had rolled and twisted herself on the sand-bank so much, that her timbers and planks had been opened, and a dangerous leak had been established. It was not a broken place, or a hole that could be stopped up, but evidently some general leakage arising from the strain to which she had been subjected.

This served, in the opinion of all, to fill up the measure of their troubles. Bad enough it was to be enclosed in the fog; bad enough to be without any knowledge of their situation; bad enough to be in the vicinity of dangerous shoals, and perhaps rocks; but in addition to all this, to have their vessel leaking, this indeed was a thing which might well cause despair. And accordingly at the first sight of the water in the hold, every one of them stood as if paralyzed, and looked on motionless and in dead silence.

Bart was the first to break the silence.

"Come, boys," said he. "We've every one of us been in worse scrapes than this. After being on a water-logged ship, we oughtn't to care for a few inches of water. Let's go to the pump, and see if we can't get rid of this."

Saying this, Bart leaped up to the deck, and sprang to the pump, followed by all the others. Only two of them could work at a time. Bart and Phil worked away first, till they were exhausted. Then Arthur and Pat took hold, and were relieved by Bruce and Tom. They worked vigorously, and with a will, in all the freshness, too, of their first efforts. Every one of them had a confident expectation that this labor would be successful, and that a half an hour, at the farthest, would be enough to pump the schooner dry. But a half hour passed, and yet that result was not accomplished. There was a difference certainly, but not anything like what they had wished. Judging from the amount of labor that they had put forth in this half hour, and the slight result, they were filled with dismay at the prospect before them.

"Well," said Tom, "it ain't what we expected; but I dare say we expected too much. Perhaps we ought to be satisfied if we find that we can keep the water under."

"But can we do it?" said Bruce.

"Of course we can. Haven't we been doing it?"

"We have—certainly. But how long can we keep at this sort of work? Why, the pump'll have to be kept going day and night."

Wade and Solomon now went to work; but their efforts made no very perceptible diminution in the water in addition to what had already taken place.

"I'm afraid," said Bruce, "that the leak gets steadily worse."

"Why so?"

"Well, because Solomon and Wade don't do more than any two of us."

"O, they don't work with such a will."

"Perhaps not. But in pumping, I dare say steady efforts like theirs amount to as much at least as our quick way of working; and besides, they're stronger, and ought to do more. I think the leak is worse."

"O, I don't believe it."

"Well, it took about two hours for the water to come in that's in her now. If it had been coming in so slowly as that, we would have pumped her dry by this time. But the fact is, the more we pump, the faster the water comes in. I think it is working its way through new seams and crevices."

There was no further reply to this; but not long afterwards, when Bruce and Tom had pumped with unusual vigor, they examined the hold once more. They found about six inches of water. The water had gained therefore. It had come back to the amount which had been there when they first began. These last efforts had gained nothing. In spite of all the water that had been poured out over the side, the quantity below was the same. There was no longer the slightest doubt that the leak was increasing, and that, too, with a rapidity that was very alarming. And while the leak thus gained power, their own efforts could not possibly increase beyond what they had already been, but, as a matter of course, would, on the contrary, rather decrease. And yet there was nothing else to be done but to pump on, for if they relinquished their efforts, they were lost. So they kept at it, taking turns as before, and while any two were at the pump, the others occupied themselves with watching the water beneath.

In one of the intervals, Solomon prepared the evening meal. It was later than usual, and any other than he would have omitted it altogether. But Solomon knew too well its importance, and felt that now it was, perhaps, of more importance than ever. The boys also, in the intervals which they had, prepared provisions for the boat. They put in oars, the boat's mast and sail, two kegs of water, amounting to about twenty gallons, a barrel of biscuit, a ham, and a few other articles. In this way they endeavored to prepare themselves for the worst, and to have everything ready when the critical moment should arrive.

All this time Captain Corbet was mooning at the helm. He occasionally offered a remark, of which, however, no heed was taken by the busy company. They had something else to do.

"Ef I'd ony a come straight along from Bosting," said he, on one of those occasions,—"ef I now at this moment was a navigatin from Bosting, I'd know whar I be. For I never know that I ever did lose my reckonin on one of them thar vyges. But comin up in this here roundabout circuous way from them outlandish seas, made me kine o' git everythin upset and jumbled together in my old head. An now where air we? 'Tis a pint I long to know. Blest if I know.

"I should be pleased," he continued, in a meditative tone, "to find out what course is the best for us jest now; though for that matter thar ain't overly much wind, and I don't seem to see how we could sail anywhars, even ef we wanted to go, an knowed jest the pint to go to. But as soon's the wind does rise, I have an idee of the course I'm goin to take."

"What's that?" asked Bart, who happened to be near and hear this last remark. It seemed to him a good sign that Captain Corbet should have any theory now about his position.

"Wal," said Captain Corbet, "it kine o' seems to me as if the best way would be to head her nothe-east. We can't head her nothe agin in this fog; r'else we'll hit another rock; but ef we keep her nothe-east, we may dodge the rocks, an fetch up somewhars."

At this utterly vague and unsatisfactory statement Bart turned away, more disheartened than ever.

That night the boys took turns till about midnight, when they all turned in, leaving Solomon, Wade, and the captain to take turns pumping till morning. The wind had gone down almost altogether, and the sea was quite smooth. The water in the hold remained at about the same level; and when the boys turned in, they had a feeling of satisfaction at this, or they would have had, if they had not been so completely worn out. Their sleeping-place was not their usual one. The water had driven them out. They brought their mattresses on deck, rolled themselves up in blankets, and curled up there the best way they could. So they passed the night.

On the following day they awaked early. There was a moderate breeze, and the Antelope was making some progress running before it. But the fog still continued, and environed them on all sides. Of this, however, they took no note just then. Their first thought was about the leak. They saw Wade working away at the pump in that dull, mechanical fashion which distinguished him in everything that he did. They said nothing to him, but at once looked into the hold.

The sight that they saw there confirmed their worst fears. The water had increased during the night, and they saw at once that either the leak had grown worse, or else that the pumping had been neglected. Things did not look well either for them or for the Antelope.

"We've all ben a takin of our turn thro the night," said Captain Corbet, who was, as usual, at the helm. "It seems to be considerable of a leak. But I dar say we'll manage to keep it down. The Antelope hadn't ought to be a leaky vessel either. I've allus took good car of her. But it's that strain she got."

"Why, there's a foot of water, at least," cried Bart, "over the floor. There must be over two feet of water in the hold."

THE TREASURE OF THE SEAS | 131

"Full that," said Arthur, gravely. "At this rate we'll have to take to the boat before long."

"O, thar's no hurry," said Captain Corbet; "the old Antelope's dreadful perseverin, and a tremenjous hand at keepin afloat."

"Well," said Bruce, "I rather think we may fight off the water to-day, at any rate, and the fog may lift before night."

"Yes," said Phil, "we'd better not take to the boat till the last moment. I'd rather be here taking my turn at the pump, than off in the boat, not knowing where we are or where we're going."

"Sure an it's a pity there wasn't another pump," said Pat. "We cud do double the work, so we cud. An I'd be proud to take me turrun at the pump twice as often, so I would."

"I tell you what, boys," said Tom. "Some of us might bale out with pails, while we're not pumping. I wish I could construct a siphon; but I suppose it couldn't be managed; so let's bale. Two at the pump, and the rest at pails. That ought to be equal to two pumps, at least."

"Sure an it'll be aqual to fower pumps, so it will, if we work hard enough."

This proposal was excellent in its way, only there was a doubt as to whether they could muster four pails. After some search two were found, and Solomon produced a tin kettle. This made three. Pat then brought forth a coal scuttle, which was well adapted for the work. With these increased resources they now set to work. Jumping down into the hold, four of them baled out the water, and poured it upon the deck, from which it ran into the sea. They worked at this most zealously and most industriously for two hours. At the end of that time they were all utterly exhausted. They had taken turns at the pump and at the pails, and the continuous work without rest had told most severely upon them all. They all felt that this would utterly use them up, if persisted in much longer. At the same time they had the satisfaction of seeing a perceptible diminution in the water, though by no means as much as they had hoped to find; and they all felt as though they had not received an adequate reward for such exhaustive labors. They saw that if they hoped to continue at the pump, it was absolutely necessary to give up the baling, and rest until the turn of each should come. And so the baling was given up.

A hasty breakfast was taken. Solomon had to give up his work as cook, and take his turn at the pump, and therefore every one had to forage for himself. Already, however, Solomon had taken the precaution to remove the stores from the hold and cabin up to the deck, where they would be out of the reach of the water, at least as long as the schooner could pretend to float. Out of these stores each one could now supply himself whenever and however he might feel inclined.

Having given up the idea of baling, the boys, in the intervals of taking turn at the pump, had nothing else to do now than to gather up strength for a new effort. While so doing, they watched the state of the water in the hold; or tried to penetrate the veil of fog that hung around; or listened, hoping to hear some sound that might tell of ships in their neighborhood. Sometimes, also, they sounded on the "fog-horn" of the Antelope—a peculiar tin trumpet with which every Down East coaster or fisher is provided, and which makes the most unearthly sound that has ever been contrived by man, not even excepting the yell of an asthmatic steam whistle. But looking, and listening, and sounding on the trumpet were alike unavailing, for no sight, or sound, or answering note of any kind came to them through that wall of mist.

All this was depressing. The fog was depressing. The fact that they had lost their way was depressing. But most of all, their own exertions proved depressing, for those exertions seemed unavailing. Still the waters crept ahead of them. They were not able to hold their own. After their vigorous and exhaustive efforts at baling, the water, held at bay for a time, came back to the assault, and this time it triumphed over the pump, and rose slowly, yet steadily. By the close of the day the water in the hold was enough to startle even the phlegmatic Wade. That personage had taken some sleep during the afternoon, after a long tug at the pump, and had snoozed away as calmly as an infant until sunset. On waking he walked to the hold, and looked down. The sight was by no means reassuring. Nearly two feet of water rolled backward and forward at the motion of the Antelope. He shook his phlegmatic, unexcitable, undemonstrative head.

"My name's Wade," he said, speaking as if to himself. "An my old 'oman's name's Gipson. An you'll not find many o' that name in this country. No, sir."

He took another look.

Again his head gave a solemn and portentous shake.

Then he said once more,—

"No, sir!"

And the pump went on.

And pump struggled with sea.

And the sea gained!

XXI.

*A miserable Night.—No one shrinks.—Their Efforts lessen.—
Morning comes.—Four Feet of Water in the Hold.—Take to the
Boat!—Come along, Captain!—The Dignity of Corbet.—The
Folly of Pat.—The Insanity of Solomon.—The Imbecility of
Wade.—The Perplexity of the Boys.—"Dat ar ole Woman!"—
An Agony of Impatience.—Four on board tempting Fate.*

Night came—a miserable—miserable night! On the previous night, the boys had slept; but this night, sleep was not thought of by any one of them. Exhausted though they all were by hard work, they yet felt the position of the Antelope to be too perilous to think of sleep. It was a time for vigilance. It was a time when each one had to keep himself wide awake, and hold himself prepared to rush to the boat at a moment's warning. The boat floated astern, as usual, and in it were all the stores that might be necessary for a lengthened row; but they wished to postpone any recourse to this boat to the latest possible moment. And all the time the Antelope held on her course, impelled by a fair, yet moderate breeze, that blew directly astern.

Exhausted though they were, yet none of them shrunk from his task. All took turns. Corbet and Wade, Wade and Solomon, Corbet and Solomon; then the boys, two by two, at the pump; each couple laboring strenuously and conscientiously, yet showing the same result. For, whoever it was that worked, or whatever was the amount of labor expended, the result seemed in each case a failure and a defeat. They were struggling against a common enemy; but the enemy was gaining. In spite of their efforts, the waters continued to rise, and there was no way by which they could bring any additional labor to bear. Had there been another pump, they would have been in a better position. At about midnight they undertook a second time to supplement the pumping with baling, but again desisted on account of the utter exhaustion which followed such severe toil. It only lessened their power of working at the pump. So once more they gave it up.

From that time on their efforts grew less and less. The long toil had told upon every one of them, more particularly upon the boys. The labors of Captain Corbet, of Solomon, and of Wade, were less vigorous certainly; yet still, they were even and well sustained; but those of the boys grew more and more fitful, irregular, and feeble. Each time that any two of them came to take their turn, they felt as though this must be the last. And so the hours and the labors of that dreary night dragged on.

Morning came.

All the boys felt that their capacity for work was well nigh exhausted. Morning came, and brought the fog. No land appeared. No ship was in sight. They sounded a blast on the fog horn, but no reply came.

Morning came, and brought, worse than all, the sight of four feet of water in the Antelope's hold,—an amount so great that further pumping was useless, and at the best could only delay for a very short time a doom that was inevitable.

Morning came, then, and brought this sight; and the four feet of water in the Antelope's hold at once forced a change in the decision of those on board.

They saw that if they continued pumping they might delay the decisive moment somewhat, but that it must come; and if it came with all of them on board, they must sink with the sinking schooner. And that the end was near, they could see. There was no time for delay. Already the signs which met their view told them that the end was near.

Take to the boat!

This was now their thought. To the boat,—before it was too late! On board the boat were all the stores necessary for a protracted voyage; and they all began to feel that this boat was now a better place than the sinking Antelope. The boat was a place of rest; a place more restricted, yet still, one which promised comparative peace and safety. To that boat, therefore, they must go, before it was too late; while yet they could embark in peace, and move away from the doomed Antelope.

Nor was a resort to the boat so hopeless an undertaking as it might appear to have been. At the worst, they were in a part of the world where ships are frequent; and some of them thought that land was near enough to be seen in some direction if only the fog should be dispelled. The stores in the boat were sufficient to sustain life for a considerable time, and they would be free from the necessity of incessant and most exhaustive labor.

There was now no time for any delay or any hesitation. They all felt this. The sight of the Antelope's hold decided them.

They must take to the boat.

"Come along, captain," said Bart. "We mustn't stay any longer. The Antelope'll go down before half an hour. If we pump any longer we'll all be used up, and won't delay her sinking more than five minutes. Come along."

"Goin doun!" said Captain Corbet dreamily. "Only think of the Antelope goin doun! Dear me!"

"Come, captain," said Bruce, taking his arm. "The boat's all ready."

"O, yes," said the captain; "and the Antelope's goin doun! Dear me! Only think of it!"

"Captain Corbet," said Arthur, solemnly, "we're all ready. Come, go aboard the boat."

"Well—well—well," said the captain. "Very well. O, all right. O, yes. You jest git into the boat. Git along. Never mind me. I'll wait a while, you know. You go ahead. I'll jest meander around here while you're gettin into the boat. All right."

At this the boys went off to the boat, and dropped in one after the other. Bruce, and Arthur, and Tom, and Phil, and Bart. Pat lingered behind. Those who had got into the boat expected that the others would follow at once, and now looked eagerly towards them.

They were afloat astern; and there, at the stern of the Antelope, stood Captain Corbet, surveying them with a melancholy air.

"Come along, captain," said Bart.

"O, all right. Wait till the rest go," said he. "Tain't right for me to clar out jest yet. The captain must allers be the last to quit the sinkin ship."

At this the boys called to the others,—to Pat, who had lingered behind, to Solomon, and to Wade.

Pat was standing by the mainmast. To their amazement, they saw that he was busily engaged in binding himself to it with ropes.

"Pat," cried Bart, "why don't you hurry up?"

Pat made no reply, but went on as before, solemnly and methodically.

"Pat," cried Tom, "what in the world are you waiting for? Hurry up! What are you doing?"

"Sure it's tyin meself to the mast, I am," said Pat.

"What," cried Bruce, "tying yourself to the mast! What nonsense! What do you mean?"

"Sure it's the right thing to do," said Pat. "It's what they allers does, so it is, wheniver a ship gits wracked. Sure I know; and I advise you to do the same."

"He's tying himself to the mast!" cried Phil. "He's mad. He's insane. Some of us'll have to drag him on board."

"Pat," cried Bart, "come along. Are you crazy? The Antelope's sinking! What do you mean? Stop that. If you tie yourself to the mast, you'll go down with her. What nonsense! Drop that rope, and come with us."

"Sure it's safer here," said Pat, calmly, "than on that bit of a boat, so it is."

"But the Antelope's sinking."

"Sure, don't I know it? Meself does."

"But you'll go down in her, if you do that."

136 | JAMES DE MILLE

"Arrah, what are you talking about? In shipwracks, doesn't everybody tie themselves to the mast?"

"What in the world shall we do?" cried Bart, in despair. "He's crazy. I never saw anything like it. He's got a craze about tying himself to the mast. Don't you remember how he did the very same on board the Petrel?"

"We'll have to go and untie him," said Bruce.

"Only see how he's fastening and knotting the rope," said Tom.

"We'll have to seize him, and bring him here by main force," said Arthur.

But from these thoughts they were now diverted by the appearance of Solomon. He had been very busy for about a quarter of an hour, and was now pulling away at a rope, as though the salvation of the whole party depended upon the successful accomplishment of his design.

"Solomon," cried Bart, "hurry, hurry! Come along! Hurry! The Antelope's going down fast! Hurry, and bring Pat along with you. The captain's waiting till you leave the Antelope. Hurry!"

"I'se jest a histin up dis yer cookin-stove," said he. "Ben tyin de ropes roun it ebery which way, an jes got her ready to be put into de boat."

"The what!" cried Arthur.

"De cookin-stove," said Solomon, gravely.

"He's mad!" cried Bruce. "He's gone crazy. Pat and Solomon have both gone mad with excitement or terror."

"You jes gib a left here, an help dis ole man put dis yer cookin-stove aboard de boat, an den you'll be all right."

"Solomon! Solomon!" cried Bart, "what horrible nonsense! What do you mean by talking about putting a cooking-stove on board the boat? Come along. Be quick."

"Tell you what," said Solomon, "dis yer stove am a nessary succumstance. How you s'pose you get you meals cooked? Mus hab a cookinstove. Mus so. You got water to bile, and things to cook."

"Nonsense," cried Bart. "Can't you see that it'll sink the boat?"

"But what'll you do?" said Solomon. "You'll suffer if you don't take it. You mus hab a cookin-stove. Mus so!"

At this obstinate persistence in such unaccountable folly the boys were in despair. The schooner was sinking lower and lower every minute, and there were those on board of her, wasting precious time and chattering nonsense. What could be the meaning of this? Had terror deprived them of their senses? It seemed so. There was Captain Corbet, absorbed in his own thoughts, evidently quite forgetful of the present danger, and unconscious of the scene around him. There was Wade, with his heavy face gaping from the windlass, where he had seated himself. There was

Pat, still tying himself to the mast; and there was Solomon, toiling away at the cooking-stove. It was like a small floating lunatic asylum. They might well feel puzzled and bewildered.

But suddenly one part of this very difficult problem was solved of its own accord. Solomon had not been very careful in the selection of his hoisting apparatus. He had picked up some bits of rope, and fastened them around the cooking-stove for slings, and into this he had passed the hook from the schooner's tackle. He pulled and labored away, hoisting the heavy stove, and succeeded in raising it about half way above the hatches. A few more pulls, and it would have been on the deck. But there's many a slip 'twixt cup and lip; and so it was destined to prove in this case. For at the very moment when the stove hung thus suspended, the slings suddenly gave way, and with a rush the heavy mass descended, falling with a loud crash to the bottom, and with a force that seemed sufficient to break through the Antelope's bottom. There it lay—a ruin!

Solomon stood and stared in silence at the scene. At length, drawing a long breath, he raised his head and looked at the boys.

"Dar," said he; "dat ar's allus de way; troubles neber comes single. Dis yer shows dat de end am come. Smash goes de cookin-stove, an shows dat dis yer scursium's a goin to tumminate in clam-ty. Dar ain't a goin to be no more eatin in dis yer party; dat's all done up."

"Solomon! Solomon!" cried Bart, "hurry up!"

"Solomon! Pat! Wade! Captain Corbet! Come! Quick! Hurry up! Quick!"

Such were the cries that now burst from those in the boat. They were floating close by the schooner, so as to be convenient for those who were yet on board. They had seen the destruction of the unfortunate cooking-stove, and were now eager to get away before the schooner should sink. But their patience was destined to be still further taxed, for Solomon continued to make observations on the fallen stove; and Pat went on winding the rope about himself and the mast; and Wade sat motionless on the windlass; and Captain Corbet stood in the same attitude as before,—in the attitude habitual with him, his hands mechanically grasping the tiller, and his mild eyes fixed before him, as though he was still steering the Antelope, and watching some shore ahead. But before him there was only fog; and what he might have seen was not visible to the material eye.

"No use" said Solomon. "Dese yer may go, but I'se boun to stay. De captain may go; an mas'r Wade, he may go; an Pat mus frow away dem ropes. But for me, I'se goin to stick to de ole Antelope."

"But she's sinking, and sinking fast," cried Bart, with feverish impatience.

"Dar's no odds to dis ole man. Ef I can't stick to de Antelope, I don't want to go no whars else. Dar's somebody a waitin for me, an I ain't a goin to 'spose mysef to her, no how."

"But you'll be drowned; you'll be drowned. O, Solomon!" cried Bart, "cut Pat's ropes, and make him come; and hurry."

"Come, come, captain. Make haste. Cut Pat's ropes, Solomon. Come, Wade. The schooner'll go down in five minutes!"

"Don't care!" said Solomon; "don't care a mite. I'se dreadful fraid ob dat ar ole woman. I'd rader be drowned here dis yar way, dan be hammered to def wid a red-hot poker. Dat's so; mind I tell you."

The boys were now in an agony of impatience and anxiety. The waters were high in the hold of the Antelope. They could see, from where they stood in the boat, the dark gleam of the rising flood, and knew that any moment might now witness the last plunge of the schooner into the depths below. And so they shouted, and screamed, and called upon every one in succession of those who still so madly lingered behind. But their cries were unheeded; for those four on the deck of the Antelope made not the slightest movement in response.

When the boys had left the Antelope, the water in her hold was about four feet in depth. All the time since then it had been increasing; yet, after all, though the time seemed long to the anxious boys, not over a quarter of an hour had elapsed in reality.

XXII.

The Waters rise.—The Boys try Force.—Attack on Pat.—He is overpowered.—My Name's Wade.—An Irish Howl.— Solomon immovable.—The Ancient Mariner at his Post.— The Boys fly.—Flight of Solomon.—"Drefful Times."— Captain Corbet sings his Death Song.—A Rhapsody on the Antelope.—The rising Waters.—The doomed Schooner.— The rolling Seas.—The Antelope sinking.—The Form of Corbet slowly disappearing beneath the raging Seas.

The waters continued to rise in the hold of the Antelope, and inch by inch the doomed schooner settled slowly down into the depths beneath. On the deck stood those four who still held aloof from the boat, and seemed to be animated by some insane or unintelligible motive. By the side of the schooner floated the boat, in which were Bruce, Arthur, Tom, Phil, and Bart. They were all standing up, and holding the Antelope's rail, and shouting, bawling, yelling, entreating, threatening, and using every possible means to save their unfortunate companions.

Suddenly Bart drew his knife.

"Boys!" said he, "we'll have to drag them off. Bruce and Arthur, come along. Tom and Phil, you mind the boat."

With these words he jumped on board the Antelope, with his open knife in his hand. Bruce and Arthur leaped on board after him.

The sight of Bart, with his open knife, thus bounding on board the Antelope, astonished the other boys, who began to think that Bart, like the others, had also lost his senses; but they did as he said—Tom and Phil holding the boat to the side of the Antelope, and watching, while Bruce and Arthur followed Bart.

Bart first rushed to Pat.

"We're not going to stand this. You're ruining us all. If you don't go aboard the boat, we'll throw you overboard, and you'll be glad to do it then. Bruce and Arthur, catch hold, and pitch Pat overboard if he don't go to the boat."

Speaking these words with breathless rapidity, Bart cut the rope with which Pat had bound himself, giving long slashes up and down. Bruce and Arthur seized him at the same moment, and as soon as the rope was severed, dragged him to where the boat was, ordering him on board, and threatening to throw him into the water if he refused. Pat was powerless. A few words of remonstrance were offered, but he was sternly silenced. He was thus overpowered, and so, yielding to necessity, he got on board the boat. There he seated himself in the stern, and, bowing his head, began a long, low, wailing Irish "keen," which is a species of lamentation in the presence of death.

This scene appeared to produce some effect upon Wade. It roused him from his lethargy. It seemed as though this man was a mere machine; and though in ordinary circumstances he was able of going through certain routine duties, in any extraordinary case he was utterly helpless, and his dull and inert nature became hopelessly imbecile. But now an idea of his situation seemed at last to have penetrated to his brain, and accordingly, rising to his feet, he went to the boat. Then he slowly and solemnly passed over the Antelope's side, and took his seat near Pat. He looked at the others with a dull stare, and then turning to Pat, he remarked, in a low, confidential tone.

"My name's Wade, an my ole 'oman's name's Gipson; an you'll not find many o' that name in this country. No, sir."

After which he heaved a sigh, and relapsed into himself. As to Pat, he took no notice of this confidence imparted to him, but went on with his Irish lamentation.

"Ow—O-o-o-o-ow—to only think—this bit ov a boat sure—an in the wide an impty say—an me a bindin meself to the only safety; for the ship-wracked sayman must always bind himsilf to a mast. And, O-o-o-o-o-o-o-w, but it was a bitter, crool thing, so it was, to tear a poor boy from his solitary rifuge—an dhrive him here into a bit ov a boat—to sail over the impty say—an from the last rifage—where safety was, an O-o-o-o-o-o-o-o-ow! but it's the croolty ov it that braks me heart!"

The summary treatment with which the boys had disposed of Pat, was not to be applied to Solomon, or to Captain Corbet. They tried to coax these, and persuade them.

Solomon, however, was obdurate.

"My 'vice to you, boys, an you, in tiklar, mas'r Bart," said he, "is to clar out ob dis yer sinkin schooner, ef yer don want to git a duckin ob de wustest sort. She's a goin down—you'd betta believe—dat's so."

"O, come, come, Solomon; we can't wait. You're making us all risk our lives," said Bart, imploringly, coaxing him as he would coax an insane man. "Come along; don't keep us here. The schooner'll sink and drag the boat down, if we don't keep farther away."

"Darsn't," said Solomon. "Couldn't, darsn't—no how."

"O, come."

"Darsn't—fraid ob dat ar ole woman, wid de broomstick, de tongs, de fence-pole, an de red-hot gridiron. Tell you what, it stings—it does, dreadful—it does so—"

"O, come. She shall never trouble you. Never."

"Who's to go skewrity fer dat ar statement? Nobody can skewer her. No. Better be drownded, dan walloped to def with hay-forks. Nobody can skewer dat ar ole woman, dough; gracious sakes, she knows how to skewer me ebery time she lay hand on a pitchfork or a meat-skewer. Yah, yah, yah!"

At this ill-timed levity Bart and the others turned away in despair and disgust.

They hurried aft.

There stood the venerable Corbet. As they drew near he gave a start, and a smile came over his reverend countenance.

"Wal, boys," said he, in a tone of kindly welcome, "how d'ye do? Pleased to see you."

He spoke precisely as if he was receiving a call from some favorite guests. The tone pained the boys, and distressed them greatly.

"Captain," said Bruce, hurriedly, "the Antelope's sinking. A moment more and you'll be lost. Come with us in the boat. Come."

And, laying his hand on the captain's arm, he sought to drag him away.

But the captain quietly though firmly, disengaged himself.

"Excuse *me*, young sir," said the venerable navigator, very politely; "but I'm captain of this here craft; an, being sich, I ain't got no call to leave her till the last man. You git to your boat, an I'll retire when the time comes."

The captain spoke with dignity. He announced a principle which involves the highest duty of every commander of a ship, and the boys knew it. His dignity overawed them.

"But come now, captain," said Bart, "there isn't a moment to lose."

"I ain't a goin ever to hev it written on my tume," said the captain, in a calm voice, "that me—Captain Corbet—ever desarted his post, or forgot his umble dooty as commander of a vessel. No, the Antelope'll see that her captain's jist as much principle an honor as any of them swell navigators that sail in clipper ships over the boosom of the briny deep."

At this moment there was a long-drawn, bubbling, gurgling sound, that came up from the hold of the Antelope, and startled the boys exceedingly.

"Come, come, captain," cried Bruce. "She's sinking now. There isn't a moment to spare."

"Wal, boys, you jist hurry off into that thar boat, an don't mind me. I know my dooty. You can't expect me to leave this here deck till the last man. It don't signify argufyin. Hurry off."

At this moment there was another sound; something between a gasp and a gurgle. It seemed like the death-rattle of the Antelope.

"She's going down, boys!" cried Bart.

Involuntarily they retreated towards the boat. But here they paused yet again, for there was a brief respite, and the Antelope was yet afloat.

"Won't you come, captain?" cried Bart.

"O, all right," said Captain Corbet, waving his hand; "all right. You jest get aboard the boat. Don't you mind me. Remember, I'm the captain, an I've got to be the last man."

This seemed to the boys like a promise to follow them.

"Come along, boys," said Bart. "He'll get into the boat if we do. He wants to be last."

Saying this, the three boys clambered over the Antelope's side, and it was with a feeling of relief that they found themselves once more in the boat.

"Now, captain," cried Bruce, "hurry up. Come, Solomon. Captain, make Solomon come on board, and then you'll be the last man."

Captain Corbet smiled, and made no reply. As for Solomon, he merely muttered something about "dat ar ole woman" and "gridiron."

The Antelope was low in the water. The deck was near the level of the sea. Instinctively, Tom, who was holding the rail, pushed away, and the boat moved off a little distance. Yet they could not leave those two infatuated men to their fate, though the instinct of self-preservation made them thus move away slightly.

"Captain! Solomon! Captain! Solomon! Make haste! O, make haste!" Such were the cries that now came from those in the boat.

Captain Corbet smiled as before, and nodded, and said,—

"O, it's all right; all right. Don't mind me. I'm all right. I know what I'm about."

At this the Antelope gave a very unpleasant roll, and settled heavily on one side; then her bows sank down, and a big wave rolled over it.

"She's sinking!" cried Tom, in a voice of horror. The other boys were silent. They seemed petrified.

But the Antelope struggled up, and gradually righted herself. Her deck was nearer the level of the sea than ever. This last incident, however, had been sufficient to shake the nerves of one of those two on board. As she settled on one side, Solomon sprang back, and, as the wave rolled over her bows, he gave one jump over the side and into the sea. He sank under, but a moment afterwards his woolly head emerged, and he struck out for the boat. There a dozen arms were outstretched to save him, and he was finally hauled in.

"Drefful times dese," said he, as his teeth chattered, either from terror or from cold. "Drefful times. Didn't 'gage in dis yer vessel to go swim-min about de Atlantic Oceum. Queer way to serve as cook—dis yer way.

An dar ain't a dry stitch ob clothin about—dat's so; an what ebber I'se a goin to do beats me. S'pose I'se got to set here an shibber de next tree weeks. Catch me ebber a 'barkin aboard sich a schooner as dis yer. Any ways, I ain't goin to sail in dis yer Antelope agin. Cotch me at it—dat's all."

But the boys heard nothing of this.

All their attention was now taken up with Captain Corbet.

He stood at the stern at his usual post, holding the tiller with both hands. He looked at the boys.

"Boys," said he, "I'm the last aboard."

"O, Captain Corbet! Come, come. Make haste!" they cried.

He shook his venerable head.

"This here," said he, "boys, air the act an the doin of Fate. I did hope that the Antelope an me'd grow old, an finally die together, though not on the briny deep. It hev allus ben a favorite idee to me, that the lives of both of us, me and the Antelope, was kind o' intermingled, an that as we'd ben lovely an pleasant in our lives, in death we'd be not divided. For the Antelope an me's knowed each other long, an lived, an ben happy together, in fair weather an foul. The Antelope's allus ben faithful and terew. She's had all my confidences. She's allus been gentle an kind, and you'll never, never find a better friend than the old Antelope. Many's the time she's bore me through sleet an snow. Many's the time she's borne me through fog an rain. Many's the time she's bore me past rocks an reefs. So long as I stuck to old Fundy, so long the Antelope was safe an sound. I used to boast as to how I could navigate old Fundy. I was wrong. 'Twan't me; it was the Antelope that navigated; for I never had a sexton aboard, nor a quadruped, nor a spy-glass, nor any of them newfangled gimcracks, savin an except a real old-fashioned, apostolic compass, as is mentioned by Paul in the Acts. And why? Why, cos the Antelope was allus able to feel her own way through rain an fog, an frost an snow—past shoals, an flats, an reefs, an was allus faithful. But, in a evil hour, I took her out of her native waters. I led her afar over the deep blue sea, up to the Gulf of St. Lawrence. There our woes began. But even there the Antelope was terew an tender. But it was too much. We come back. She had never ben thar before. She lost her way. Then she found it. We got to Sable Island an Chester. Then we put out agin. An then agin she lost her way. It was my fault, not hern. She lost her way in this fog, an she went aground. She couldn't help it. In Fundy she never ran aground, 'cept when nessary; an it was me that brought her to this. An now what hev I got to do? I've got this to do—that if I've led my Antelope to ruin, I won't survive her. No. We've been lovely an pleasant in our lives, an in death we ain't goin to be divided."

144 | JAMES DE MILLE

The boys did not hear one half of this, but interrupted the speaker constantly with their entreaties that he would save himself. Captain Corbet, however, was too much taken up with his own thoughts to notice what they said. He was like one who soliloquizes.

"O, captain!" cried Bart, with a final effort; "think of your wife—think of your, your, a—baby—"

"My babby!" said Captain Corbet. "My babby! Ah, young sir, when you mention my babby, you don't know that you tetch a cord in this parentual heart that throbs responsive. That thar is the strongest emotion that inspires this aged breast; but, young sir, dooty air powerfuller than love, an even that pe-recious infant has less claims on me at this moment than my Antelope. For my Antelope has ben the friend that's ben faithful in thousand perls; that's ben my refuge an my solace in times of persecution. Yes, young sirs, in the days when a bold an violent woman disturbed my peace, by dashin a pail full of cold water over my head—at such times the Antelope hav took me to her heart; an can I ever cease to be affectionate an kind to thee, who's ben so terewly kind to me—my Antelope? No, no; young sirs. Go, an tell my beloved one—my offspring—my inspired babby—that his parent, the aged Corbet, died a marchure's death; died like a hero, a standin' at his post; which post was the rudder-post of the Antelope. Tell him that; an tell him, tew, that, though dooty bound the feyther to the Antelope, yet still that feyther's last thoughts was of his belessed babe."

At this point the Antelope gave another lurch, and rolled far over. Captain Corbet stopped abruptly, and stiffened his sinews, and clutched the tiller with a tighter grasp. The boys looked on with horror in their faces and in their hearts.

It was a moment of awful expectation.

They had cried, and bawled, and yelled till they were hoarse. They had prayed and entreated Captain Corbet to save himself. All in vain.

But now the time for entreaty had passed.

Suddenly the Antelope rolled back, and then her bows sank. A huge wave rolled over her, followed by others, which foamed from bow to stern. Then all the sea settled itself over the sinking schooner.

The Antelope was going down!

The hull disappeared!

The rail sank under water!

But Captain Corbet stood at his post, erect, rigid, his hands clasping the tiller. Beneath him the Antelope sank down into the sea. Around him the waters rolled.

They rolled about his knees; about his thighs; about his waist. His venerable hair fluttered in the breeze; his eyes were fixed, with a rapt and abstracted air, on vacancy.

The boys looked on in horror. Instinctively they pushed the boat back out of the reach of the waters that ingulfed the Antelope, so as to avoid being carried down into that vortex.

The waters rolled about the form of the aged navigator, and so he descended with his beloved Antelope, till they were above his waist.

The boys could no longer cry to him. They were petrified with horror. They sat, with white faces, awaiting the end.

XXIII.

Watching with pallid Faces.—The Torso of Corbet.—A sudden and unaccountable Break in the Proceedings.— Great Reaction.—Unpleasant Discovery.—Pat and the salt Water.—The Rheumatiz and kindred Diseases.—Where to go.—Where are we?—Sable Island.—Anticosti, Bermuda, Jamaica, Newfoundland, Cape Cod, or Owld Ireland.—A land Breeze.—Sounding for the Land.—Land ahead.

A painful thing it was to see the Antelope thus sinking into the sea; to view the waters thus rolling over her familiar form from bows to stern; to see the boiling foam of the ingulfing billows; but how much more terrible it was to see the sacrifice of a human life; the voluntary self-destruction of a human being, and of one, too, who had been their guide, their revered and beloved friend! They had no cause for self-reproach. They had done all that they could. His own will had brought him to this. Still the spectacle was no less terrible to all of them, and there was no less anguish in their souls as they saw him—the meek, the gentle, the venerable Corbet,—thus descending, by his own free will, and by his own act, into the dark abyss of this unknown sea.

And so they watched with pallid faces, and with agonized hearts for the end.

The ancient mariner sank down, as has been said, with his sinking schooner, and his feet were overwhelmed by the rushing flood, and his ankles, and his knees, and his thighs, and at length he stood there with the waters about his waist, and his mild eyes fixed upon vacancy.

Another moment, and they expected to see that venerable and beloved form disappear forever from their gaze.

But that venerable form did not, in fact, disappear.

That venerable form remained stationary,—the waters reaching as far as the waist: thus far, but no farther. The lower half had disappeared beneath the sea, but the upper half still remained to bless and cheer their eyes. Corbet still lived! But it was what an artist might call a Torso of Corbet.

Corbet thus had sunk into the unfathomable depth of ocean up to his waist, but after that he sank no more. Higher than that the waters did not rise. He stood in that rigid attitude already described, grasping the tiller, and thus steadying himself,—upright, firm as a rock, and so he stood after the waters had risen to his waist.

The hull of the Antelope had disappeared. But still her masts and rigging rose above the waters, and above the head of Corbet, and these sank no farther, but remained at the same height above the sea.

Astonishment seized upon all of them, Corbet included. What was it that had caused this wonder? Was it because the hull was too buoyant to sink any farther? Was it because there was still some air left inside the hull which prevented the schooner from sinking altogether? This they might have thought had they not been made wiser through their recent experiences. By these they now knew that on these seas there were sand banks and shoals; and, therefore, what was more natural than that, the Antelope had sunk in some place where there happened to be, just beneath her, a convenient shoal which had received her sinking hull? It was certainly a very curious sea,—a sea which seemed to abound in such shoals as these; but whatever might be the character of that sea, this fact remained, that the Antelope had sunk in less than a couple of fathoms of water.

And so it was that the heroic and devoted resolve of the venerable and high-minded captain was baffled, and his descent into the depths of the ocean was arrested. For there lay the Antelope, resting upon some place not far beneath the sea, with her masts still high above water, and with the person of her gifted commander half submerged and half exposed to view; and there stood that venerable commander up to his waist in water, but unable to descend any farther; a singular, a wonderful, an unparalleled spectacle; unaccountable altogether to those whose eyes were fastened upon it.

But the thought of a shoal or sand bank soon came, and so they began to understand the state of affairs. The Antelope had sunk, not into an unfathomable abyss in mid-ocean, but upon some sand bank. Where or what that sand-bank might be, they did not then take time to consider. Whether it was some part of one of the Banks of Newfoundland, or the slowly declining shore around Sable Island, or some other far different and far removed place, did not at that time enter into the sphere of their calculations. Enough it was for them that the terror had passed; that the grim spectacle of death and destruction before their very eyes had been averted; that Corbet was saved.

Till this moment they had not been aware of the greatness of their anguish. But now the reaction from that anguish made them acquainted with its intensity, and in proportion to their late sufferings was now their joy and rejoicing. At the first movement of the Antelope towards a descent into the sea, they had instinctively and very naturally moved their boat farther away, so as to avoid being sharers of the fate which Captain Corbet seemed to desire; but now, after the first danger was over, and the first emotions of amazement and wonder had subsided, they rowed nearer. They believed that now Captain Corbet would listen to reason, and that, having done so much in obedience to the call of duty, he would be willing to save himself.

And now, as they rowed nearer, the boat floated over the rail of the sunken schooner, and came close up to the half-submerged commander.

"Come, captain," said Bart, in a voice that was yet tremulous with excitement, "jump in. There's plenty of room. You—you—don't—don't want to be standing in the water this way any longer, of course."

To this remark Captain Corbet made no reply in words, but he did make a reply in acts, which were far more eloquent. He seized the side of the boat at once, and scrambling in, sank down, wet and shivering, in the stern, alongside of those other obstinate and contumacious ones—Pat, Wade, and Solomon. And so it was that at last, after so much trouble, those four, who had at first been so unmanageable, now were assembled on board the boat into which they had once refused to enter.

The delight of the boys was as great as their grief had been a short time before, and no other thought came into their minds than that of the happy end that had occurred to a scene that had promised such disaster. The fact that their situation was one of doubt and uncertainty, perhaps peril, did not just then occur to them. It was enough joy for them that Captain Corbet had been snatched from a watery grave; and so they now surrounded him with careful attention. Bruce offered him a biscuit; Bart asked about his health; Tom urged him to wring out the water from his trousers; and Phil, who was next to him in the boat, fearing that he might feel faint, pressed upon him a tin dipper full of water.

Captain Corbet took the proffered draught and raised it to his lips. A few swallows, however, satisfied him, and he put it down with some appearance of haste.

"As a gen'ral thing," said he, in a tone of mild remonstrance, "I don't use sea water for a beverage. I kin take it, but don't hanker arter it, as the man said when he ate the raw crow on a bet."

"Sea water!" exclaimed Phil. "Did I?"

He raised the water to his own lips, and found that it was so.

"Then we've taken sea water in this keg," he cried, "and we haven't any fresh."

At this dreadful intelligence consternation filled all minds.

"Who filled that keg?" asked Bruce, after a long silence.

"Sure I did," said Pat.

"You! and how did you happen to make such a mistake?" cried Bart.

"Sure ye said to fill the kegs with wather, an didn't say what kind; so I jist tuk the say wather, because it was most convaynient."

THE TREASURE OF THE SEAS | 149

At this amazing blunder the boys were dumb, and stared at Pat in silence. Words were useless. The mistake was a fatal one. The fresh water had gone with the Antelope to the bottom. Where or when could they hope to get any more? Who could tell how long a time, or how great a distance, might now separate them from the land? Bad enough their situation already had been, but this opened up before them the prospect of unknown sufferings.

"O, don't talk to me about water," said Captain Corbet, in lugubrious tones, squeezing his hands, as he spoke, over his thighs and shins, so as to force the water out of his clothes. "Don't you go and talk to me about water. I've hed enough, an don't want ever to see any agin. Why, it kem up as high as my waist if it kem a inch. An now what's to hender me a fallin a helpuless victim to rheumatiz. O, I know it. Don't tell me. I know what's a goin to come to this ferrail body. Thar's rheumatiz acute and chronic, an thar's pleurisy, an thar's lumbago, an thar's nooralgy, an thar's fifty other diseases equally agonizin. An dear, dear, dear, dear! But how dreadful wet it did feel, to be sure! dear, dear, dear, dear! An here am I now, with my tendency to rheumatiz, a settin here in my wet clothes, an not a dry stitch to be had for love or money. Wal, I never knowed anythin like this here, an I've lived a life full of sturrange vycissitudes—from bad to wuss has ben our fate ever sence we sot foot on this here eventfual vyge; an ef thar's any lesson to be larned from sech doins an car'ns on as this here, why, I ain't able to see it. An now what am I to do? What's a goin to become of me? No dry clothes! No fire to dry myself! Rheumatiz before me! lumbago behind me! pleurisy on each side o' me! such is the te-rific prospect of the blighted bein that now addresses you."

The boys paid but little attention to Captain Corbet's wailings. They had other troubles more serious than these prospective ones. They could not help, however, being struck by the thought that it was a little odd for a man who had just been snatched so narrowly from a terrible death to confine all his attention and all his lamentations to such a very ordinary circumstance as wet clothes. He who had announced so firmly, a short time before, his calm and fixed intention of perishing with the Antelope, now seemed to have forgotten all about her, and thought only of himself and his rheumatiz. Could this be, indeed, Captain Corbet? Strange was the change that had come over him; yet this was not the only singular change that had occurred on this eventful day. They had witnessed others quite as wonderful in Solomon and Pat. These two, however, had now resumed their usual characteristics.

There they were, in a boat, all of them, but where? That was the question. The masts of the sunken Antelope rose obliquely out of the water, showing that she was resting on her side at the bottom. But what was that bottom, and where? Was it some lonely rock or reef? Was it some sand-bank or shoal like that upon which they had already gone aground, and where the Antelope had received those injuries which had at length wrought her ruin? None of them could answer this.

And where should they go? In what direction should they turn? This was the question that pressed upon them, and required immediate decision.

"It's impossible to even guess where we are," said Bart. "We've been going in the dark all along. We may as well be off Sable Island as anywhere else. And if so, all I can say is, I've seen worse places."

"Sure an thin it's as likely to be Anticosti as Sable Island," said Pat. "We've ben a turrunin around ivery way, so we have, an we may have fetched up there, so we may, an if that's so, we may as well dig our graves an lay ourselves down in thim."

"Well, if you're going so far as that," said Bruce, "I'd put in a claim for Bermuda. I don't see why we mayn't be off Bermuda as well as Anticosti. If so, we may be sure of good accommodations."

"Well, while you're about it," said Arthur, "why don't you say Jamaica?"

"At any rate," said Bruce, "I shouldn't wonder if it should turn out to be Newfoundland. This sou'-west wind would take us there."

"Yes, but there's been a calm," said Arthur, "for some time, and we've got into some current. I dare say it's taken us west, and that this is close by Cape Cod."

"Pooh!" said Phil. "If we've been drifting with any current, there's only one current hereabouts. That's the Gulf Stream. I tell you what it is, boys; we've crossed the Atlantic, and this place is off the coast of Owld Ireland; and there ye have it."

"Arrah, go way wid yer deludherin talk," said Pat. "We want a sinsible opinion."

"The more I think of it," said Tom, "the more I'm inclined to be of Bart's opinion. We've been tacking and drifting, and going backward and forward, and it seems to me most likely that this is Sable Island. If so, we may be glad that we came here when the water was so calm."

"Wal," said Captain Corbet, thoughtfully, "I don't b'lieve that this here air Ireland, nor Iceland, nor Africky, nor Jamaiky, nor any other sech. 'Tain't unpossible for it to be Sable Island. We drifted there onst, an may heve done it agin. Far be it from me to dispute that thar. But then again it might be Newfoundland. 'Pears to me as ef we've got off some land whar thar's woods, for I got jest now a kine a scent o' trees, an 'peared to me of spruce an sech. I shouldn't be s'prised ef the wind was to haul round. It often doos, specially when it's ben an done its wust, an you don't care. So now we don't care what it doos, or which way it blows; an consekently it's goin to turn an blow away the fog."

At this moment, and while the ancient mariner was yet speaking, there came a breath of wind, very gentle, yet quite perceptible, and there was in it an unmistakable odor of forest trees—balmy, delicious, most fragrant, bringing with it hope, and joy, and delight.

"The land must be close by," cried Bart. "Hurrah!"

"Don't hurrah too soon," said Tom. "It may be Anticosti."

"Pooh! Anticosti could never send out such a smell of spruce and pine."

"Well, it may be Newfoundland, and that won't help us much."

"The wind's going to change," said Arthur. "I think the fog isn't so thick as it was."

"Come, boys, this bottom shoals in some direction. Let's sound, and row on in the direction where it shoals. That'll bring us to the shore."

This suggestion, which came from Bruce, was at once acted on. Bart and Tom took the oars. Bruce took a hatchet which had been flung into the boat, and tying a line to it, used this as a sounding lead.

"Row gently," said he.

The boys did so, following Bruce's direction, while, holding his sounding-line, he tested the bottom. After a little while he had satisfied himself.

"It shoals in this direction," said he. "Row straight on a dozen strokes."

They did so.

Bruce sounded again.

"All right," said he. "Row on."

They rowed farther.

Bruce sounded again. The bottom was much shallower.

They rowed farther.

But now no sounding was any longer necessary, for there, straight before them, looming through the now lessening fog, they all descried the welcome sight of land.

XXIV.

*Rowing ashore.—Nearer they come.—The Fog dispels.—
Strangely familiar.—A Man advances towards them.—
Wild Shouts from Bart and Tom.—Wilder, Shouts from the
other Boys.—Confused Rejoicings.—A hearty Welcome.—
Explanations.—The receding Tide.—A Visit to the Antelope.—
Mournful Remembrances.—The Speech of Captain Corbet.*

At the sight of land a cry of joy burst forth from all in the boat, and
Bart and Tom bent to their oars with all their force. As they drew nearer,
they saw, to their intense delight, that this strange land was no wilder-
ness, no desolate shore, but an inhabited place, with cultivated fields,
and pasture land, and groves. One by one, new features in the landscape
revealed themselves. There was a long beach, with a grand sweep that
curved itself away on either side, till it joined steep or precipitous shores.
Behind this were fields, all green with verdure, and a scattered settlement, whose white houses, of simple, yet neat construction, looked most
invitingly to these shipwrecked wanderers. At one end of the winding
beach rose the fabric of a large ship in process of construction.

Nearer they came, and yet nearer. The tide was high on the beach,
and the waters almost touched the green fields that fringed the shore with
alder bushes. Here a boat was drawn up, and beyond this stood a neat
farm-house. On a fence nets were hanging, showing that the occupant
of this house united the two callings of farmer and fisher. Beyond the
settlement, the land rose into high hills, which were covered with forest
trees, and from these had been wafted that aromatic breeze which had
first made known to them the neighborhood of land.

All this time the breeze had been slightly increasing, and the fog had
been steadily diminishing. Now the shores appeared in fuller outline.
Looking back over their course, they could see the masts of the Antelope, where they projected above the water. They could see that they had
drifted into a bay, and the Antelope had sunk into its shallowest part.

There was something in this scene which appeared to them strangely
and most unaccountably familiar. All had the same feeling, yet not one of
them expressed it. Each imagined that it was his own fancy; and so disturbed had their minds been for the past few days, that they felt unwilling
now to indulge this fancy. Yet every moment the fancy grew stronger,
and brought fresh wonder with it. In this way they rowed along, and
every moment brought the boat nearer and nearer to the shore.

At length they saw a man come forth from the house before them, and advance towards the beach. His face was turned towards them; he was staring at them most intently. As the boat advanced, he advanced; and thus the two parties approached. Every moment revealed more and more of the opposite party to each.

Bart and Tom were rowing, and thus had their backs turned to the shore and their faces towards the sea outside. Here the fog was fast dispelling; and as it fled, there opened up mile after mile of the coast, and the sea horizon. There, on that horizon, there came forth out of the fog to their eyes a solitary object, that appeared to float upon the sea. It revealed itself more and more; and first, magnified and distorted by the mist, it seemed like a lofty table land of cloud then like a giant rock, but at length resolved itself into a wooded island with precipitous sides. There it lay full before them.

As it thus revealed itself, Tom uttered a wild shout. Bart instantly uttered another.

"Boys! Boys! Look! Look! Hurrah! Hur-ra-a-a-a-a-a-ah! Hurra-a-a-a-a-a-a-a-a-a-a-a-a-ah!!"

But at that very instant there arose a wild out cry—a clamor worse than theirs—from all the others in the boat. Solomon gave a yell, Captain Corbet started up, and ceased to stroke his legs. Bruce, Arthur, Phil, and Pat, with one wild cry, started erect to their feet, regardless of the swaying and rocking of the boat. And "Hurrah!" they cried. "Hurra-a-a-a-a-a-a-ah!! Hurra-a-a-a-a-a-a-a-a-a-a-a-a-ah!!!"

"Scott's Bay! Ile Haute!" cried Tom and Bart.

"Scott's Bay! Benny Grigg!" cried all the others.

"Scott's-Grigg."

"Benny-Haute."

"Ile-Bay."

"Benny-Bay."

"Ile-Grigg."

"Scott's Haute."

Such was the medley of cries that arose from all, shouting and yelling at once. While all the time there stood on the shore the man that had come down to meet them; who first had started and stared with amazement,— and who then, recognizing them all, and seeing the masts of the sunken schooner beyond, understood the whole situation, and rejoiced over it accordingly—showing his joy, indeed, in a less noisy and demonstrative manner than theirs, but in a way which was thoroughly characteristic.

For Benny suddenly turned, and started off to the house on a full run. Then he disappeared.

The boat drew nearer.

Benny appeared once more.

The boat touched the beach.

At that very instant Benny touched the beach also, and, plunging into the water, began shaking hands with every one of them, in the most violent, and vehement manner.

"Come along! Come along! Come right up! Come along! Don't mind the boat. I'll see to that. Come along to the house. Blowed if I ever see the likes o' this in all my born days! Come along!"

Such was the welcome of Benny Grigg.

And in this way Benny dragged them all up to his house. Here he gave them another welcome, characterized by a lavish hospitality, and a warm-hearted friendliness that was truly delightful to his guests; in all of which he was seconded by Mrs. Benny. The table that was spread before them was loaded down with everything that the house could furnish, and the shipwrecked guests ate with an appetite such as is only known to those who have labored hard and fasted long.

After which Benny questioned them all closely, and made them tell him how it was that they had come here. Great was his astonishment, but greater still his amusement. Though it had so nearly been a tragedy, to hear it seemed like a comedy. There is but one step between the sublime and the ridiculous—the terrible and the grotesque—tragedy and comedy. Benny chose to regard it all from the lighter point of view, and accordingly he laughed with unrestrained hilarity, and made merry with exceeding mirth.

But after the story was all told, he grew more serious, and, producing a well-worn chart, he explained to them his theory as to their wanderings. He pointed out to them the probable place where the Antelope had struck, described the character of the tides and currents, and showed how it was that, with such a wind, and under such circumstances, they, very naturally, had drifted into this particular part of the Bay of Fundy. Benny's explanation was indeed so very lucid, and so satisfactory, that they all expressed their regrets at not having known this before, in which case they would have been saved from much anxiety.

When they arrived at Scott's Bay it was high tide, but by the time that they had finished their story and the conversation that had been caused by it, the tide was far down on the ebb. On going forth they could see that the deck of the Antelope had been uncovered by the retreating waters. In two or three hours more the tide would be at the lowest ebb, and they could see that it would be possible for them to visit the sunken schooner. It lay about a mile away from the beach, between which and her there extended long mud flats, which could easily be traversed at low water.

They waited till the tide was low, and then they all walked down to her.

There she lay—the Antelope—the vessel that had carried them so far, through strange seas, amid so many dangers and perils—the vessel associated with so many memories. They climbed on board. They saw that her hold was still full of water; for, though the crevices were numerous, and wide enough to let in the sea, they could not let it out with sufficient rapidity to keep pace with the fall of the tide. Still, the water streamed out in small jets, or trickled out, drop by drop, in a hundred places, affording them a very impressive sight of the true condition of the Antelope, and of the danger against which they had struggled so long and so laboriously.

"If the water'd ony get out of her," said Captain Corbet, in a melancholy voice, "she might float ashore."

"Yes," said Benny, "she might float, perhaps, as far as the shore, but no farther, 'Tain't no manner of uthly use a tryin to repair that thar craft, cos she's ben an gone an got done for. She's wore out, the wustest kind. That thar vessel ain't wuth a tryin to repair her. It's a mussy she held out so long, an didn't go to pieces all of a suddent, somewhars in the middle of the sea."

To this Captain Corbet made no reply. He felt keenly the truth of the remark, and could see that the Antelope was indeed beyond the reach of human aid.

The boys all climbed on board of the beloved, though battered old craft, to take a last look and a last farewell. It was with unconcealed sadness that they looked around. They could not go down into the cabin, or the hold, for the water was there; yet the deck was enough to remind them of that eventful past which they had experienced here. This was the schooner that had borne them on their cruise around Minas Bay; which had taken them around the Bay of Fundy when Tom was lost; which had afterwards taken them to the Bay de Chaleur. This was the schooner for whose appearance they had so watched and waited on board the waterlogged Petrel, and which had lately borne them over so many miles of watery sea, through so many leagues of fog. And this was the end.

Captain Corbet it was that first broke the solemn silence.

"It air gone," he said; "the derream hev bust! The berright derream of fortin, of wealth, an of perosperity. Gone, tew, air the ole Antelope—companion of my toils, my feelins, an my fame. Boys, you hev ben the confidants of my feelins towards this here Antelope, an knows how I loved her, yea, even as the apple of my aged eye! I stood here, not long sence, by yon rudder, fixed firm an solemn; resolved to perish with her; ready to sink into the deep blue sea. From that fate I was spared; yet still my feelins air the same; the heart's the same—'twill ne'er grow cold. An now I feel to mourn. I feel that I am indeed a growin old. The days of my navigatin air brought to an end. Henceforth the briny deep will be traversed by the aged Corbet no more forever. From this time I retire from the heavin biller, an take refooge in my own vine an fig tree. My navigatin arter this'll be, with my belessed babby in my arms, up an down the room. The only storms that await me now, an the only squalls, air to be of a sterictly domestic characture. Weak human natur, boys, might be tempted to repine, an to indulge in vain lamintations over this here; but the time hev passed. I've made my lamintation, an that's enough. I'll lament no more. Peace to her ashes. Let her lie, an may no rude hand go a disturbin of the beloved Antelope in her last restin-place. Let her lie buried here beneath the ocean. Let the billowy main sound her requem, an chant her foon'ral dirge. An now, farwell! an may you be happy! Good by, Antelope—ole friend—an receive, as your last legacy an benediction, the belessin of the mournful Corbet!"

He ceased. Silence followed, and in that silence they all retired from the Antelope, and returned to the shore.

XXV.

Discussing the Situation.—By Land or by Sea.—Conferences with Bennie.—The Offer of Bennie.—The last Meal at Scott's Bay.—The Boat is on the Shore, and the Bark is on the Sea.—Last Words of Solomon, and Farewell Speech of the Ancient Mariner.

On reaching the shore they found it necessary to take into consideration the course of action that was now most advisable.

"We've got a few weeks yet of vacation, boys," said Bart, "and if we want to enjoy ourselves, we'd better get out of this as fast as possible."

"We ought, at any rate, to write to our fathers and mothers," said Phil; "I don't know what they'll think."

"Write!" said Bruce; "we'd better hurry off home our own selves, and not send letters. For my part, I'm ready to start off this evening for Grand Pré."

"Grand Pré? But why Grand Pré?" asked Arthur.

"O, I don't know," said Bruce: "what other way is there to go? We'll have to get away from this, of course; and it seems most natural to cross the mountain to Grand Pré, and then go on by stage. Bart could leave us at Windsor, and take the steamer for St. John."

"Sure an the stage goes the other way altogether," said Pat.

"How's that?"

"Why, down the valley to Annapolis; an the steamer starts from that to St. John, so it does; an' it's twice as near, so it is."

"No, it isn't."

"Yes, it is. St. John is only sixty mile from Annapolis, and it's more'n a hundred an twinty from Windsor."

"But Annapolis is seventy or eighty miles from this place, and Windsor's only thirty."

"At any rate, it's easier goin by the way of Annapolis."

"No, it isn't."

"Yes, it is; you go down the valley, so you do, an the other way you have to go up."

"Pooh! nonsense! The Annapolis valley isn't a hill. The fact is, from here to St. John it's easier to go by the way of Windsor."

"It's further thin."

"Yes," said Phil, "it's a hundred and fifty miles by the way of Windsor, and only a hundred and forty-seven by the way of Annapolis."

"For my part," said Bart, "I don't fancy either way. What's the use of talking about a hundred and fifty miles, when you need only go half that distance?"

"Half that distance? How?"

"Why, across the bay."

"Across the bay? O! Why, that completely alters the case," said Bruce. "Of course."

"Sure, but how can we go on fut across the bay? or by stage?" objected Pat.

"There don't seem to be any schooner here," said Arthur, looking all around.

All the others did the same, searching narrowly the whole line of coast. Nothing, however, was visible of the nature of a vessel. Boats there were, however, in plenty, quite commodious too, but none of them sufficiently large to take them so far as St. John.

"I'm afraid, Bart, your idea of getting to St. John by water won't do," said Bruce. "You'd better make up your mind to come along with us."

"O, I'll go, of course, along with you; we must stick together as long as we can; but we must settle, first of all, which is the best way to go. You'll find it most convenient to come to St. John. You can go from there up the bay, and then go over to Prince Edward Island, easier than by any other route."

"Well, I don't know but that we can, at least as easy as any other way, and so I've no objection; but won't it be best to go to Windsor, or, if you prefer it, to Annapolis?"

"Well, let's find out, first of all, whether there is any chance of going by a more direct way. Old Bennie can tell us all about it."

"Yes, yes," said Tom, who had thus far taken no part in the discussion, "let's ask old Bennie; he can tell us what's best to do."

With these words the boys walked on faster towards where old Bennie was sauntering about with Captain Corbet and Solomon. At the first mention of their wish Bennie energetically refused to say anything about it.

"You've got to stay here, boys—you've *got* to, you know; an thar's no use talkin, an that's all about it—thar now."

This the good Bennie said over and over again, persisting in it most obstinately. At length Bart managed to secure his attention long enough to convey to him an idea of the circumstances in which they were, and especially the regard which they had for their respective parents. At the mention of this Bennie's obstinacy gave away.

"Wal, thar, boys", said he, "that thar does knock me, an I give up. The fact is, when I regard you, and think on what you've ben a doin on, an how you've ben adoin of it, an what sort of a craft you've ben a navigatin in, I feel as though the parients an guardins of sech as youns had ort to be pitied."

In fact, Bennie's commiseration for these anxious parents was so great that he changed his tactics at once, and instead of trying to keep the boys with him, he exhibited the utmost eagerness to hasten their departure.

"You can't go straight off to St. John, boys, from this place, for there ain't a schooner in jest now; but there's a way of goin that'll take you to that place faster, mebbe, than you could go if you went direct in a sailin craft. It's to get off to the nighest place where the steamer touches."

"What's that?"

"Parrsboro'."

"Parrsboro'? and how far is it?"

"O, only a few miles; it's only jest round thar;" and Bennie swung his arm round over towards the right, indicating a vast extent of the earth's surface.

"O, we all know Parrsboro' perfectly well," said Bart; "but when can we catch the steamer there?"

"Why, to-morrow, some time, at about half tide. The steamer comes up to-night, and goes down to-morrow. So, if you go to Parrsboro' an take the steamer thar, you'll be able to be in St. John quicker than if you went any other way."

This intelligence at once settled the question completely. They all saw that to go by land part of the way would take up much longer time. Parrsboro' was so near that it needed only to be mentioned for them all to adopt at once this plan. The only question now remaining was how to get there.

"Wal, there ain't no trouble about that," said Bennie. "Thar's my boat—a nice, clean, roomy one; and I'll engage to put you over in Parrsboro' quick sticks. 'Tain't big enough, quite, to take you to St. John; not because she couldn't go there, for I'd a precious sight sooner cross the bay—yes, or the Atlantic Ocean—in her than in that old Antelope; but because she hain't got good sleepin accommodations in case we was to be delayed, as would be very probable. She's ony an open boat—a beautiful one for sailin in by day, an in fine weather, but not overly good for long vyges for reasons above mentioned, as you'll observe, young gentlemen."

"And can we get over there to-day?"

"Wal, let me see. The tide's a leetle agin us, but bein as you're anxious, I don't know but what we might do it. There ain't much wind about, an we may have to pull a bit; but we'll do what we can, an then, you know, we've got all night afore us. Even at the wust we're sure to get to Parrsboro' before the steamer doos; for if the tide's too much for us we can wait till it turns, and then go up with the flood. An so, if you're bound to be off, why, here am I, in good order and condition, an at your service."

Bennie now led the way to his boat, which was drawn up on the beach. It was an open fishing boat of large size, with one mast and sail. It was, as Bennie had said, quite clean and comfortable, and afforded a very pleasant mode of dropping over to the Parrsboro' shore. Having once seen the boat, the boys were now all eager to be off. Bennie, however, insisted on their taking their dinner before starting. This they all consented to do very readily. The dinner was almost ready, and Bennie prepared for the voyage, which preparation consisted chiefly in moving the boat down over the beach to the water, which was some distance away.

Then followed the dinner, which was served up in the usual sumptuous style peculiar to Mrs. Bennie. After this followed a kindly farewell to their motherly hostess, and the boys followed Bennie to the beach, accompanied by the venerable Corbet and the aged Solomon.

It had been no slight task to move the heavy boat from the place where she had been lying all the way down to the water, for the tide was quite low, and the space intervening was considerable; but Bennie had accomplished the task with the help of some of his neighbors, and the boat now lay so that a slight push might suffice to set her afloat; and inside were some provisions prepared by the forethought of Mrs. Bennie, together with some wraps put there with an eye to some sudden assault of the fog. Everything was, therefore, very well ordered to secure the comfort of the travellers.

On the way to the boat the venerable Corbet and the aged Solomon were silent, and appeared overcome with emotion. This silence was first broken by Solomon.

"Tell ye what, chilen," said he; "it am drefful hard for a 'fectionate ole nigga like me to hab to undergo dis yer operatium. Can't stan it, no how; an donno what on erf I'se a gwine to do. Here I ben a romin ober the mighty oceam, feelin like de father an garden ob all of youns; and now it 'mos stracts dis yer ole nigga to tar his sef away. Blest if I ain't like to break down like a chicken; an I ain't got nuffin else to do. Darsen't go on wid you, Mas'r Bart—darsen't, no how. Fraid ob dat ar ole woman wid de gridiron. De aged Solomon hab got to become a pilgrin an awander on de face ob de erf. But I ain't gwine to wander yet a while; I pose to make a bee-line for de Cad'my. I hab a hope dat de ole 'oman hab not got dar; an if so I be safe, an tany rate de doctor'll take her in hand—he's de boy—dat ar's de identical gemman dat kin overhaul her an teach her her 'p's' an 'q's.' But what you'll do, chilen, widout me to cook, and to carve, an to car for you, am more dan I can magine. Ony I truss we'm boun to meet agin afore long, an jine in de social band; an so you won't forgit ole Solomon."

The boys all shook him warmly by the hand, advising him to go by all means back to the Academy, and put himself at once under the protection of the doctor, who would defend him from all possible dangers arising out of his "ole 'oman."

The mate, Wade, also received their farewells.

Thus far the venerable Corbet had been a mute spectator; his heart was full; his mind seemed preoccupied; he seemed to follow mechanically. At last he saw the moment come which must once more sever him from them, and with a long breath he began to speak.

"It air seldom, young sirs," said he, "that I am called on to experience a sensation sich as that which this moment swells this aged boosom; an I feel that this is one of the most mournful moments of my checkered career. Thar's a sadness, an a depression, an a melancholy, sich as I've seldom knowed afore. 'Tain't altogether the loss of the friend of my youth. That air passed and gone—'tis o'er. I've met that grief an surmounted him. But it was a sore struggle, and the aged Corbet ain't the man he once was. Consequently, I'm onmanned; I'm all took aback. It's this here separation, boys dear, comin as it doos, hard an fast on the heels of the great calamity of the loved and lost Antelope. But it's got to be."—He paused and sighed heavily. "Yes," he continued, pensively, "it's got to be. You ain't my sons; you've got parients an gardens that's anxious about you an wants to see you, and no doubt hain't got that confidence in me which they might have in some. But go you, boys dear, and tell all them parients an gardens that there ain't a pang, an there ain't a emotion, an there ain't a anxiety, an there ain't a grief that they've ever had for any of you that I haven't had for every one of you. Tell them that there ain't a tear that they've shed over you, but I've shed too; an there ain't a sigh they've heaved what I haven't heaved, and ain't a groan they've groaned that I ain't groaned too. Tell them that Corbet, with all his faults, loves you still, an that if you run into dangers and trials, thar wan't a moment when he wouldn't hev shed his heart's blood to get you off safe and clear. Don't let em run away with the idee that I'm a stony-hearted monster that's ben a endangerin of your lives in divers places. I'm ready to be blamed for carlessness an ignorance, boys dear, but not for lack of affection. You know it, an I know that you know it, an what I want is for you all to make them know it too. For, boys dear, I'm a father, an I know a father's heart, an I wouldn't have the heart of any father made bitter against me."

How long the venerable navigator would have gone on talking, it is impossible to say; indeed, it seemed now as if, after his long silence, his tongue, having once found voice, had become endowed with perpetual motion, and was ready to wag forever. But Bennie Grigg put on a stopper, and abruptly interrupted.

"All right, all right, my hearty," said he; "I'll engage that they'll do all that; but thar ain't no time to lose; so tumble in, boys, tumble in, and let's get off so as to round the pint an take the flood tide as it runs up."

Upon this the boys all shook hands hurriedly with Captain Corbet, one after another, and then each one "tumbled" into the boat. Captain Corbet, thus suddenly silenced, remained silent as he seized each one's hand. Then Bennie called upon him and Solomon to help him shove off the boat. Then Bennie jumped in and hoisted the sail. Then the boat moved slowly away, bearing the "B. O. W. C." and their fortunes.

"Good by, boys," wailed Captain Corbet.

"Good by," murmured the aged Solomon.

"Good by! Good by!" cried all the boys.

"We'll meet soon," said Captain Corbet.

"O, yes—in a few weeks," cried Tom.

And so with frequent good bys the boat moved slowly from the beach, and slowly passed over the water till the forms of the aged Solomon and the ancient mariner were gradually lost to view.

XXVI.

A hard Pull.—Wind and Tide.—Bennie's "Idee."—Jolly under creditable Circumstances.—The Triple Promontory.—The Advance of the Fog.—The Line of Cliff.—The foaming Sea.—The slow Passage of the Hours.—The Strait of Minas.—Land at Last.—Bennie triumphant.

The tide was coming up; some time had elapsed since the Antelope had sank, and it had sufficed for the ebb of the tide and its return to its flood. The wind also was light, and as they sought to get out of Scott's Bay, they had the tide against them, and very little wind to favor them. At first they moved rather along the line of the shore than away from it, and though they lost sight of the figures on the beach, they did not therefore make any very great progress.

Scott's Bay is enclosed in a circle of land formed by the Nova Scotia coast, which here rises high above the Bay of Fundy, and throws out a long, circling arm, terminating in a rugged, storm-beaten, and sea-worn crag, known as Cape Split. It was necessary to double this cape, and then go up the Strait of Minas to Parrsboro', which place was at the head of the strait, inside Minas Basin, and rig opposite Cape Blomidon. In order to do this, either the wind or the tide ought to favor the navigator; but, unfortunately, on the present occasion, they were not thus favored.

"I had an idee," said Bennie, after a long silence, "I had an idee that the wind would come up a leetle stronger out here, but it don't seem to; an now I've a notion that it's goin to turn. If so we'll be delayed, but still you'll be landed in Parrsboro' time enough to catch the steamer. Only you may have to be longer gettin thar than you counted on."

"O, we don't care. Only get us there in time for the steamer, and we won't complain."

"Wal, it's best to make up one's mind for the wust, you know. The wind may change, an then we may be out half the night, or even all night. But, at any rate, I'll put you through."

"You needn't think about any inconvenience to us. We're only too grateful to you for putting yourself out so much, and none of us would care whether we were out all night or not. We've learned to rough it during the last two or three weeks."

Bennie now diverted his gaze to the surrounding sea, and kept his eyes fixed upon it for a long time in silence, while the boys chatted together in the light-hearted manner peculiar to those who feel quite comfortable, and have no particular aversion even to a moderate amount of discomfort. Yet Bennie did not seem altogether at ease. There was a slight frown on his noble brow, and he did not show that genial disposition which generally distinguished him.

The wind was light and fitful. At first it had been favorable, but before long it changed. It did not grow stronger, indeed; yet still, though it continued light, the fact that it was acting against them made their prospects worse, and justified Bennie's fears that they might be out all night. The distance was not great, being not more than fifteen miles or so; but their course was in such a direction that the opposition of wind and tide might delay them to a very uncomfortable extent. The spur of the coast line, which terminated in Cape Split, as has been said, and formed the bay, ran for about five miles, and this distance it was necessary to traverse before they could go up the Strait of Minas.

"I think, boys," said Bennie, at last, "we'd best try the oars, for a while at least. We may save a tide. I don't know, but at any rate we'd best try an see; for, you see, we've got the wind agin us now,—what thar is of it,—an thar's no knowin how much wuss it may grow. If we could ony git around that pint afore the tide turned, we might save ourselves from spendin the night aboard. I did hope that the wind might favor us; but it's changed since we started, an now I see we'd best prepar for the wust."

"All right!" cried Bruce, cheerily; "we're in for anything. We can pull as long as you like."

Upon this the boys took the oars which were in the boat, and began to row. There were four oars. Bennie lowered the sail, and took the stroke oar, Bruce and Arthur took the next oars, and Bart the bow oar. They rowed in this way for about an hour, and then they changed, Arthur taking the stroke oar, Tom and Phil the next oars, and Pat the bow oar. Bruce soon relieved Arthur, and thus they rowed along.

The labor at the oars, far from being unpleasant, served to beguile the time. Those who were not rowing sang songs to enliven the labor of the rowers. Bennie was anxious to row all the time, but after the first hour he was not allowed to row any more, the boys declaring that it was enough for him to come with them, and that it was no more than fair that they should work their own way.

As they went, the wind increased somewhat, and, as the tide was strong, the two powers combined to oppose their progress. They therefore did not make the headway which was desirable, and after one hour of steady pulling they did not find themselves more than half way to Cape Split. Still, they did not become discouraged, but rowed bravely on, making the change above mentioned, and anticipating a turn for the better when once they had doubled the cape.

At length they reached the cape. More than two hours of hard rowing had been required to bring them there, and on reaching this place they saw Bennie's face still covered with gloom and anxiety. What that might mean, they did not at first know; but they soon found out. At first, however, they were too much taken up with their own thoughts, and the natural pride which they felt at having attained the aim of so long and anxious an endeavor, to notice particularly any expression which Bennie's face might assume. Besides, there was something in the scene before them which was sufficiently grand to engross all their thoughts.

Among the freaks of nature, so called, few are more extraordinary, and at the same time more impressive and sublime, than that which is afforded by this Cape Split. The whole northern shore of Nova Scotia, which borders on the Bay of Fundy, consists of a high ridge, known as the North Mountain. With one or two great chasms, like that at the entrance into Annapolis Basin, it runs along until it arrives at the Basin of Minas, where it terminates at the sublime promontory of Blomidon. Yet it hardly terminates here. Rather it may be said to turn about and seek once more to invade the water, which, for so many miles, it has defied; and thus turning, it advances for some miles into the Bay of Fundy, forming thus, by this encircling arm, Scott's Bay, and finally terminating in Cape Split. Here, where the tides are highest, and the rush of the waters strongest, Cape Split arises,—wild, rough, worn by the sea, and scarred by the storm,—a triple series of gigantic peaks that advance into the profoundest depths of the Bay of Fundy, whose waters, at every ebb and flow of their tremendous tides, roll, and foam, and boil, and seethe about the base of the torn promontory. The cliffs of Blomidon rise precipitously, and Blomidon itself is the centre of attraction in the scenery of a vast circuit of country; but Blomidon itself, to a near observer, shows less wildness of outline and less of picturesque grandeur, than that which is revealed in the terrific outline of Cape Split. Taken in connection with all the surrounding landscape as its centre and heart, Blomidon is undoubtedly superior; but taken by itself alone, without any adjuncts save sea and sky, it is Cape Split that the artist would choose to portray upon the canvas, or the lover of the picturesque and the sublime to feast his eyes upon.

This, then, was the point which they had reached, and they saw before them a series of giant rocks towering aloft from the depths of the sea hundreds of feet into the air,—black, rough, without a trace of vegetation, thrusting their sharp pinnacles into the sky, while thousands of sea-gulls screamed about their summits, and myriads of sea-waves beat about their bases. There the tide rolled, and the ocean currents streamed to and fro, and the billows of the sea kept up perpetual war, assailing the flinty rock, and slowly wearing away, as they had been doing through the ages, atom by atom and fragment by fragment, the forms of these mighty bulwarks of the land.

This was the scene upon which they gazed as they reached Cape Split and prepared to enter into the Strait of Minas. But Bennie's brow was dark, and Bennie's brow was gloomy, and there were thoughts in Bennie's mind which had no connection with any grandeur of scenery or beauty of landscape. For Bennie was thinking of the practical, and not of the picturesque; and so it was that the question of reaching Parrsboro' was of far more importance to him than the glories and the grandeur and all the sublime attractions of Cape Split.

"Tell you what it is, boys," said he, after a long and thoughtful silence, "we've missed it, an we've got to look sharp, or else we'll miss it agen."

"Missed it? Missed what?"

"What? Why, everything."

"Everything. What do you mean?"

"Wal, it's this con-founded tide."

"What about it?"

"Why, you see," said Bennie, scratching his grizzled head, "I thought we might git round the cape in time to catch the flood tide, and if so, it would carry us straight up to Parrsboro'; but, unfort'nately, we've jest missed it. We've took so much time in gittin here that we've lost the flood. The tide's now on the ebb, an it's clear agin us. What's wuss, it runs down tremenjus, an it'll be a leetle hard for us to git up anyhow; an, what's wusser, thar's goin to be a fog."

"A fog!"

"Yes, a fog, an no mistake. See thar,"—and Bennie pointed down the bay,—"see thar. The wind's ben a shiftin an's finally settled into a sou-wester, an thar's the fog a drawin in all round us, an before another half hour we'll be all shut in, an won't be able to see the other end of the boat. What's wuss still, the fog is goin to be a reglar settled fog, an may last a fortnight; an the ony thing that I can see in our favor jest now is, that the wind is fair for us; but, unfortinately, the wind don't seem to promise to be strong enough to carry us up agin the tide."

"What! Can't we get to Parrsboro' in time for the steamer at all?"

"The steamer? O, yes, no doubt about that. But what I'm afeard on is, that we'll be all night about it."

"O, well, that can't be helped. We can stand it. We've had worse things than this to stand of late, and this is mere child's play."

"Child's play? Wal, I don't know about that altogether," said Bennie. "For my part, I don't seem to see how goin' without sleep's child's play, as you call it; but still I'm glad all the same that you look on it in this way; I am railly."

"O, you needn't give any thought to us. We're old stagers. We've been shipwrecked and we've lived on desert islands. We've risked our lives a dozen times in a dozen days. Fellows that have been cast ashore on Anticosti and on Sable Island, can't be frightened at anything that you can mention."

"After my life on Ile Haute out there," said Tom, looking at the dim form of Ile Haute, which was even then being enveloped in the gathering fog, "I think this is mere child's play."

"And after my adventures in the woods," said Phil, "I'm ready for anything."

"Pat and I," said Bart, "have known all the bitterness of death, and have felt what it is to be buried alive."

"An meself," said Pat, "by the same token, have known what it is to bathe in the leper wather, so I have; an what's fog to that?"

"Well," said Arthur, "I've had my turn off Anticosti in the boat, Tom and I."

"And I," said Bruce, "have had my turn at the Five Islands; so you see you've got to do with a lot of fellows that don't care a rush for fogs and tides, and all that sort of thing."

"Wal, young fellers," said Bennie, "I knock under, I cave in. I won't say anything more. You're all the right sort, an are ready for anything. So come along; an here goes for Parrsboro'. You've got to be up all night; but arter all, you've got wraps and rugs, an bread an butter, an pie, an can keep yourselves warm, an can have enough to eat,—'so what's the odds, as long as you're happy?' I ain't a croaker, I ain't, but go in for bein cheerful, an if you ain't goin to knock under, why I ain't, an so let's be jolly an move on."

Saying this, Bennie hoisted his sail once more. The wind was light, but fair, and the only question now was, whether that wind would be strong enough to carry the boat against the tide. As to the tide, that was certainly sufficiently strong, but unfortunately it was unfavorable. The tide had turned, and was running down the Strait of Minas, up which they wished to go. The tide was thus adverse, and in addition to this was the fog.

The fog!

Yes, the fog, the dreaded, the baleful fog, was coming on. Already Ile Haute was concealed from view. Soon the opposite shore would be veiled. Worse than all, the night was coming on. With fog and darkness united, their way would be uncertain indeed.

Fortunately for them, the way was a straight one, and the wind, though not very strong, and though opposed by the tide, was yet fair. This much was in their favor.

And so they spread their sails. And the wind filled the sails, and the boat went on. The tide was against them, but still the boat advanced. Some progress, at last, was made. Hour after hour passed, and still they went on. Bennie seemed to be quite encouraged. At last they came to a wide beach.

"Hurrah!" said Bennie, "we're here at last. This is the place, lads. We're at Parrsboro'! Hurrah!"

XXVII.

The Village by the Sea.—The Village Inn.—A hospitable Landlord.—Making Inquiries.—Astounding Intelligence.— Dismay followed by Despair.—A Search without Result.—A mournful Walk.—A Sail! A Sail!—Boat, Ahoy!—An old Friend!—Great Jubilation.—Conclusion.

It had been a most eventful day for all the boys, and when they stepped ashore it was nine o'clock in the evening. They looked around with some curiosity, for they saw no signs of houses just here, though the fog had diminished greatly, and it was not so dark but that they could see the outline of the shore.

"Now, boys," said Bennie, "here you are. You see that island in front,—well, Parrsboro' is just behind that, and not more'n half a mile off by land. It's too far to go round it in the boat; so we'll leave her here, and I'll show you the way along the shore."

With these words, Bennie drew up the boat a little distance, and secured it by putting the anchor out upon the beach. After this he started off, and the boys followed. Bennie walked along the beach, occasionally explaining the different objects around, pointing out Blomidon, Partridge Island, and other places, all familiar enough, and needing only to be mentioned to be recognized by the boys.

At length they came in sight of a number of houses on the side of a hill close by a cove. Lights shone in the windows, and everything had a most inviting appearance.

"Here you air, boys," said Bennie, "an here I'll leave you, for you can find your way on easy enough. You've only got to foller your noses. I've got to go back an drop down with the tide so as to git to Cape Split before the wind goes down. An so I'll bid you good by."

The boys made no effort to detain him, for they knew well that the return would be tedious, and had no desire to keep him away from his home any longer than they could help. So they all shook hands with him, thanking him earnestly, and promising, in obedience to his reiterated request, to pay him a visit on their return to school. Bennie now left them and returned to his boat, in which he embarked and set sail for Scott's Bay. The boys went on. The village was reached in a short time, and they walked to the inn.

On entering the parlor of the inn, they were accosted by the landlord, and the following conversation took place.

"Can you give us accommodation for the night?"

"O, yes."

"And get us some tea as quick as you can, for we're starving?"

"You can have it in half an hour."

"That's right. We've just come over from Scott's Bay, and have had no end of a tug. We want to take the steamer here to St. John."

"O, ye'll be wantin to wait for the steamer."

"Yes; it's the only thing for us to do; and I'm precious glad we've got such good quarters."

"O, ay. Parrsboro's a good place to stop at. There be people that stops here weeks an months, an says as how it's one of the best places goin. I can put yes on the way to the best streams for salmon an trout in the country; an ye can have a nice boat if ye want to go over to Blomidon; it's a mighty fine place over there, and folks finds cur'ous minerals; an if ye want deep-sea fishin, why, out there a mile or two in the bay ye can get no end of cod."

"O, for that matter, we haven't any idea of sporting. We're in too much of a hurry. Just get us a tea and bed, and I suppose we'll have time to get breakfast to-morrow?"

The landlord stared.

"Time? Breakfast?"

"Yes; before the steamer comes, you know."

"Before the steamer comes?" repeated the landlord, dubiously.

"Yes; I suppose she won't touch here too early but that we'll have time for breakfast?"

"Breakfast? When? To-morrow?"

"Yes."

"Why, there's no steamer comes to-morrow."

"What!"

At that astonishing intelligence, all the boys started up to their feet from the easy lounging attitudes into which they had flung themselves, and surrounding the landlord, stared at him with speechless amazement.

"What's that?" cried Bruce, at last; "no steamer to-morrow?"

"No; O, dear, no."

"Why—why—when does she come here?"

"Why, she was here this morning, and won't be here again till this day week."

"This morning?"

"Yes; she was here about ten o'clock."

"This morning! Ten o'clock!"

"Jest so."

Once more the boys subsided into silence. All was plain now. Bennie had utterly mistaken the day of the steamer. It was not an unlikely thing for him to do, living as he did in an out-of-the-way place, and having no interest in the steamer's movements. But the mistake had been made, and there was the stolid fact that no steamer would touch at Parrsboro' for a whole week to come.

The landlord now went off to prepare their tea, and the boys, left to themselves, discussed the situation in a low, melancholy, and utterly dispirited way. At length tea made its appearance—a bounteous repast. The well-loaded table gave a new turn to their thoughts, and as they sat down with ravenous appetites to partake of the same, they felt that they had something still left to live for.

After tea they resumed the discussion of the situation. It seemed to them now not by any means so forlorn and gloomy as it had done before tea, for then they were weary, worn out, and half starved; but now, thanks to the generous repast, they all felt life, and strength, and hope, and looked out upon life and its vicissitudes with the utmost equanimity. So great is the effect which is produced upon the mind by a good dinner! They now invited the landlord to take a share in their discussion, and in order to enable him to do so to the best advantage, they enlightened him as to the immediate cause of their presence here, informing him about the voyage of the Antelope, her mournful fate, and Bennie Grigg's kindness in bringing them to Parrsboro'. Bennie had indeed been very kind, and had put himself to no end of trouble for their sakes, and was even at that time, perhaps, thinking, with a glow of satisfaction, of them, little dreaming how completely, though unintentionally, he had deceived them.

The first thing the landlord advised, after hearing all this, was, that they had better wait till the steamer came. He offered, if they did so, to put them in the way of all the sport that the country could afford,—fishing of all kinds, shooting too, and excursions to places of interest. But the landlord's offer was not very gratefully received. It was, in fact, rejected at once most peremptorily. Wait a week! And in Parrsboro'! Impossible! It was not to be thought of for a moment.

What else was there to do?

To this question the landlord showed two answers. One thing to do was to go by land; another thing, to try to find some schooner, and go by water. As to the land route he had much to say. There was a mail stage that ran every week to New Brunswick, but as it went only on steamboat days, and as it would not go for another week, they found no help here. The landlord, however, pointed out to them the fact that they could hire a wagon and travel in that way. He offered to furnish them with a commodious wagon, and a very nice pair of ponies that would take them through to Dorchester, in New Brunswick, where they could catch the steamer for St. John, or go in the mail stage. But, unfortunately, on reckoning up the time and distance, they found that it would take about four days to perform their journey in this way.

The water route still remained. Could they not find a schooner that was about leaving? The landlord rather thought they could. One way would be to wait till some schooner passed by on its way down the bay, and board her. He felt certain that any coaster would land them at St. John. Another way would be to go to Mill Village,—a part of Parrsboro', which lay about a mile off, behind a hill,—and look up a vessel among the numerous ones which at that time happened to be in port. Both of these suggestions seemed good, and the boys felt sanguine that something might result. They therefore dismissed the idea of going by land, and resolved to wait at least one day, to see whether they might not find some schooner which would take them down the bay.

It was very late when this discussion was finished, and the boys, whom excitement had thus far sufficed to keep awake, now yielded to the combined influence of fatigue and sleepiness, and retired for the night. That night passed in profound slumber, and the dawn of day still found them in deep sleep. It was after ten o'clock before any one of them awoke; and even then, so sleepy were they that they did not feel inclined to get up. But they had work before them, and so they managed to dress themselves and put in an appearance at breakfast, which had been waiting for them for two or three hours.

Then followed a journey to Mill Village. It was a beautiful day; all the fog was gone; there was not a cloud in the sky; the water was rippled by a gentle breeze from the north, and its blue surface seemed more inviting than ever. It seemed to promise them a pleasant return to their home if they would only trust themselves once more to it.

The landlord had a wagon all ready for them, and a short drive brought them to Mill Village. It was rather larger and busier than the little settlement where the inn was, and they noticed with delight three schooners in port. On reaching the place they hurried about, making inquiries. But the result of the inquiries was not very cheering. The first schooner which they visited was about leaving for Windsor, to take in a load of plaster, which would occupy a week, after which she would sail for Boston. Schooner the second would not leave for a fortnight, for she was waiting for a cargo of deals. Schooner the third was even worse. She was not seaworthy, and the skipper was hesitating between repairing her and condemning her. On making inquiries further as to the probability of other vessels being available along the coast, they could learn nothing. And this was the result of their journey, and with this they had to satisfy themselves as best they might. There was nothing now left but to return to the inn.

It was one o'clock when they reached the inn. They were all disheartened, and did not know exactly what to do. Dinner over, they began once more to discuss the situation; and the more they discussed it the more they found it necessary to hire the landlord's team and set out to make the long, roundabout land journey. But it was now too late to set out on this day, and it would be necessary to wait till the morrow. This, then, was the conclusion to which they came; and having reached it, they began to feel more settled in their minds.

It was about three o'clock when this question was at last settled, and weary with their long discussion, they all went out to stroll about the village and along the beach. The village was not much to speak of. Some half dozen houses, with their attendant barns, comprised it all. The beach, however, was very much indeed. To the right, Partridge Island arose, lofty, rugged, wooded, projecting into the Strait of Minas. Opposite was a long line of precipitous cliff, which terminated in Blomidon. The beach began at Partridge Island, and ran on in a long, curving line for more than two miles, covered with pebbles, and sloping gradually to the water. The view was remarkably beautiful. On the right, the rugged, wooded island; in front, the long line of cliff on the opposite side of the strait; farther in, the sublime form of Blomidon; on the left, the beach, winding far away till it terminated in a promontory, beyond which spread the wide waters of the Basin of Minas, terminated in the dim distance by the far-off line of coast.

And there, as they strolled along the beach, they became aware of an object on that wide sheet of water which filled them all with the most intense interest. A sail!

Yes; there was a sail there, and it was moving towards them—towards the Strait of Minas. Doubtless it was some vessel on its way down the bay. It was a schooner bound, perhaps, for Boston—or perhaps for St. John. What mattered it? Enough that it was going down the bay.

One wild shout of joy burst forth from all that forlorn party as they recognized the truth. Here came deliverance; here came a way of escape; they were saved. Other times they had known when the sight of an approaching vessel would have been the assurance of escape from something worse than this, of course; but their situation now, though not perilous, was monotonous, and wearisome, and doleful, and altogether miserable; and so they naturally hailed this new appearance with shouts of joy.

But how to get to her was now the question.

How? Easily enough. Had not the landlord already suggested a way? Had he not promised to furnish them with a boat, with which they might board any passing vessel? Boats there were, in plenty, along the shore, and any one of these would suffice for their purpose. There was no time to lose. The schooner was coming quickly on, borne by wind and tide; they must make haste.

And they did make haste.

Hurrying back to the inn, they acquainted the landlord with the new state of affairs. That worthy, though loath to lose his lodgers, was still honest and sympathetic enough to use all energy towards furthering their desires, and proposed at once to take to the boat. As for the boys, they all felt perfectly sure that this schooner would take them; and so they insisted on paying their bills and taking a final leave of the inn.

The boat was launched without any trouble, and soon was passing over the waters, impelled by oars in the hands of Bruce, Arthur, Bart, and Tom. The schooner came on, nearer and nearer, and finally came within hail.

"Schooner, ahoy!"

"Boat, ahoy!"

"Where are you bound?"

"Schooner Dart—St. John."

"All right. We want to go aboard."

In a few moments the boat was alongside, and the boys were all aboard. They waved a farewell to the landlord, who dropped astern, and then turned to the skipper to make known their wants.

The first look which they gave to the skipper, who was standing there before them, was enough to fill them with surprise and delight. In that broad, thick-set frame, and that honest, jovial face, they recognized an old friend and a cherished one—one, too, who was associated with the memories of former adventures; in fact, no other than Captain Pratt. At so strange and unexpected a meeting they were all filled with amazement. One cry burst from them all,—

"Captain Pratt!"

The worthy Pratt, on his part, was no less surprised, and, it must be added, no less delighted.

"Why, boys, where in the world have you sprung from? Have you been a cruisin about Minas Basin ever since? It looks like it; but railly now—it can't be—it can't railly."

"Well, not exactly," said Bart, who then and there began to give a brief outline of the adventures of the "B. O. W. C." since the time of their visit to Pratt's Cove, where they had last parted with their worthy friend.

Never was there a pleasanter meeting. It was altogether unexpected, yet not unnatural, for Captain Pratt was a frequent cruiser over these waters, and was now, as he informed them, on his way to St. John with a cargo of deals. The jovial captain made them tell the whole story of all their adventures since they had last parted with him, in the Bay of Fundy, in the country about the Bay de Chaleur, in the Gulf of St. Lawrence, at Anticosti, Sable Island, and Mahone Bay, and thus acquainted himself with every particular of the wonderful story which they had to tell. The worthy captain regarded it all as a joke, and at every fresh incident his homeric laughter burst forth in long, irrepressible peals.

But such a story occupied some time in the narration, and before it was ended the schooner was far out of the Strait of Minas, beyond Ile Haute, in the Bay of Fundy. On one side lay the Nova Scotia shore, on the other the coast of New Brunswick. Before them extended the waters of the bay.

Night came, and they all slept. On the following day, in the afternoon, they reached St John.

Their adventures for a time were over. Bart took all his friends to his own home, where they spent two or three days.

Then they separated, Phil going to Nova Scotia, and Bruce, Arthur, and Tom to Prince Edward Island. Pat remained with Bart for the rest of the holidays.

www.ingramcontent.com/pod-product-compliance
Lightning Source LLC
Chambersburg PA
CBHW020642180626
46816CB00003B/1080